THE
SILENT
WATERS

THE ELEMENT SERIES, BOOK 3

BRITTAINY C. CHERRY

Published: Brittainy C. Cherry 2016
brittainycherry@gmail.com

Editing: Editing by C. Marie, Ellie at Love N. Books
Copy Editing: Librum Artis Editorial Services
Proofreading: Virginia Tesi Carey, Lawrence Editing
Interior Formatting: Elaine York, Allusion Graphics, LLC/
Publishing & Book Formatting, www.allusiongraphics.com
Cover Design: Quirky Bird
Cover Model: Luke Ditella

Dedication

TO THE DRIFTERS LIKE ME WHO FLOAT AWAY.
TO THE ANCHORS WHO ALWAYS BRING US HOME.

Moments.

Humans always remember the moments.

We recall the steps that led us to where we were meant to be. The words that inspired or crushed us. The incidents that scarred us and swallowed us whole. I've had many moments in my lifetime, moments that changed me, challenged me, moments that scared me and engulfed me. However, the biggest ones—the most heartbreaking and breathtaking ones—all included him.

It all began with a rocket ship nightlight
and a boy who didn't know me.

PROLOGUE

Maggie

"It's going to be different this time, Maggie, I swear. This time is forever," Daddy promised, as he pulled up to the yellow brick house on the corner of Jacobson Street. Daddy's soon-to-be wife, Katie, stood on her front porch watching our old station wagon pull in the driveway.

Magic.

It felt like magic, coming up to the house. I'd moved from a small place to a palace. Daddy and I had lived in a tiny two-bedroom apartment all our lives, and now we were moving into a two-story home with five bedrooms, a living room, a kitchen the size of Florida, two and a half bathrooms, and an actual dining room—not a living room where Daddy set up TV dinner trays at five in the afternoon each night for supper. Daddy told me they even had an inground pool in their backyard. A *pool*! In their *backyard*!

I went from living with one person to becoming a part of a family.

The family part was nothing new, though. Since I could remember, I'd been part of many families with Daddy. The first one

I hadn't really known, since my mama had walked out on Daddy and me before I'd even spoken my first word. She'd found someone else who made her feel more loved than Daddy, which was hard for me to believe. Daddy gave his all to love, no matter how much it cost him. After she left, he gave me a box of photographs of her so I could remember her, but I thought that was a weird thing. How could I remember a woman who was never even there? After her, he became good at falling in love with women, and oftentimes, they fell in love with him, too. They'd move into our tiny world with all their belongings, and Daddy would tell me it was forever, but forever was always shorter than he hoped it would be.

This time was different.

This time, he had met the love of his life in an AOL chat room. Daddy had his share of bad relationships after my mama left us, so he thought trying to meet someone online would've been better, and it worked. Katie had lost her husband years before and hadn't dated until she signed online and met Daddy.

And unlike all the times before, this time Daddy and I were moving in with Katie and her children, not the other way around.

"This time is forever," I whispered back to Daddy.

Katie was beautiful like all the women on TV. Daddy and I watched television when we ate our supper together, and I'd always notice how beautiful the people were. Katie looked just like them. She had long blonde hair and crystal blue eyes, kind of like me. Her nails were painted a bright red color that matched her lipstick, and her eyelashes were thick, dark, and long. When Daddy and I pulled into her—*our*—driveway, she was waiting there in a pretty white dress, wearing yellow high heels.

"Oh, Maggie!" she cried, rushing over to me and flinging the car door open so she could wrap her arms around me. "It's so nice to finally meet you."

I raised an eyebrow, wary about hugging Katie back, even though she smelled like coconuts and strawberries. I never knew coconuts and strawberries went together until I met Katie.

I looked over at Daddy, who was smiling my way, and he nodded once, giving me permission to hug the woman back.

She hugged me so tight and lifted me out of the car, squeezing the air from my lungs, but I didn't complain. It'd been a long time since I'd been hugged that tight. The last time had probably been when Grandpa had come to visit and wrapped me up in his arms.

"Come on, now. Let me introduce you to my kids. We'll stop by Calvin's room first. You two are the same age, so you'll be going to school together. He's right inside with a friend of his."

Katie didn't bother putting me down, instead carrying me over to the steps as Daddy grabbed a few pieces of our luggage. As we walked through the front door, my eyes widened. *Wow.* It was beautiful, something straight out of Cinderella's palace, I was sure. She took me upstairs, to the last room on the left, and opened the door. My eyes fell on two boys playing Nintendo and shouting at each other. Katie placed me down on my feet.

"Boys, pause," Katie said.

They didn't listen.

They kept arguing.

"*Boys*," Katie repeated more sternly. "*Pause.*"

Nothing.

She huffed and placed her hands on her hips.

I huffed and copied her stance.

"BOYS!" she shouted, unplugging their video game system.

"MOM!"

"MS. FRANKS!"

I giggled. The boys turned to face us, utter shock in their stare, and Katie smiled. "Now that I have your attention, I want you to say hello to Maggie. Calvin, she's staying with us, along with her father. Remember me saying you were gonna get a sister, Calvin?"

The boys stared blankly at me. Calvin was clearly the blond one, who looked identical to Katie. The boy sitting next to him had dark messy hair and brown eyes, along with a hole in his pale yellow t-shirt and potato chip crumbs on his jeans.

"I didn't know you had another sister, Cal," the boy said, staring my way. The more he stared, the more my stomach hurt. I stepped behind Katie's leg, my cheeks heating up.

"Me neither," Calvin replied.

"And, Maggie, this is Brooks. He lives across the street from us, but tonight he's sleeping over."

I peeked around Katie's kneecap at Brooks, who gave me a small smile before eating the crumbs off of his pants.

"Can we play the game again?" Brooks asked, going back to his controller and staring at the blank television screen.

Katie snickered to herself, shaking her head back and forth. "Boys will be boys," she whispered to me as she plugged their game back in.

I shook my head and giggled, too, just like Katie. "Yeah. Boys will be boys."

Next, we stopped by another room. It was the pinkest room I'd ever seen, and a girl was sitting on the floor, drawing, wearing bunny ears and a princess dress, and eating Doritos out of a pink plastic bowl.

"Cheryl," Katie said, walking into the room. I hid behind her leg. "This is Maggie. She's gonna be staying with us, along with her father. Remember I told you about this?"

Cheryl looked up, smiled, and stuffed more Doritos into her mouth. "Okay, Mom." She went back to drawing, and her red curly hair danced back and forth as she hummed a song to herself. Then she paused and looked up again. "Hey, how old are you?"

"Six," I said.

She smiled. "I'm five! Do you like playing with dolls?"

I nodded.

She smiled again and went back to drawing. "Okay. Bye."

Katie laughed and walked me out of the room, whispering, "I think you two are going to be really good friends."

She showed me to my room next, where Daddy was putting my

bags. My eyes widened at how big the space was—and it was all for me. "Wow…" I took a deep breath. "This is mine?"

"This is yours."

Wow.

"I know you two must be tired from the long drive, so I'll let you get Maggie ready for bed." Katie smiled at Daddy and kissed his cheek.

As Daddy pulled out my pajamas, I asked, "Can Katie maybe tuck me in?"

She didn't argue.

As she did, I smiled at her, and she smiled at me. A lot of smiling happened and a lot of talking, too. "You know, I've always wanted another daughter," she said, brushing my hair.

I didn't say it, but I had always wanted a mama, too.

"We're going to have so much fun together, Maggie. You, Cheryl, and me. We can get our nails done, and go sit down by the pool, and drink lemonade, and flip through magazines. We can do everything guys hate doing."

She hugged me goodnight, then she left and shut off the light.

I didn't sleep at all.

I tossed, turned, and whimpered for a long time, but Daddy couldn't hear me because he was all the way on the first floor, sleeping in his bedroom with Katie. Even if I wanted to go find him, I couldn't, because the hallway was dark, and I hated dark places more than anything. I sniffled a bit, trying my best to count sheep in my head, but nothing was working.

"What's the matter with you?" a shadowy figure standing in my doorway said.

I gasped and sat up straight, hugging my pillow.

The shadow moved closer, and I let out a small sigh when I saw it was Brooks. His hair was wild and standing up on his head, and he had sleep wrinkles on his cheek. "You gotta stop crying. You keep waking me up."

I sniffled. "Sorry."

"What's the matter, anyway? You homesick or somethin'?"

"No."

"Then what is it?"

I lowered my head, embarrassed. "I'm scared of the dark."

"Oh." He narrowed his eyes for a second before leaving the room.

I kept hugging my pillow, and I was even more surprised when Brooks came back. He had something in his hand and walked over to the wall to plug it in. "Calvin doesn't need a nightlight. His mom just put it in his room." He arched an eyebrow. "Is that better?"

I nodded. *Better.*

He yawned. "Okay, well, night…er…what's your name again?"

"Maggie."

"Night, Maggie. You don't really gotta worry 'bout nothing here in our town, either. It's always safe. You're safe here. And if that ain't better, I'm sure you can come sleep on Calvin's floor. He won't mind." He left, scratching his messy hair and still yawning.

My eyes fell to the nightlight shaped like a rocket ship just before they started to close. I felt tired. I felt safe. I felt protected by a rocket ship given to me by a boy I'd just met.

Before, I wasn't sure, but this time I knew.

Daddy was right.

"Forever," I whispered to myself, falling deeper and deeper into my dreams. "This time is forever."

Part One

1

Maggie

JULY 25TH, 2008 — TEN YEARS OLD

A note to the boy who's in love with me
By: Maggie May Riley

Dear Brooks Tyler,

I spent a lot of time upset with you the other day after you called me a name and pushed me into a puddle. You ruined my favorite dress and my pink and yellow sandals. I was so ~~made~~ mad at you for pushing me.

Your brother Jamie told me you're mean to me because you love me. You call me names because that's what boys do when they are in love. You pushed me only because you wanted to be close to me. I think that's ~~stiupid~~ stupid, but I also know that my mama says all men are stupid, so it's not your fault. It's in your DNA.

So, I accept your love, Brooks. I allow you to love me forever and ever and ever.

I started planning the wedding.

It's in a few days, in the woods, where you boys always go fishing. I always wanted to get married by the water like my mama and daddy.

You better wear a tie and not that ugly mud-colored one you wore to church last Sunday. Get some of your dad's cologne, too. I know you're a boy, but you don't have to smell like one. I love you, Brooks Tyler Griffin.

Forever and ever and ever.

Your soon-to-be wife,
Maggie May

P.S. I accept your apology that you never gave me. Jamie said you were sorry, so you don't have to worry about me being mad.

***

A note to the girl who is crazy
By: Brooks Tyler Griffin

Maggie May,
I. Don't. Like. You! Go away forever and ever and ever.

Your NOT soon-to-be husband,
Brooks Tyler

A note to the boy who is funny
By: Maggie May Riley

My Brooks Tyler,

You make me laugh. Jamie said you'd reply like that.

What do you think about the colors purple and pink for the ceremony? We should probably move in together, but I'm too young to have a mortgage. Maybe we can stay with your parents until you get a ~~steddy~~ steady job to support me and our pets.

We'll have a dog named Skippy and a cat named Jam.

-Your Maggie May

A note to the girl who is still crazy
By: Brooks Tyler Griffin

Maggie,

We are not getting married. We are not having pets. We aren't even friends. I HATE YOU, MAGGIE MAY! If your brother wasn't my best friend, I'd never talk to you EVER! I think you're crazy.

Skippy and Jam? That's stupid. That's the stupidest thing I've ever heard. Besides, everyone knows Jif is the best peanut butter.

NOT YOURS,
Brooks

A note to the boy who has bad taste
By: Maggie May Riley

Brooks Tyler,

Mama always says that a great relationship is about two main things: loving the ~~similariaties simliariates silimiaiities~~, stuff the couple has in common and then also respecting the different things.
I love that we both like peanut butter, and I respect your opinion about Jif.
Even if your opinion is wrong.

Always,
Maggie May

P.S. Did you find a tie?

A note to the girl who is still, STILL crazy
By: Brooks Tyler Griffin

Maggie May,
I don't need a tie, because we're never getting married.
And it's spelled 'similarities', you idiot.

-Brooks

A note to the boy who made me cry
By: Maggie May Riley

Brooks,

That was mean.

-Maggie

A note to the girl who is still, STILL crazy, but shouldn't ever cry
By: Brooks Tyler Griffin

Maggie May,

I'm sorry. I can be a real jerk.

-Brooks

A note to the boy who made me smile
By: Maggie May Riley

Brooks Tyler Griffin,
I forgive you.
Go with the mud-colored tie if you want to. No matter how bad you dress, I'll still love becoming your wife.
See you next weekend at five between the two twisty trees.

Forever and ever and ever,
-Maggie May Riley

Brooks

I hated Maggie May.

I wished there were a bigger word to describe my feelings for the annoying, loud-mouthed girl who had been following me around lately, but hate seemed to be the only thing that came to mind whenever she stood near me. I should've never given her that nightlight all those years ago. I should've just pretended she didn't exist.

"Why is she coming?" I groaned, packing fishing line, floats, sinkers, and hooks into my tackle box. For the past two years I'd been on fishing trips with my dad, my older brother, Jamie, Calvin, and his new dad, Eric—or Mr. Riley as I called him. We'd go up to Harper Creek, 'bout a fifteen-minute walk away, and sit on Mr. Riley's boat, laughing and joking with one another. The lake was so huge that if you looked across it, you could hardly see the other side where the town's shops were located. Calvin and I often tried to point out the buildings, like the library, the grocery store, and the mall. Then, we'd try our best to catch some fish. It was a dudes' day where we ate too much junk food and didn't care if our guts were close to bursting. It was our tradition, and it was currently being ruined by a stupid ten-year-old who always sang and never stopped dancing in circles. Maggie May was the definition of annoying. That was the truth, too. I looked up her name in the dictionary once and the meaning was: 'Calvin's annoying stepsister.'

I might've added the definition myself and gotten yelled at by my mom for writing in a book, but still, it was true.

"My parents said she had to come," Calvin explained, lifting his rod. "Mom is taking Cheryl to the doctor, so there ain't nobody to watch her for the next few hours."

"Can't she just be locked in the house? Your parents could leave her a peanut butter and jelly sandwich and a juice box or something."

Calvin smirked. "I wish. It's so stupid."

"She's so stupid!" I exclaimed. "She has this idea that she's gonna marry me in the woods. She's crazy."

Jamie snickered. "You're just sayin' that because you secretly love her."

"I do not!" I shouted. "That's disgusting. Maggie May makes me sick. The thought of her gives me nightmares."

"You say that because you love her," Jamie mocked.

"You better shut your mouth before I shut it for you, jerk. She said you were the one who spread the rumor about me liking her! You're the reason she thinks we're getting married."

He laughed. "Yeah, I know."

"Why would you do that?"

Jamie slugged me in the shoulder. "'Cause I'm your big brother, and big brothers are supposed to make their younger brothers' lives terrible. It's in the sibling contract."

"I never signed a contract."

"You were underage, so Mom signed it for you, duh."

I rolled my eyes. "Whatever. All I know is Maggie is going to ruin today. She has a way of ruining everything. Besides, *she doesn't even know how to fish!*"

"I do, too!" Maggie yapped, barging out of their house wearing a dress, yellow sandals, and holding a Barbie fishing rod.

Ugh! Who goes fishing in a dress, and with a Barbie fishing rod?

She combed her fingers through her stringy blond hair and flared her gigantic nose. "I bet I catch more fish than both Calvin and Brooks could ever catch! Not you, Jamie. I bet you're good at fishing." She gave him a smile that made me gag. She had the ugliest smile.

Jamie grinned back. "I bet you ain't so bad, either, Maggie."

Insert eye roll here. Jamie always did that—made super nice with Maggie because he knew it annoyed me. I knew there was no way he liked her at all, because she was so unlikeable.

"Are you boys gonna sit here all day, or are we going to get walking down to the creek?" Mr. Riley asked, coming out of the house carrying his tackle box and fishing rod. "Let's get a move on."

We all started walking down the road—well, the guys walked. Maggie skipped, and twirled, and sang more pop songs than anyone should've had to hear. I swear, if I had to watch her do the Macarena one more time, I'd go crazy. Once we reached the woods, I imagined us dudes climbing onto Mr. Riley's boat, and Maggie somehow getting left behind.

What a perfect daydream.

"We're gonna need some bait," Mr. Riley said, pulling out a small digging shovel and his metal pail. "Whose turn is it?"

"Brooks," Calvin said, pointing toward me. Each time we went fishing, one person was in charge of going digging through the dirt in the woods to collect some worms. I grabbed the shovel and pail and didn't complain. Truth was, digging for the worms was one of my favorite parts of fishing.

"I think Maggie should go with him." Jamie smirked, winking at Maggie. Her face lit up with hope, and I was seconds away from knocking my brother over the head.

"No. I'm good. I can do it myself."

"I can go, though." Maggie grinned ear to ear.

Such an ugly smile!

"Daddy, can I go with Brooks?"

My eyes darted to Mr. Riley, and I knew I was doomed, because Mr. Riley suffered heavily from DS—daughter syndrome. I'd never once seen him say no to Maggie, and I doubted he had any plans to start that afternoon.

"Sure, darling. You two have fun." He smiled. "We're gonna get the boat set up, and once you're both back, we'll get out on the water."

Before we headed out into the woods, I made sure to give Jamie a hard slug in the arm. He slugged me harder, making Maggie laugh. As she and I headed into the woods, I put in the earbuds attached to my MP3 player and hurried my pace, hoping to lose her, but her skips and twirls were surprisingly fast.

"So, have you found a tie yet?" she asked.

I rolled my eyes. Even with my music playing, I could still hear her loud mouth. "I'm not marrying you."

She giggled. "We're getting married in two days, Brooks. Don't be silly. I'm guessing Calvin is your best man, or will it be Jamie? Cheryl is going to be my maid of honor. Hey, you think I can listen to some of your music? Calvin said you have some of the best music ever, and I think I should know what kind of music you listen to if we're getting married."

"We aren't, and you're never gonna touch my MP3 player."

She giggled as if I had told a funny joke.

I started digging around in the dirt, and she swung on tree branches. "Are you going to help me dig or what?"

"I'm not touching a worm."

"Then why did you even come out here?"

"So we could finish planning together, duh. Plus, I was hoping we could go look at the cabin not far from here. It could be our house, if you wanted it to. We could fix it up for us, Skippy, and Jam. Ain't nobody living there, anyway. It's big enough for our family."

This girl was a lunatic.

As I kept digging, she kept talking. The quicker I dug, the faster she spoke about girly crap I didn't care about—shoes, makeup, first dances, wedding cakes, decorations. She even talked about how the abandoned cabin could be used to put the food inside for a reception. The list went on and on. I considered ditching the shovel and pail and running for my life—it was pretty clear that Maggie was out to kill me. When she mentioned the naming of our first child, I knew things had gone too far.

"Listen!" I shouted, knocking over the pail with the few worms I had found. They wiggled around, trying to find their way back into the dirt, and I didn't even care. I puffed out my chest and shuffled my feet in her direction. My fists thrust in the air, and I screamed straight into her face. "We are not getting married! Not today, not tomorrow, not ever! You disgust me, and I was only nice to you in the last letter because Jamie said if I wrote you any meaner letters, he'd tell my parents and I'd get in trouble. Okay? So just shut up already with all this wedding talk."

Our faces were inches apart. Her fingers were clasped behind her back, and I saw the small tremble in her bottom lip. Maggie narrowed her eyes, studying me, as if trying to decipher the clear-as-day words I had just delivered to her. For a second she frowned, but then she found that ugly smile again. Before I could roll my eyes, she leaned in toward me, grabbed my cheeks with both of her hands, and pulled me closer to her.

"What are you doing?" I asked with smooshed cheeks.

"I'm going to kiss you, Brooks, because we have to work on our first kiss before doing it in front of our family and friends."

"You definitely aren't going to kiss—" I paused and my heart thudded. Maggie placed her lips against mine and pulled me in closer to her. Without hesitation, I yanked away from her. I wanted to say something, but speaking seemed hard, so I stared, awkwardly and uncomfortably.

"We should try again," she said, nodding to herself.

"No! Do not kiss—" Again, she kissed me. I felt my whole body heating up, with…anger? Or maybe confusion? No. Anger. Definitely anger. *Or maybe…*

"Will you stop that?" I hollered, ripping myself away again and stepping backward. "You can't go around kissin' people who don't want to be kissed!"

Her eyes grew heavy and her cheeks reddened. "You don't want to kiss me?"

"No! I don't. I don't want nothin' to do with you, Maggie May Riley! I don't want to be your neighbor anymore. I don't want to be your friend. I don't want to marry you, and I most certainly don't want to kiss—" I was cut off again, but this time by myself. Somehow, during my rant, I had stepped closer and closer to her, and my lips stole her next breath. I placed my hands against her cheeks and smooshed them together, kissing her hard for a whole ten seconds. I counted each second, too. When we pulled away, we both stood still.

"You kissed me," she whispered.

"It was a mistake," I replied.

"A good mistake?"

"A bad mistake."

"Oh."

"Yeah."

"Brooks?"

"Maggie?"

"Can we have one more bad mistake kiss?"

I kicked my shoe around in the grass and rubbed the back of my neck. "It won't mean I'm going to marry you."

"Okay."

I cocked an eyebrow. "I mean it. It will just be ten seconds and that's it. We'll never kiss again. *Ever.*"

"Okay," she replied, nodding.

I stepped in closer, and we both smooshed each other's faces. When we kissed, I closed my eyes, and I counted to ten.

I counted slowly, as slow as the worms moved.

1...

1.3...

1.5…

2…

"Brooks?" was muttered into my mouth, and my eyes opened to find Maggie staring my way.

"Yes?" I asked, our hands still smashed against each other's cheeks.

"We can stop kissing now. I'd already counted to ten five times."

I stepped back, embarrassed. "Whatever. We need to get back to the boat, anyway." I hurried to try to recollect the worms, failing terribly, and out of the corner of my eye, I saw Maggie swaying in her dress, humming away.

"Hey, Brooks. I know I said you could wear the mud-colored tie for the wedding, but I think you'd look better in a green one. Bring the tie for our rehearsal tomorrow. Meet me right here at seven." Her lips curved up, and I couldn't help but wonder what had changed about her in that moment.

Her smile didn't look completely ugly anymore.

As she started off, I stood quickly, knocking over the worms again. "Hey, Maggie?"

She swung away on her heels. "Yes?"

"Can we maybe try the kissing thing one more time?"

She blushed and smiled, and it was beautiful. "For how long?"

"I don't know…" I stuffed my hands into my pockets and shrugged, looking down at the grass as a worm wiggled across my shoestring. "Maybe just for ten more seconds."

3

Maggie

I loved Brooks Tyler.

I wished there were a bigger word to describe my feelings for the handsome, rude boy who had been kissing me lately, but love seemed to be the only thing that came to mind whenever he stood near me.

As I lay on my bed, thinking and thinking about our last ten-second kiss, I heard a loud, "You have to be kidding me!" from Cheryl.

I wasn't certain what was howling more, the wind outside or Cheryl. "I don't know how to be a maid of honor!" Cheryl whined as she plopped down next to me. Her curly red hair bobbed up and down as she bounced on my mattress. Cheryl had been my best friend since I'd moved in with her family, on top of being my stepsister. Therefore, she had to be my maid of honor.

"You don't have to do anything, really, except everything I don't want to do, and when I'm stressed over wedding planning, you're the girl I get to yell at nonstop. Oh, and you have to hold the back of my dress while I walk down the aisle."

"Why do I have to hold your dress?'

I shrugged. "I don't know, but my aunt's maid of honor held hers, so I think that's just part of getting married." In the middle of my bedroom floor I'd set up the whole layout of the wedding ceremony with my Barbie dolls, stuffed animals, and My Little Pony toys. Ken was standing in for Brooks in the position of groom, and Barbie was standing in for me.

"How'd you even get a boyfriend, anyway?" Cheryl asked, still bouncing.

"*Fiancé*," I corrected. "And it's pretty easy really. I'm sure you could get one. You just twirl your hair and write a letter telling him he's going to marry you."

"Really?" Cheryl's voice heightened. "That's all it takes?"

I nodded. "That's it."

"Wow." She sighed, sounding a bit amazed. I didn't know why, though. Boys were pretty easy to get. Mama said it was the gettin' rid of them that was the trouble. "How do you know all of this?"

"Mama told me."

She pouted. "Why didn't she tell me? I'm her daughter, too. Plus, she was *my* mom first."

"You're probably just too young. She'll probably tell you next year or something."

"I don't want to wait a year." Cheryl stopped her bouncing and started twirling her hair. "I need a pen and paper. Or, well…are you sure Brooks wouldn't want to marry me, too?"

My hands slammed against my hips, and I cocked an eyebrow. "What's that supposed to mean?"

She kept twirling. "I'm just saying. I've seen him smile at me a lot."

Oh. My. Gosh.

My sister was a tramp. Mama said I wasn't allowed to say that word, but I had heard her call her sister it once for going after a married man, and Aunt Mary hadn't been happy about it. Cheryl was pretty much trying to do the same thing.

"He's friendly. He smiles at everyone. I saw him smile at a squirrel once."

"You're comparing the smiles he gives me to the smiles he gives squirrels?" she asked, her voice heightened. I hesitated for a moment, thinking on it. Cheryl and squirrels had a few things in common. For example, squirrels liked nuts, and Cheryl was completely nuts if she thought for a second Brooks would like her before me.

Cheryl stood up and huffed, still twirling her hair. "You took too long to answer! Wait until I tell Ma what you said! I could get any boyfriend I wanted, Maggie May, and you ain't gonna tell me no different!"

"I don't care. You just can't have my fiancé."

"I could!"

"Couldn't!"

"Could!"

"Shut up and stop twirling your stupid hair!" I screamed.

She gasped, teared up, and whined, storming off. "I'm not coming to your wedding!"

"You aren't even invited!" I hollered back her way.

It only took a few minutes before Mama walked into my room with narrowed eyes. "You girls had another fight, huh?"

I shrugged. "She was just being dramatic again."

"For two best friends, you sure get annoyed with one another quite often."

"Yeah, well, that's kind of what girls do."

She smiled and agreed completely. "Well, just remember, she's younger than you, Maggie, and Cheryl doesn't have it as easy as you do. She's a bit of a loner and an oddball, and doesn't quite fit in. You're her only true friend and her sister. She's family, and what does family do?"

"Look out for each other?"

Mama nodded and kissed my forehead. "That's right. We look out for each other, even on the tough days." Whenever Cheryl and I got into fights, Mama always said that to me. *Family looks out for each other.* Especially on the tough days when it was hard to even look *at* each other.

I remembered the first time she had said it, too. She and Daddy had sat Calvin, Cheryl, and me down in the living room and told us all it was okay to call them Mama and Dad if we wanted to. It was the night of their wedding, and we were officially a family. As we sat there, Mama and Daddy had us pile our hands on top of one another and make a promise to always look out for each other. *Because that's what families do.*

"I'll apologize," I whispered to myself, talking about Cheryl. She was, after all, my best friend.

I spent the rest of the afternoon planning the wedding. I'd been dreaming of my wedding since I was seven years old, so a super long time. I wondered what kind of music Brooks liked. Since he wouldn't let me listen, I had to guess on my own. He and Calvin had been messing around with Daddy's guitars a bit each night and said they were going to be famous musicians someday. I didn't much believe them at first, but the more they practiced each night, the better they got. Maybe they could play at the wedding. Also, maybe I'd pick his favorite song to walk down the aisle to. Then again, he and my brother had been singing "Sexy Back" by Justin Timberlake for the past week, and that didn't seem wedding-y enough for me.

Maybe for our first dance, though.

Each night after Mama and Daddy put us all to bed, I'd hear music playing downstairs in the living room. It was the same song every single time: Sam Cooke's "You Send Me"—their first dance song. Tiptoeing out of my room, I went to the top of the staircase and looked downstairs. The lights were dimmed, Daddy took Mama's hand and asked her a question. "Dance with me?" he asked her every night before they started to dance. Daddy was spinning Mama around in circles, both of them giggling like they were kids. Mama had a glass of wine in her hand, and as Daddy swayed her, the wine flew from the glass and onto the white carpet. They giggled even more at the mess and pulled each other closer. Mama's head rested against Daddy's chest as he whispered into her ear, and they danced so slow.

That's what true love meant to me.

True love meant you could laugh at mistakes.

True love meant you could whisper secrets.

True love meant you never had to dance alone.

The next morning, I woke ready for the day ahead of me. "Today is the rehearsal for my wedding day!" I shouted, stretching my arms out and jumping up and down on my bed. "It's my rehearsal! It's my rehearsal day!"

Calvin stumbled into my bedroom, rubbing his hands over his sleepy eyes. "Gosh, Maggie, can you shut it? It's three in the morning," he griped, yawning.

I smirked. "It doesn't matter, because it's my rehearsal day, Calvin!"

He grumbled some more and called me a name, but I didn't care.

Daddy stumbled into my room almost exactly how my brother had, rubbing his eyes and yawning. He walked over to my bed, and I wrapped my arms around his neck, forcing him to hold me up in the air.

"Daddy, guess what? Guess what?" I shrieked with excitement.

"Let me guess, you're having your wedding rehearsal today?"

I nodded quickly and laughed as he tiredly spun me around in a circle. "How did you know?"

He smirked. "Lucky guess."

"Can you make her stop yelling so we can go back to bed?" Calvin groaned. "It's not even a real wedding!"

I gasped and went to sass him for his lies, but Daddy stopped me, whispering, "Someone's not a morning person. How about we all go back to bed for a few hours, and then I'll cook you a day-before-wedding-day breakfast?"

"Waffles with strawberries and whipped cream?"

"And sprinkles!" He smiled.

Calvin stomped his grumpy butt back to his room, and Daddy laid me back down on my bed, giving me Eskimo kisses. "Try to get a few more hours of sleep, okay, honey? You have a big day ahead of you." He tucked me in, the same way he did each and every night.

"Okay."

"And, Maggie May?"

"Yes?"

"The world keeps spinning because your heartbeats exist." He'd said those words to me every single day, as long as I could remember.

When he left the room, he shut the light off, and I lay in bed, staring up at the glow-in-the-dark star stickers on my ceiling, smiling wide with my hands over my chest, where I felt each and every one of my heartbeats that kept the world spinning.

I knew I was supposed to be sleeping, but I couldn't, because it was the day before my wedding day, and I was about to marry a boy who didn't know it yet, but was going to be my best friend once we made it to our ten-year anniversary.

He'd probably need those ten years to realize he did indeed want to be my husband.

And we'd obviously live happily ever after.

When morning came, I was the first one up, waiting downstairs for my waffles. Daddy and Mama were still sleeping when I creeped into their bedroom.

"Hey, you guys awake?" I whispered. Nothing. Poking Daddy in the cheek, I repeated myself. "Hey, you awake, Daddy?"

"Maggie May, it's not time to get up yet," he murmured.

"But, you said you'd make waffles!" I whined.

"In the morning."

"It is morning," I groaned and walked over to their windows, pulling back the drapes. "See? The sun is out."

"The sun is a liar, that's why God created curtains," Mama yawned, rolling on her side. She opened her eyes and glanced at the clock on her nightstand. "Five-thirty a.m. on a Saturday is not the morning, Maggie May. Now get back to bed, and we'll come wake you up."

They didn't wake me until eight in the morning—but surprisingly I was already up. The day went slower than I wanted it to, and my parents made me go watch Cheryl's dance recital, which lasted longer than it should've, but once we got home, I was ready to head out to Brooks.

Mama told me I could only go off to play if I took Cheryl with me, but even after I apologized to her, she still didn't want to be my maid of honor, so I had to sneak off on my own to go meet Brooks in the woods. I skipped down the streets of the neighborhood, taking in the perfectly mowed lawns and perfectly planted flowers. Harper County was a small town where everyone knew everyone, so it wouldn't be long before Mama got a call saying so-and-so saw me skipping down the street alone. Therefore, I had to be quick.

Just not *too* quick, because I always had to stop on the corner of my block, look both ways down the road, then cross the street to Mrs. Boone's house. Mrs. Boone's lawn was the complete opposite of everyone else's. She had flowers growing everywhere, with no kind of order at all. Yellow roses, lavender, poppies—you named a flower, and it was probably growing in Mrs. Boone's yard.

Nobody ever bothered stopping by the old lady's house. Everyone called her rude, grumpy, and standoffish. Mostly she sat alone on her front porch, swaying back and forth in her rocker, mumbling to herself as her cat, Muffins, rolled around in the yard.

My favorite time of the day was when Mrs. Boone went inside to make herself some tea. She drank more tea than anyone I'd ever seen. One day Cheryl and I watched her from across the street and were blown away by the number of times Mrs. Boone left her rocker and came back with a cup of tea.

Whenever she disappeared into the house, I'd sneak into her front yard, which was guarded by a white picket fence. I'd smell as many flowers as possible then roll around in the high grass with Muffins.

That night, I hurried into her yard, because I didn't have much time before I had to meet Brooks.

"Hey! Eric's girl! Get off my lawn!" Mrs. Boone hissed, pushing open her screen door with a cup of tea. I'd told her my name hundreds of times, but she refused to ever acknowledge it.

"Maggie," I said, standing up and holding a purring Muffins in my hands. "My name is Maggie, Mrs. Boone. *Maggie.*" I said it slow and loud the second time, to make sure she understood.

"Oh, I know who you are, you little rascal! Now get away from my flowers and my cat!"

I ignored her. "Gee, Mrs. B, you got the prettiest flowers I've ever seen in your yard. Did you know that? My name's Maggie, again, just in case you forgot it. You can call me Maggie May if ya want. A lot of my family calls me that. Speaking of family and flowers, I thought I might ask…do you think I can borrow some of your flowers for my wedding tomorrow?"

"Wedding?" she huffed, narrowing her eyes, which were covered in too much makeup. Mama always said less was more. Mrs. Boone obviously said the opposite of that. "Aren't you a bit young to be getting married?"

"Love knows no age, Mrs. B." I reached for a poppy, picked it, and placed it behind my ear as Muffins leaped out of my arms.

"Pick one more flower and you'll never be able to pick another thing in your life," she warned, giving me a grumpy frown.

"I'll even toss in some ice cream for the flowers, Mrs. B! I can pick them all now, so you won't have to worry about—"

"Leave!" she shouted, her voice sending chills down my spine. I stood up straight, my eyes wide with panic and stepped backward.

"Okay. Well, if you change your mind, I'll be passing by tomorrow, too, before the wedding. You can even come if you want. It will be between the two twisty trees in the woods at five tomorrow night. Mama's making cake, and Dad's making punch. You can bring Muffins, too! Bye, Mrs. B! See you tomorrow!"

She grumbled some more as I hurried out of her yard, picking two yellow roses to take with me. I skipped along and waved goodbye to the grumpy lady who probably wasn't really grumpy, but just liked to live up to the rumors her neighbors made up.

The closer I got to the twisted trees, the more my heartbeat increased. Each breath was filled with more and more urgency, more and more thrill. Each step was a step closer to Brooks. *It's happening.* It was finally coming true. I was going to get what Daddy and Mama had. I was going to be his, and he was going to be mine.

This time is forever.

He was late.

I knew he had clocks in his house, and I knew he was capable of telling time, yet still, Brooks was late.

How could we live happily ever after if he didn't show up on time?

My eyes glanced at my Barbie watch, and my chest tightened.

7:16 p.m.

He was late. I'd told him seven, and he was sixteen minutes late.

Where was he? Was he standing me up? *No, he wouldn't.*

Did he not love me the way I loved him? *No, he did.*

My heart hurt as I walked through the woods, searching the forest for a dumb boy with beautiful eyes. "He's just by the wrong two twisty trees," I assured myself, listening to the crunching leaves under my steps. "He's coming," I swore, watching the bright sky grow darker and darker.

I was never allowed to be out past the streetlights turning on, but I knew it'd be okay, because I was getting married the next day, and I wouldn't be alone in the darkness, because Brooks was coming to join me.

7:32 p.m.

Which direction had I come from? And where had the two twisty trees gone? My heart was beating faster and my palms were sweaty as I stomped through the forest. "Brooks," I shouted, more nervous because I'd lost my way. He'd find me, though. *He's coming.* I kept walking. Was I going deeper into the forest? Farther from the trees? How could I tell? I couldn't find my way. Where were the trees?

7:59 p.m.

The water.

I'd find the water where the boys went fishing. Maybe that's where Brooks would be. But which way was the water? I started running. I ran and ran, hoping I'd see the water swaying back and forth, reminding me of where I was and how I'd get home, or how I'd find Brooks. Maybe he had gotten lost, too. Maybe he was alone, and scared, and sweaty. Maybe he was searching for me, too. I had to find him, because I knew I'd be okay when we were standing near one another.

8:13 p.m.

The water.

I found it.

I found the ripples, and stones, and calm sounds.

I found the water, and I found him.

"Don't walk away, please, Julia. Listen to me."

Brooks?

No.

Not him.

Someone else, who wasn't alone. A man was there with another.

A woman. She kept telling him no, saying she couldn't be with him anymore, and he didn't like that.

"We have a life together, Julia. We have a family."

"Will you listen? I don't want to be with you anymore."

"Is this about that guy from work?"

The woman rolled her eyes. "Don't start this again. This is what I'm talking about. You have all these anger issues. I can't keep our son around that. We can't keep doing this."

He raked his hands through his hair. "You're fucking him, aren't you? You're fucking the guy from work." Before she could respond, he grew more and more upset, his chest puffing in and out.

The man was someone who made my breaths harder to swallow, and my fear more fearful. I had been less afraid when I'd stood alone by the wrong twisty trees. I should've stayed by the wrong trees.

He screamed at her, his voice cracking. "You fucking whore!" he shouted, slapping her hard across the face. She stumbled backward and whimpered, her hand flying to her cheek. "I gave you everything. We had a life together. I just took over the business. We were getting on our feet. What about our son? What about our family?" He slapped her again and again. "We had a life!" He shoved her to the ground and his eyes popped out of his head, as if he was crazy—disturbed.

My throat tightened as my eyes stared across the way, where the man who reminded me of the dark sky wrapped his hands around the woman's neck. "You can't leave me," he said, almost begging her as he choked and shook her. She screamed, clawing at his hands. He shook her. She screamed, trying to gasp for air. He shook her. She screamed, and I felt his hands.

It felt as if his hands were around me. Choking me. Shaking me. Dragging me.

My fingers wrapped around my neck and I begged for air, knowing that if I felt like I couldn't breathe, the woman was hurting even more.

Then the evil man started dragging her body toward the water.

In that moment I knew who he was.

The devil.

The devil pulled the woman's body toward the water and shoved her head beneath its waves.

And I stopped breathing.

He drowned her.

He drowned her.

The devil drowned a woman on the bank of Harper Creek.

I knew she was dead. She fought back as the devil kept holding her head beneath the water. The devil held her at the edge of the lake and kept shoving her head under the water.

The woman fought at first, clawing her fingers at him, trying her best to attack the devil. The woman's body pushed against his, but each time the devil brought the woman's head back from under the lake, her mouth inhaled and exhaled, choking on water, struggling to breathe. The devil pulled her deeper into the waters, splashing loudly. The water was up to the devil's neck, and I couldn't even see the woman anymore.

"Don't leave me," he begged her, pleaded. "Don't leave me, Julia."

I should've stopped looking.

I couldn't stop looking.

She was fully submerged, and all I saw was the devil's darkness.

He pulled the limp woman from the water, back to the shore, and he wouldn't stop talking to her. "How could you? How could you do this to us?" He reached for the woman's left hand and removed the wedding band from her finger. He slid it onto his own finger.

He killed the woman.

He killed her.

I saw it, too—the realization of his actions, him realizing what he had done. He started to shake the woman, her body limp. "Julia," he whimpered. "Julia, wake up." He fell to the ground beside her and shook her, trying to bring her back, but he couldn't. He sobbed over her body. "Please, come back."

I stepped backward and broke a branch.

He looked up.

He killed that woman, and he was looking at me.

Don't look at me.

My hands clamped up, my mind spun. I stumbled backward, breaking each and every branch my flip-flops hit along the way. My back slammed against the closest tree trunk as the devil's chocolate brown eyes danced across my body. A petrified look swam in his eyes, and he dropped the lady. "Hey!" he shouted, looking at me. "Hey, what are you doing?" He moved in closer to me.

His feet dragged my way, his clothing dripping wet.

Don't wander off on your own, Maggie May. Do you understand? You mustn't wander off without your sister.

Mama's words kept circling in my mind. He grew closer and closer, and I screeched, turning away from him. I started running as fast as I could, flying through the branches, feeling my heart pounding against my chest.

His footsteps grew louder, but I couldn't look back. He was running after me. Closer, closer, closer. *Run, Maggie.* Faster, faster, faster. *Run!*

A sharp yank to my dress sent me backward, the poppy in my hair flying to the forest floor. His fingers were wrapped around my dress and he tossed me to the ground. My breaths weaved in and out and I screamed as he tackled my body, placing all of his weight on top of me, his filthy hands covering my mouth, muting my shouts.

I kicked and screamed, screamed and kicked. He was going to kill me.

He'd kill me.

No, please.

Tears streamed down my cheeks as I struggled.

"You weren't supposed to be here," he hissed, starting to sob. "You weren't supposed to see that. It was a mistake. I didn't mean to..."

No!

He placed a hand around my neck, choking me, making it harder and harder to breathe. He cried. He cried so much. He cried and apologized. He apologized for hurting me, apologized for pushing a few fingers into the side of my neck, making it harder and harder for me to find my next breaths. He told me he loved her, told me love did it to him, to her. He swore he'd never hurt her. He promised he wouldn't hurt the woman he already killed.

"You weren't supposed to be here, but now you are," he said, lowering his face down to me. "I'm sorry. I'm sorry." He smelled like tobacco and licorice, and his forearm had a big tattoo of two praying hands with a person's name beneath it. "How did you get here?" he asked.

His mouth was inches away from mine, and he shook his head as I parted my mouth to scream for Brooks, praying for him to hear me, to find me. He placed his finger against my mouth, then pushed his lips against his fingers, too, and made a quiet shushing sound.

"Shh," he whispered. My eyes were wide with fear. "Please, don't yell. It was an accident." He moved his lips to my forehead and pressed his mouth against my skin. "Shh," he said again. His lips traveled to my earlobe and I felt his mouth touching me before he hissed one last time. "Shh..."

I lost myself.

He stole me from myself in that moment.

I felt dirty.

I felt used.

I felt trapped.

"Maggie May! Where are you?" Brooks hollered, his voice breaking the devil from his thoughts.

He pushed himself away from me and took off in a sprint.

I stumbled to stand and didn't bother to dusk off the dirt, leaves, and sticks tangled all over me. I was wet. His wet clothes had soaked me, and I had wet myself, too. I struggled, but I ran. I ran. I ran as fast as I could toward the sound of Brooks' voice. The louder his sounds grew, the more my heart raced.

"I mean, geez, Maggie! I went with the stupid purple tie because you were so against the mud tie, and then you stand me up! I can't believe this!"

When my eyes saw his back, he was kicking around the grass and muttering to himself.

Brooks.

When he turned to face me, any irritation he felt disappeared and was replaced with heavy intense concern. As I ran toward him, I tripped over my own feet and his arms reached out, catching me.

"Whoa, Maggie, what's going on?"

I opened my mouth to speak, but all I heard in my head was the sound of the devil shushing me, pressing his skin against my skin, pressing his finger against my lips. Against my forehead. Against my earlobes. Against me. *He was going to kill me.*

There was a rustling behind us and I jumped, my eyes wide as I pushed myself against Brooks hard, clamoring for protection.

"Maggie, it's fine. It's just a squirrel. What freaked you out? What happened to you?" No words could leave me. My fingers grasped Brooks' shirt, pulling him closer to me. He didn't ask any questions, but he did hold me tight. "It's okay, Maggie. You're okay."

I sobbed into his t-shirt, and he just held on tighter.

Maggie

I blinked.

The lights were already bright, and the nurse kept shining her flashlight into my eyes. Into my nose. Into my ears. Into my mouth.

I blinked.

Daddy had tears in his eyes, but they weren't falling. He leaned against the wall, his hand in a fist, his fist resting against his mouth, his mouth speaking no words.

Blink.

Mama cried when the nurse mentioned an SAK. I didn't know what it was, but it made Mama sob.

Blink.

The nurse swabbed me all over. My lips, my cheeks, my thighs, my…

Blink.

She combed through my hair. Leaves fell out. She found blood. Daddy began to cry softly.

Blink.

She cut my dress and shook it out. There was dirt. My dress was dirty. I was dirty. Everywhere. My poppy was gone. Where had my poppy flower gone? She picked at my nails. My nail polish was ruined. My nails were ruined. I was ruined.

Blink.

They carried me to the car. I crawled into a ball. The streetlights flashed reds and greens. The yellows blurred. I saw his face in my mind.

Blink.

Calvin and Cheryl were on the porch when I got home. They didn't speak. I didn't either.

Blink.

Mama and Daddy took me to their bedroom, and I cried into their sheets, shaking, feeling dirty, broken, used. Scared. So scared.

Shh…

Shh…

Did the nurse get it? Did she get his taste on my lips? Did she get his skin on my skin? Did she…?

Blink.

I shut my eyes. I didn't want to feel. I didn't want to be. I didn't want to blink anymore. I kept my eyes closed. I didn't want to see, but, I still saw. I saw him. I felt him. I tasted him.

Everything grew darker.

Everything became shadows.

Everything went black.

Maggie

Mama kept pacing around her and Daddy's bedroom, twisting her hands. I sat on the edge of their mattress, listening to her high heels tap against the hardwood floor. The bed felt like sitting on a pile of a million feathers, and it was almost impossible to not melt into the softness. I felt tired, too, so it was a bad combination. My eyes fought to stay open, though lately dreams seemed better than staying awake. The only problem with dreams was that sometimes they became nightmares, and nightmares were what I'd been drowning in lately.

"You haven't spoken in days, Maggie May," Mama scolded. "Not one single word. Your father and I are terrified." Her butterscotch-colored hair hung past her shoulders, and she kept combing it behind her ears. When she wasn't moving her hair, her manicured nails danced against her forearms, digging into her skin. Worry attacked her spirit as she kept a quick pace. I wished Daddy were home and not off at work. He was normally able to keep Mama from having her panics.

"What happened out there, Maggie?" she asked. "What were you doing out in those woods? Your father and I told you… We asked you not to wander off."

My fingers dug into the side of the mattress and my head stayed lowered.

"It was past your curfew," she whispered, a tremble in her voice. "And I begged you to be home when the streetlights came on, didn't I?" She began to stutter, which was weird because Mama was always so composed and well-spoken. "I to-told you yo-you shouldn't be out at night, Maggie May."

My lips parted to speak again, but no words came out. Mama turned my way and bit her bottom lip. Her arms crossed and she tucked her hands beneath her underarms before walking in my direction. I broke my stare away from her. "Look at me, Maggie," she ordered.

I shook my head.

A few tears fell down my cheeks and my body shook.

"Maggie May, when I tell you to look at me, you must listen!" Her voice was laced with panic, almost as if she was fearful that her little girl was gone and would never come back.

Maybe I won't. Maybe I'd fallen so deep into the back of my mind that I'd never have to remember what it was like to feel, to hurt, to break, to breathe. My eyes hurt from being awake for so long, but that hurt was nowhere near the ache in my chest. In my ears, I could still hear the screams of the person being attacked. In my head, I could still see her fighting for her life, and in my heart, I could still feel the monster against my soul.

A few tears fell down my cheeks and my body shook.

"Oh, honey," Mama cried. Her fingers slipped beneath my chin and she tilted my head up. "Word by word, tell me what happened. What happened to you in those woods?"

Out of the corner of my eye I saw Calvin and Brooks in the hallway, listening in on the conversation between Mama and me. They were leaning against the wall, staring at us. Brooks' eyes looked sadder than I thought eyes could've ever looked. Calvin's fingers were folded tightly into fists, which he tapped repeatedly against the wall behind him. Mama followed my stare, and when she saw the boys, they hurried away. I was certain they hadn't gone far, though. Those two boys hadn't left my side for the past few days.

Cheryl was the opposite, though. She seemed afraid to come near me. She acted as if I had some kind of disease and she'd catch it if she looked my way. I had heard her crying the other night because she had to miss her dance recital. It was my fault, because our parents didn't want to leave my side.

"Maggie May," Mama whispered.

I turned my head away from her, and she sighed once more.

"Please, Maggie. Speak. I don't know how to help you if you won't tell me what happened." She kept begging and begging me to say something to her, but I couldn't. My throat was dry. I needed ice water, maybe. I needed something to loosen me up, something to make words fly from between my lips, but I couldn't move. "I don't understand! I don't understand why you won't speak to me. You need to tell me, baby, because my mind is thinking the worst things. Did someone hurt you? Did someone…" She couldn't say the words, but I knew what she was asking me. "You just tell me what happened, even if someone hurt you, honey. I won't judge you, I swear. Mama just wants to know if someone hurt you." She swallowed hard. "You can nod your head if someone hurt you, honey. You can tell me," she whispered. "Remember when we spoke about being safe? And how people weren't allowed to touch you, and if they did, you'd have to tell your father and me? Did that happen? I mean, I know the doctors checked, but those tests…they take time. Did somebody…" Her words faltered once more.

I lowered my head. The stranger hadn't physically raped me, and I knew that was what she was asking. Even so, truth be told, he had raped me in almost every other way possible. He had raped my innocence.

My youth.

My voice.

He had stolen so much of me away when I'd witnessed his act of horror and when he'd tried to end me. He had stolen so much of my soul.

I shook my head no for Mama, though. He hadn't physically raped me.

Mama let out a sigh of relief before she broke down into uncontrollable sobs. Her hands covered her face as she violently shook, and her words were tough to understand. "Why won't you speak?" she asked.

Because I have nothing left to say.

"I think that's enough for now, Katie," a voice said.

I looked up to see Daddy standing in the doorway, staring at Mama and me. He must've come home early from work to take care of her. Mama always did better when he was around.

She walked over to him, and within seconds, Daddy's arms were wrapped around her tiny frame. He whispered something into her ear, and it seemed to be the right words, because Mama's crying came to a halt, and she nodded in agreement with Daddy's soft voice.

After a few minutes, she said she needed air and headed out of the room.

Daddy stepped over to me, kneeled down, and gave me his best crooked smile. "Maggie May?"

Yes, Daddy?

"The world keeps spinning because your heartbeats exist," he promised. His nose brushed against mine, giving me his Eskimo kisses. "And everything's gonna be okay. You know why?"

I shook my head, and he continued.

"Because none of us are ever alone. You've got a family that loves you and will be there for you always. Okay, sport?"

Okay, Daddy.

He smiled as if he heard the words I didn't say. "How about we go out for some frozen yogurt later tonight? I think it will be good for us to get out and about. What do you say?"

Yes.

He smiled wider, as if he understood me again.

Maybe parents always knew the things their kids were thinking. Maybe it was some kind of sixth sense. I was thankful for Daddy's superpowers.

He went off to check on Mama, and I stayed in their room, sitting against the mattress made of feathers, and I began to allow myself to sink into the softness. I lay back, my legs dangling from the edge of the bed, and I closed my eyes. Lately my ears were more aware of every noise that came near me, from the wind slapping against the apple trees in the backyard, to the fly buzzing around in the bathroom down the hall.

My eyes shot open before words even left Brooks' mouth. I heard his soft footsteps coming my way. Calvin's steps were always heavy, as if he put his full weight into every step, but Brooks' were much more gentle, almost as if he tiptoed across the floors. I wondered if his steps were always like that, or if he had adopted the gentle movements the past few days. I would've been lying if I'd said I'd ever noticed the sounds of his footsteps before. I wondered how many things people missed when they were busy talking too much.

"Are you okay, Maggie?" he asked, standing in the doorway. I didn't sit up, but my head tilted in his direction. When we met one another's stare, his chest caved and his shoulders rounded. His hands were stuffed tightly into his jeans. "Calvin and your pops are outside checking on your mom. She asked me to go home, and I told her I would, but I couldn't without stopping by to see you, to see if there's anything I can do."

I shrugged. He frowned.

"Can I come in?" he questioned.

I nodded. He frowned some more.

Brooks sat on the bed before lowering himself down to lie beside me. My head was still tilted toward him, and his was now facing me. "Your mom said you're not speaking. She said you have nothin' to say, but I think that's a lie. I think you have a lot to say, but you don't know how to say it."

A single tear fell down my cheek, and I turned in the other direction to avoid him seeing me cry. He still witnessed the single tear. I kept the rest running down my face to myself and Mama's pillow.

He quietly spoke. "It's my fault, you know. I was supposed to meet you in the woods for our rehearsal, but I was wastin' too much time trying to pick out a tie you'd like. I know you probably thought I was standing you up, but I wasn't, Maggie May. I swear I was gonna come meet you, and when I got out there, you weren't anywhere to be found. I'm so sorry."

More tears fell from my eyes as I listened to Brooks sniffle.

He continued talking. "I'm just so sorry. I'm sorry, I'm sorry…"

We stayed there for a few more minutes. Tears kept falling from my eyes, and he didn't try to convince me to stop crying. It might've been my imagination, but I thought Brooks cried right beside me for a little bit.

"Who's up for some ice cream?" Daddy said, barging into his bedroom, the room Brooks and I hadn't left. I didn't know when it had happened, but at some point, Brooks and I had started holding hands, and I hadn't found the power to pull away from his grip yet.

We both sat up, and Brooks quickly pulled his hand from mine. "I'd love some ice cream!" he bellowed.

Mama came and frowned behind Daddy. "Brooks, you haven't been home in a while. Maybe you should head back. We probably need a bit of family time alone if that's all right." She didn't mean to be rude, but I could tell Brooks' feelings were a little hurt by the way he smiled.

Most people probably thought it was a normal smile, but I knew it was the smile he gave when he was a bit embarrassed.

"Sure, Mrs. Riley. Sorry. I'll get going." He turned to me and gave me a lopsided grin. "You okay today, Maggie May?" Since the incident, he'd been asking me that each day. I nodded slowly.

I'm okay, Brooks.

He stood up from the bed and started to walk out of the bedroom, but Daddy cleared his throat. "I think it might be okay for Brooks to join us for a bit of ice cream."

"Eric," Mama protested, but Daddy placed a comforting hand on her shoulder.

"That is, only if Maggie thinks it's okay," he finished, looking at me.

Brooks' eyes shot up to me, filled with hope, and there was no way I could say no to him. He listened to my silence, after all. After I agreed, we all put on our shoes and headed to the front of the house. As everyone walked outside, I paused in the doorway.

My mind grew panicked and my chest tightened. What if he was still out there? What if he was waiting for me? What if he was waiting to hurt me? Or was hurting someone else, or…?

"Maggie," Mama said, staring my way. She raised an eyebrow. "Come on, honey."

I tried my best to step out of the house. I tried my best to move forward, but the panic was overwhelming. Each time my mind told me to move forward, I somehow stepped backward.

"What are you doing?" Calvin asked, looking at me as if I'd lost my mind.

Everyone was staring at me like that.

Had I?

Had I lost my mind?

I can hear him shushing me, I thought to myself. *He can see me. He can hurt me.*

I stepped backward farther and farther, and I ran into a wall, which made me jump with fright. I couldn't go outside. It wasn't safe out there. I knew it wasn't, and all I ever wanted to feel was safe.

The world was scary, and I had more fear than strength lately.

"Come on, Maggie," Cheryl groaned. "You're ruining it for all of us."

Mama pinched Cheryl's arm. "Knock it off, Cheryl Rae!"

She was right, though. I was ruining it for everyone. *I'm sorry. I'm sorry.* I backed up another step and before I knew it, my feet took off, running back to my parents' bedroom. It was the safest place I knew, and I wasn't sure how to leave. Crawling under their blankets, my body shook violently. I couldn't breathe. I couldn't shut out all the noises in my head. I couldn't shut off my brain.

When the blankets moved, I gripped the edges, fighting to keep him out. *He found me, he found me.*

Relief rushed through me as I met Daddy's eyes. My stare was wide and panicked, and I could almost feel the worry dancing off his skin. He climbed under the blankets and sat beside me. I couldn't stop trembling.

Shh…

Shhh…

The devil's sounds poisoned my memories. Every thought I had was followed by the memory of his shushing noises attached to them. I couldn't leave the house. If I did, he'd see me. I couldn't speak. If I did, he'd hear me.

"We'll figure this out, Maggie," Daddy said, wrapping me into his arms. "No matter what, we're gonna fix this."

It was the first time Daddy had ever lied to me.

When he stood up to go speak to Mama in the hallway, I pulled the covers tighter around me. I couldn't stop my trembles from taking over as I listened to Mama speak her deepest fears. "What if she never comes back from this? What if she'll never be herself again? What will people think? What will people say?"

"Since when do we care what people say?"

"Always, Eric. We always care what people think of us."

It was the first time I'd ever felt a crack in the foundation of my parents' love.

And it was all because of me.

Brooks

"Stupid mud tie. Stupid purple tie. Stupid, stupid, stupid!" I muttered, tossing all the ties into my top dresser drawer. I hated ties, because they had made me late. I hated myself for being the reason Maggie had been alone in the woods.

As I pushed to close my dresser drawer, I grew angrier and angrier again when it wouldn't shut due to being too full. "UGH!" I hollered, slamming my fist against it. "I hate you! I hate you!" I kicked the dresser hard, which only led to me limping and rubbing my toe.

"Everything okay, Brooks?" Mom asked, walking in with concerned eyes. She was already dressed in her scrubs to go to work at the hospital, where she was a nurse, and the way she glanced down at her watch told me she was running behind.

"I'm fine," I huffed, hobbling over to my bed and sitting before rubbing my toes some more.

She walked over to me and placed the back of her hand to my forehead. "What's wrong, babe?"

"Nothin'," I muttered. "You're gonna be late."

She took off her watch and placed it behind her back. Then she gave me a smile. "No worries. Let's talk before I go. I know you've been going through a lot of stuff after what happened to Maggie."

"No. That's not it. I just couldn't get my drawer to shut." My face was heating up and my hands were gripped into tight fists. "It's the stupid ties' fault," I whispered through my gritted teeth.

"The ties?"

"Yeah! I took all the stupid ties out of that drawer, and now I can't get them to fit back in, so I kicked it and hurt my foot."

"Why were your ties out to begin with?"

"Because..." I hesitated and raised an eyebrow at Mom. "You're gonna be super late."

"Don't worry." She smiled and ran her fingers through my hair. "I'll be okay. Tell me what's really bothering you."

"Well...I was supposed to meet Maggie out in the woods for our rehearsal."

"Rehearsal?"

"For our wedding."

"You two were getting married?"

My face heated up even more, and I looked down at the ground. How had I not told my mom I was getting married? Maggie had told everyone, and me? Nobody. "Yeah, well, I don't know. It was Maggie's stupid idea. I was just going along with it because Jamie made me. Anyway, Maggie told me to pick out a tie and meet her in the woods, which was supposed to be easy, but I spent too much time picking out a tie. So, she was in the woods by herself, and whatever happened to her out there was because of me. I was the reason she got freaked out, because I was late to the twisted trees."

"Oh, honey." Mom sighed and started rubbing my back. "It wasn't your fault."

"Yeah, it was. It was my fault for not being there to protect her, and now she ain't talking or leaving her house because something scared her, and I should've been there to stop it, to save her."

"Brooks..." Mom lowered her voice and clasped her hands together. "Whatever happened to Maggie is tragic, but it wasn't your fault. If I've learned anything in life, it's that it doesn't help to sit and play a situation over and over again in your head. You can't change the past, but you can shape the future with the right now. You know how you can help Maggie now?"

"How?" I asked eagerly, sitting up straight. I'd do anything to fix her.

"Be her friend. She's probably pretty scared right now and confused. Lonely, even. She doesn't need you to feel sorry for her, honey. She just needs a friend. Someone who stops by and checks in on her every now and again. Someone to ask if she's okay. Someone to let her know she's not alone."

Yeah. A friend. "I can do that. I can be a good friend, I think."

She snickered slightly and bent forward, kissing my forehead. "I know you can. One second, let me get something for you." She hurried out of the bedroom and when she returned, her left hand was in a fist. She sat beside me and opened her hand to reveal an anchor charm on a string. "Your father gave it to me when we were young, after my father died, and he made a promise to always be there for me whenever I needed him. He said he'd be my anchor when I felt like I was drifting away. He was always an amazing friend to me, and he still is. Maybe you can give it to Maggie, to make her smile."

I took the necklace from my mom and thanked her. She helped me more than she knew, and if this anchor would make Maggie smile, then it was hers. I'd do anything to bring her beautiful ugly smiles back to the world.

"You okay today, Maggie May?" I asked with my hands holding my MP3 player as I stood outside of her bedroom door. She was standing by her window, staring down at the street when I arrived. She turned slowly my way and wrapped her arms tightly around her body. Her eyes looked sad, which made me sad, but I didn't show it. I just gave her a small smile. "You okay today?" I repeated.

She nodded slowly, and I knew it was a lie, but that was okay. She could take all the time she needed to be okay, I didn't mind. I wasn't going anywhere.

"Can I come in?"

She nodded again.

When I stepped in, I straightened my tie—the green one she loved. My palms were sweating against my MP3 player, and my nose sniffled as we both sat on her bed. I didn't know what to say. I mean, most of the time when people had a friendship, both sides talked. The more silence there was, the more nervous I became. My feet started tapping on the floor, and I watched as Maggie's hands stayed clasped together in her lap. Her skin was extra pale, her eyes were extra heavy, and in that moment, I missed it. I missed the one thing that had annoyed me for so long.

I missed her voice.

"Can I hold your hand again?" I asked.

She slid her left hand into my right, and I sighed. Her fingers felt like ice.

"Squeeze my hand once if the answer is no, and twice if it's yes, okay?"

She agreed and closed her eyes.

"Are you scared?"

Two squeezes.

"Are you sad?"

Two squeezes.

"Do you want to be alone?"

One squeeze.

"Do you think maybe...do you think I could be your friend?" I whispered.

Her eyes opened and locked with mine. I wondered if her heartbeats matched mine—wild, dizzy, panicked.

She looked down at our hands and squeezed once. Then she squeezed again, and my heart exploded.

I released the breath I had been holding.

With my free hand, I reached into my pocket and pulled out Mom's necklace. "This is for you. It's a friendship necklace. An anchor. I promise to be your friend, and be a good one, too. I mean, I'll try my best. I'll be your anchor. I'll help you stay grounded when you feel like you're drifting away. I just..." I sighed, staring down at the charm in my hand. "I want you to smile again. I want you to have the things you always wanted, and I'm gonna work hard to make sure you get them, too, even if it's a dog named Skippy and a cat named Jam. I want you to know..." I sighed again, because whenever her eyes watered over, my chest hurt so much. "I need you to know that even if you decide to never speak again, you'll always have someone around to hear you, Maggie. All right? I'll always be there to listen to your silence. So do you want it? Do you want the necklace?"

She squeezed my hand twice, and a tiny, almost nonexistent smile found her.

"And if you want, we can listen to my music together. I know I said I'd never let you listen, but I mean, you can, if you want. Jamie made me a new playlist on his computer last night, and I put it on my MP3 player. I don't know what he put on it, but we can listen together."

She squeezed my hand twice again. I gave her one of the earbuds, and I took the other. We lay backward on her bed with our feet dangling off the edge. I hit play on the MP3 player and the song that started playing was "Low" by Flo Rida featuring T-Pain. *Geez, Jamie.* Not the perfect song for the moment. I went to change it, but Maggie squeezed my hand once, stopping me. Her eyes were closed and a few tears fell down her cheeks, but I swore I saw it: a tiny smile. It was so tiny some people would probably think it was a frown, but I knew it wasn't.

My chest hurt, seeing the almost smile on her lips. I closed my eyes, and a few tears fell from my eyes, too, as we listened to Flo Rida. I didn't know why, but whenever she cried, I did, too.

In that moment, I knew she had been right about everything all along.

She was right about me, and her, and us.

She'd be the one girl I'd love until forever.

No matter how life tried to change us.

Part Two

Maggie

MAY 15TH, 2016 — EIGHTEEN YEARS OLD

Mama and Daddy never danced anymore.

Over the past ten years, I'd noticed a lot of changes between the two, but that was the saddest one. They still hugged each other each morning, and Daddy always kissed her forehead before he went to work at the university each day. As he walked out the front door, he always said, "I love," and Mama would finish his sentence, "You."

They still loved each other, but they never danced.

Normally at night, Mama spent time on the telephone, talking to her college best friends about me, different therapists, reading articles online, or paying bills. Daddy sat in the living room grading a stack of his papers from his graduate students or watching *The Big Bang Theory*.

In the past, Daddy used to try to turn on their wedding song, but Mama was too tired to sway with him.

"Dance with me?" he'd asked.

"Not tonight. I have a headache, Eric," she'd reply.

She never knew it, but I always saw how Daddy frowned when she walked away.

"I love," he'd say, staring at her back.

"You," she'd murmur out of routine.

When she'd glance up the staircase, she'd see me and frown. She always frowned at me, as if I were the crack in the family portrait. "Bed, Maggie May. Then up early for school."

Sometimes she'd stand there looking at me, waiting for some kind of reply. Then, when one wasn't given, she'd sigh and walk off, more tired than she had been a moment before.

It was hard knowing how much I exhausted her.

It was harder knowing how much I exhausted myself.

"You okay, sport?" Daddy asked, peeking his head into my bedroom.

I smiled.

"Good, good." He rubbed his hand against his beard, which was now peppered with gray. "Joke time?" he asked. My father was a nerd in the best way. He was an English professor at Harper Lane University and knew more about literature than most, but his real talent was knowing the worst jokes in the whole wide world. Each night he delivered me something awful.

"What would you find in Charles Dickens' kitchen?" He patted his legs as a drum roll and then shouted, "The best of thymes, the worst of thymes!"

I rolled my eyes, even though it was the funniest thing I'd ever heard.

Walking over to me, he kissed my forehead. "Goodnight, Maggie. The world keeps spinning because your heartbeats exist."

As I lay in my bed each night, I listened to Calvin playing music down the hallway. He always stayed up late, listening to music while doing homework or hanging out with his girlfriend, Stacey. I could always tell when she was over because she giggled like a girl who was madly in love with a boy. They'd been together for so long that they each wore promise rings that pledged them to one another forever.

Around eleven at night, I'd wake up to hear Cheryl tiptoeing out of the house to go visit her boyfriend, Jordan. Jordan was the classic bad boy type I'd read about in so many books, and Cheryl was much better off without him, but I couldn't tell her that. Even if I could, she wouldn't listen.

Each of my family members had found a certain way of dealing with me and my silence over the past ten years. Calvin became one of my best friends. He spent a lot of time with me, along with Brooks, playing video games, watching movies we weren't supposed to watch, and discovering the best music before the rest of the world.

Mama kind of shut me out after she realized I wasn't going to speak again. She left her job to homeschool me, but she hardly spoke to me about anything that wasn't school-based. Truth was, I could tell she kind of blamed herself for what had happened to me. Seeing me each day seemed a bit hard for her, so she built up a wall. She didn't know exactly what to say to me, so after some time, the blank stares were a bit too much for her. Sometimes, when I walked into a room, she'd go the other way. I didn't blame her, though. Seeing me was a reminder of how she hadn't noticed that I'd left the house to meet Brooks all those years ago. Seeing me hurt her.

Daddy was always the same, though, if not even goofier and more loving than before. I was thankful for that. He was my one constant. He never looked at me as if I were broken, either. In his eyes, I was completely whole.

Cheryl, on the other hand, she hated me. Hate might've seemed like a strong word, but it was the only one that came to mind. She had plenty of good reasons to dislike me, though. Growing up, she was sort of put on the backburner because of my issues. There were family trips that couldn't be taken, talent shows that had to be missed due to my in-home therapy appointments, money that wasn't available because of the cash my parents spent on me. Plus, since Mama couldn't look at me, she was always looking at Cheryl, yelling at her for little things, blaming her for everything. It wasn't a surprise that when Cheryl became a teenager, she began to rebel against the world. Jordan was her biggest rebellion, her perfect mistake.

I'd fall back to sleep to Calvin's music, then wake back up around three in the morning when Cheryl snuck back in.

Sometimes I'd hear her crying, but I couldn't check on her, because she liked me more when I acted invisible.

***

"Will you hurry up already?!" Calvin said, standing in the hallway and banging on the bathroom door the next morning. His hair stood up on top of his head, and his pajama pants were wrinkled, one leg scrunched up while the other dragged across the floor. He had a towel tossed over his shoulder as he banged on the door again. "Cheryl! Come on! Brooks is gonna be here any minute, and I'm gonna be late. Get out already. No amount of mascara is going to fix your face."

She swung the door open and rolled her eyes. "And no amount of water is going to fix your odor."

"Oh, good one. I wonder what Mom would think about it, along with the fact that you snuck out last night."

Cheryl narrowed her eyes and shoved past him. "You're the most annoying person in the fucking world."

"Love you too, sis."

She flipped him off. "I used all the hot water." As she stomped to her room, she looked at me since my door was wide open. "What are you looking at, freak?"

Then into her room she went, where she slammed the door.

Calvin looked at me and snickered. "What a ray of sunshine she is. Morning, Maggie."

I waved.

My routine for getting ready for school was pretty simple. I woke up, read some of my favorite book, brushed my teeth, combed my hair, and then walked down to the dining room to get to my classes.

My favorite part of each day was when Brooks stopped by to visit. He drove Calvin to school every day, and seeing as how Cheryl always hogged the bathroom, Calvin was always late getting ready in the morning.

Brooks was one of those people everyone instantly loved. Even with his hipster edge, he was still one of the most popular kids at his school. It wasn't shocking; he was such a people person. People were addicted to his charm, which was why he always had a girlfriend. Lacey Palmer was the lucky girl of the moment, but there was a list of girls eagerly awaiting their turn. No surprise there, since he was not only charming, but gorgeous, too. He had the perfect tan color to his skin, muscular arms, and wavy hair that had the perfect amount of shag.

His smile was perfect, too. He always smiled out of the left side of his mouth and laughed out of the right. His outfits consisted of indie rock band t-shirts he collected from shows he traveled to with Calvin and their two friends, Oliver and Owen. His jeans were always torn and held up with a leather belt that displayed small pins with lyrics from his favorite musicians. In his front pocket, there were always a few guitar picks he'd randomly flicker through his fingers throughout the day, and his white Chuck Taylors were always unlaced and colored in with highlighters.

Also, he had a thing for mismatched socks. If he was ever wearing a pair of socks that matched, it meant he had gotten dressed in the dark.

"You okay today, Magnet?" he asked me. I nodded. He asked me that question each day whenever he came by to visit. After the incident years ago, Brooks had promised to look after me, and he held onto that promise. Lately he had started calling me Magnet, because he said he was drawn to our friendship. "There's this magnetic pull of friendship between us, Maggie May. You're my magnet." Of course, the nickname had come after a night of going to some party and getting wasted with my brother then throwing up on my floor, but still, the name stuck.

"Can I come in?" he asked. He always asked permission, which was weird. The answer was always yes.

He hopped into my room—even at seven in the morning he was an energized bunny. "I got something I want you to hear," he said, walking over to me and reaching into his back pocket to pull out his iPod. We both lay down on my bed, our legs hanging over the edge, our feet touching the floor. He placed one earbud in his ear, and I took the other, then he hit play.

The music was airy and light, but there was a solid bass sound that slicked throughout the song. It felt romantic and free—wild. "'All Around And Away We Go' by Mr. Twin Sister," he said, tapping his finger on the mattress beside me.

Brooks was my human jukebox. He told me to never turn on the radio to find tunes, because it was a bunch of Hollywood brainwashing bullshit. So, each day, morning and night, he delivered to me what he considered to be music gold.

We'd lie in my bed, staring at the ceiling and listening to music, until Calvin came dashing into my room with wet hair and a muffin stuffed in his mouth.

"Ready!" he shouted, getting crumbs on my carpet.

Brooks and I sat up, and he took his earbuds back, winding them up around his iPod. "All right, I'll come back with some more stuff for ya after school, Magnet," he said, smiling my way. "Remember, say no to drugs unless they're the good ones, and stay in school, unless you don't want to."

Off they'd go.

My eyes darted to the ticking clock on my wall.

Sigh.

Only eleven or so more hours until the music came back to me.

Maggie

Each day at five in the afternoon, I took an hour-long bath. I'd sit in the tub with a novel in my grip and read for forty-five minutes. Then, for ten minutes, I'd put the book aside and wash up. My fingers wrinkled like raisins as I closed my eyes, and ran a bar of lavender soap up and down my arms. I loved the smell of lavender, almost as much as I loved gardenias. Gardenias were my utmost favorites. Each Wednesday, Daddy went to the farmer's market and bought me a fresh new bouquet of flowers to sit against my bedroom windowsill.

The first time he brought the gardenias, he could tell I loved them most, maybe by the way my lips turned up, maybe by the number of times I nodded my head as I breathed in the scent, or maybe simply because he had learned how to read my silence.

My father knew almost everything about me, based on my small gestures and tiny movements. What he didn't know was that each day at the end of my bath, when the scalding hot water became chilled, I'd slip my head under the water and hold my breath for the last five minutes.

Within those five minutes, I remembered what had happened to me. It was important for me to do it—to remember the devil, how he looked. How he felt. If I didn't remember, some days I'd blame myself for what had happened, forgetting that I had been a victim that night. When I remembered, it wasn't so hard to breathe. I did my best thinking when I was beneath the water. I forgave myself for any guilty feelings when I was submerged.

She couldn't breathe.

My throat tightened as if the devil's fingers were wrapped around my neck instead of the woman's.

The devil.

He was the devil in my eyes, at least.

Run! Run, Maggie! *My mind kept screaming, but I stayed still, unable to look away from the horror before my eyes.*

"Maggie!"

I emerged from the water at the sound of my name and released a deep breath before taking a deeper inhale.

"Maggie, Mrs. Boone is here to see you," Daddy hollered from downstairs. I stood up in the bathtub and unblocked the drain, allowing the water to swirl clockwise down the pipes. My long, stringy blond hair hung down to my buttocks, and my skin stayed ghostly pale.

My eyes met the clock on the wall.

6:01 p.m.

Mrs. Boone was late. Really late.

Years ago, when she had heard about my trauma, she'd asked if she could meet with me once a day so I could interact with someone. Secretly, I thought she met with me each day to hide her own loneliness, but I didn't mind. When two lonely souls found one another, they held on tight, no matter what. I wasn't certain if that was a good or bad thing yet. One would think when two lonely people came together, the two negatives would cancel out and make a positive, but that wasn't the case. The two seemed to make an even deeper level of loneliness, one they loved to drown in.

Mrs. Boone often brought her cat, Muffins, along with her to entertain me at lunchtime. She always came by at noon, and we'd sit down in the dining room for sandwiches and tea. I hated tea, and Mrs. Boone knew I hated tea, yet each day she found the need to bring it to me from the local bakery, Sweetest Addictions.

"You're young, which means you're stupid, so you don't truly understand how wonderful tea is for you. It will grow on you," she promised—a promise that was always a lie. It never grew on me. If anything, I hated it more and more each time.

She had lived in Britain when she was young and in her prime, and I had to assume that was where her love for the mucky drink came from. Since the death of her husband years ago, she had always dreamed of moving back to England. He was the reason she had come to America, but after he passed away, I guessed as time went by she'd lost her nerve to go back to England.

"Stanley was home," she'd always say about her late husband. "It didn't matter where we lived, because as long as he was there, I was home." After he passed, it was almost as if Mrs. Boone became homeless. When Stanley packed his bags and went off to the afterlife, he took Mrs. Boone's safe haven with him—his heartbeats. I often wondered if she ever closed her eyes for a few minutes and remembered those heartbeats.

I knew I would.

"Maggie!" Daddy shouted, shaking me from my thought.

I reached for the oversized white towel on the counter and wrapped it around my body. Stepping out of the tub, I moved in front of the mirror and grabbed my hairbrush. As I began to get the knots out of my hair, I stared at my blue eyes that matched Dad's and the sculpted cheekbones I had also received from him. The small freckles across my nose came from my grandma, and the long eyelashes, my grandpa. So much of my ancestry could be seen each day simply by staring into a mirror. I knew it was impossible, but sometimes I swore I had Mama's smile and her frown.

"Maggie," Daddy hollered again. "Did you hear me?"

I debated not responding, because I was pretty irritated that Mrs. Boone thought it was okay to drop by so late in the afternoon as if I hadn't other things to do. Twelve noon was when she was supposed to come. We had a routine, a planned schedule, and she had gone against it that afternoon. I didn't even truly understand why she bothered to stop by each day, or why I allowed her to come over for lunch. She was ruder than rude most of the time, telling me how stupid I was and how ridiculous it was that I wouldn't speak a word.

Childish, she called it.

Immature, even.

I guessed I kept dealing with her each afternoon because she was one of my few friends. Sometimes her rude comments were so harsh they'd pull a reaction from me—a small grin, tiny, silent chuckles only I could hear. The seventy-year-old fart was one of the best friends I ever had. She was my favorite enemy, too. Our relationship was complicated, so the best word to described us was frenemies—friendly enemies. Plus, I still loved her cat as much as I had when I was a child, and she still followed me around the house, rubbing her soft fur against my legs.

"Maggie May?" Daddy hollered again, this time knocking on the bathroom door. "Did you hear me?"

I knocked on the door twice. One knock meant no, two knocks meant yes.

"Well, let's not keep Mrs. Boone waiting, okay? Hurry downstairs," he said.

I almost knocked once against the door to show my sassiness, but I refrained from the act. I braided my still soaked hair into one giant braid that hung over my left shoulder. I put on my underwear, then slipped my pale yellow dress over my head. I grabbed my novel from the side of the tub before opening the bathroom door, then hurried down the stairs toward the dining room to see my favorite frenemy.

Mrs. Boone always dressed as if she were off to meet Queen Elizabeth. She wore jewels and gems around her neck and her fingers, and they always sparkled against the faux fur she wore around her shoulders. She always lied and said it was real fur, but I knew better.

I'd read enough books based on the forties to know the difference between real fur and fake.

She always wore dresses and tights with sweaters and short heels, and then she'd place a shimmering colorful collar around Muffins' neck to match her outfit.

"It's rude to keep the elderly waiting, Maggie May," Mrs. Boone said, tapping her fingers against the cherry oak table.

It's rude to keep the young waiting, too, Mrs. Boone.

I gave her a tight smile, and she cocked an eyebrow at me, displeased. I sat down beside her, and she pushed my cup of tea toward me. "It's Black Earl Grey tea. You'll like it this time," she said.

I took a sip and gagged.

Once again, she was wrong. She smiled, satisfied by my displeasure. "Your hair looks awful. You really shouldn't let it air dry like that. You'll catch a cold."

No, I won't.

"Yes," she huffed. "You will."

She always knew the words I didn't say. Lately I wondered if she were a witch or something. If perhaps when she was a child, an owl showed up to her windowsill and dropped her an invitation to attend a school for witches and wizards, but then somewhere along the way she fell in love with a Muggle and came back to Wisconsin to choose love over true adventure.

If it were me, I'd never choose love over adventure.

I'd always accept the owl's invitation.

That idea was ironic, seeing as how the only adventure I'd ever lived was through the pages of novels.

"What have you been reading?" she asked, reaching into her oversized purse and pulling out two turkey sandwiches. I couldn't see the sandwiches because they were still in the brown paper Sweetest Addictions wrapped all their food with, but I knew they were turkey. Mrs. Boone always kept our sandwiches the same: turkey, tomato, lettuce, and mayo on rye bread. Nothing more, nothing less. Even on the days I wanted tuna, I had to just pretend my turkey was fish.

She set one in front of me and the other she unwrapped, taking a large bite. For a tiny lady, she sure knew how to take big bites of food.

I placed my novel in front of her, and she sighed. "Again?"

Yes, again.

For the past month, I'd been rereading the Harry Potter series, which might've had something to do with the fact that I believed Mrs. Boone to be a witch. To be fair, she did also have the classic witch mole next to her nose.

"There are so many books in this world, and you find a way to read all the same ones over and over again. There's no possible way the stories still surprise you after all this time."

Obviously she hadn't ever read or reread Harry Potter.

Each time was different.

When I had first read the books, I'd seen the excitement in the story.

As I reread them, I saw much more of the pain.

A person never reads an outstanding book twice and walks away with the same beliefs. An outstanding book always surprises you and awakens you to new ideas, new ways of looking at the world, no matter how many times the words have been read.

"I'm going to start believing you're into Wicca," she said, chowing down on her sandwich and sipping her tea. A peculiar thing for a witch to say to a Muggle, if you asked me.

Muffins came from under the table and rubbed against my leg to say hello. I bent down to pet her. *Hello, friend.* Muffins meowed before turning on her side for me to pat her belly. When I didn't pat her the way she wanted me to, I swore she muttered a curse word at me in cat language, then she wandered off, probably to find my mother, who was a professional at petting Muffins.

"What's wrong with your face?" she barked, narrowing her eyes at me.

I raised an eyebrow, confused.

She shook her head back and forth. "Your eyes look awful, like you haven't slept in days. You should really have Katie bring you some makeup. You look horrid."

I touched below my eyes. It was always worrisome when someone said you looked tired but you didn't feel that way.

"Listen, Maggie. We must talk." Mrs. Boone sat up straighter in her seat and cleared her throat. "What I mean is you must listen as I speak."

I sat up straighter, too. I knew it must be serious because whenever she was going to be stern, her nostrils flared, which they were doing at that moment.

"You have to leave your house," she said.

I almost laughed.

Leave home?

What a ridiculous idea. She knew my situation—well, she didn't *know* my situation, but she knew well enough. In the past ten years, I hadn't left home. Mama and Daddy had enrolled me in homeschooling years ago, and whenever I needed a doctor or a dentist, my parents arranged for them to come to us. Mrs. Boone knew these facts; it was why we never had disgusting tea at her house.

Her brows furrowed. "I'm not joking, Maggie May. You have to leave. What are you going to do? Stay here forever? You're about to graduate high school. Are you not interested in college?"

I didn't have an answer to that.

Mrs. Boone frowned. "How do you expect to ever live your life? How will you ever fall in love? Or hike a mountain? Or see the Eiffel Tower at night? Jessica, we can't keep supporting you like this," she said.

I paused and raised an eyebrow. *Jessica?*

"Your father and I are being pushed to the limit, and there's not much more we can take. Don't you want to be something? Do something?"

The room filled with silence, and Mrs. Boone's brows lowered, as if she was going deep into thought. A cloud of confusion washed over her as she pressed the palms of her hands against her eyes. She shook her head slightly before reaching for her tea and taking a sip.

Her eyes were filled with a state of bewilderment when she looked up at me. "What were we saying?" Where had she just traveled? "Oh right. You must leave, Maggie May.

"What about your parents? Are they just supposed to spend the rest of their days sitting in this house with you? Do they never get a chance to be married without kids in their home? They didn't sign up for this."

I turned my back to her, angered and hurt, but mostly ashamed, because she was right. Out of the corner of my eye, I could still see her frowning. The more I saw her frown, the angrier I grew.

Leave.

"Oh. You're grumpy now and throwing a tantrum," she muttered.

I knocked on the table once. *No.*

She knocked on it twice. "Yes. A teenage girl who is emotional and throwing a tantrum, how original. Finish your sandwich, grumpy. I'll be back tomorrow."

Whatever, old fart. Don't be late again. I rolled my eyes and stomped my feet hard against the floor. God, I was throwing a tantrum. *How original.*

"You're mad at me, which is fine," she said, rolling her brown paper into a ball. She stood up from her chair, placed her purse on her shoulder, and lifted up my novel. Her steps brought her closer to me and she lifted my chin with her finger. "But you're only mad because you know I'm right." She placed the book in my lap. "You can't just read these books and think that means you're living. It's their story, not yours, and it's heartbreaking to watch someone so young toss away their chance at writing their own story."

74

9

Maggie

"You're really starting to piss me off, Cheryl."

Cheryl was fighting with her boyfriend, Jordan, across the hall from my bedroom as I sat on my bed reading a novel.

Correction: Cheryl was fighting with her *ex*-boyfriend Jordan across the hall from my bedroom as I sat on my bed reading a novel.

"I'm just saying," Cheryl groaned, tapping the heel of her shoe against the wall. Her arms were crossed and she kept smacking her bubble gum. "It's not me, it's you. I'm just not into you like that anymore."

"You gotta be shitting me," Jordan huffed, his feet storming back and forth in the hallway. "I broke up with my ex for you! I paid more than a hundred bucks for our prom tickets—a fucking dance I didn't even want to go to—for you. I've bent over backward to treat you right. I've ditched parties to watch chick flicks with you."

Cheryl twirled her hair on her finger and shrugged. "Nobody told you to do all those things."

Jordan chuckled, flabbergasted. "Yes! You did! You even smoked my weed every night."

"That was me being nice to you," she explained. "You smoking pot alone would've just made you a pothead. You smoking with me made you a social butterfly."

"This is bullshit," he snapped, raking his hands through his hair. "Prom is tomorrow. What the hell am I supposed to do?"

"Go by yourself."

Cheryl was beautiful, that was a given fact. Over the years, she had grown into her body—big chest, thick hips, slim waist—a lot faster than I had grown into mine. In my mind, she had the perfect body, and from years of braces, a perfect smile to go with it. After years of feeling like an outsider, she'd created this persona where she was determined to fit in—even if that meant extreme measures to lose weight for an ounce of attention.

Another given fact about my sister was that she knew her beauty existed, and she used it in almost every situation to get whatever she wanted in the world—no matter who it hurt. Then, she'd come to my bedroom and tell me about how many guys she used and abused, just to get things from them. Dates, money, presents, sex—anything and everything.

Sometimes I thought she told me so much because she resented me for making her miss out on so many things as a kid. Other times, I thought she felt guilty about what she did, and my silence gave her a bit of confidence that what she did was okay.

She was a professional fake lover of love. She made guys believe in the love, too, which wasn't easy for boys our age—especially for a bad boy turned good like Jordan. He literally went from the biggest jerk ever to a puppy dog whenever he was around Cheryl. He always seemed as if he was begging her to love him—except for when she pissed him off. When she pissed him off, his true colors showed. People could hide their true selves for a while, but over time, the masks always fell off.

"No. Screw that. You said you loved me," Jordan choked out, almost close to tears.

"Yeah, loved—*past tense.*"

I peeked over the top of my book and stared at them. Jordan's face was red, and Cheryl seemed more than amused by the fact that he was upset.

"No," Jordan hissed, grabbing her tightly by the arm.

I put my book down.

"No. You don't get to do this. Not without a real reason."

"You want a real reason? Fine." Cheryl yanked her arm from his grip, and she stood up tall, staring him square in the eyes. "I slept with Hank."

Jordan's eyes grew wide. "What? No, you didn't."

"I did." Her eyes widened too, and a wicked grin found her lips.

Oh no. She was about to crush his spirit, the same way she'd crushed many other guys in our hallway.

"I screwed him at Tim's party when you were sick, and at his house when I told you I was getting my hair done, and in my room yesterday when—"

Jordan closed his eyes and his hands wrapped into fists. "Hank is my best friend."

She snickered and lightly shoved him in his chest, forcing him to step away from her. "You should choose your friends more carefully."

Her laughter faltered as her head flew sideways when Jordan's hand slapped her hard. Her back slammed against the wall and her body slid down to the floor.

I hadn't a clue how it happened, but the next thing I knew, I was standing in the hallway, holding my novel in my hand, ready to knock Jordan out if he stepped an inch closer to my sister. Cheryl's face reddened from his hit, and her hand gripped her skin.

"You're a fucking whore," Jordan said, spitting at her, his words hitting me hard, his actions hitting me harder.

He screamed at her, his voice cracking. "You fucking whore!" he shouted, slapping her hard across the face. She stumbled backward and whimpered, her hand flying to her cheek. "I gave you everything. We had a life together. What about our son? What about our family?" He slapped her again and again. "We had a life!" He shoved her to the ground and his eyes popped out of his head, as if he was crazy—disturbed.

"You'll come to your senses, trust me," Jordan told my sister. "And I'll be waiting when you come running back to me."

I raised my arms up high, seconds away from hitting him. I stomped my feet, my mind traveling from past to present day with each blink of my eyes. Over and over again I stomped my feet until Jordan turned to look my way. When our eyes met, I stepped back.

Jordan's dark side was showing. Everyone had a dark side, their own personal devil that they kept chained up most days. The devil whispered lies into individuals' ears, filling them with fear and doubt, pushing them to do dark things. The main goal was to control the sounds of the devil, to only allow it to peek out of the closet where it was chained up. The devil could only truly take over one's mind if the person freed him, and allowed him inside.

Jordan's devil broke free of his chains that night.

His darkness scared me.

Shh…

I blinked slowly, and when I reopened my eyes, Jordan had a sly smile on his face. "What the hell are you gonna do, freak? Are you going to silently beat me to death with a book?" He came toward me and launched forward like he was going to hit me.

A sharp yank to my dress sent me backward, the poppy in my hair flying across the forest floor. His fingers were wrapped around my dress and he tossed me to the ground. My breaths weaved in and out and I screamed as he tackled my body, placing all of his weight on top of me, his filthy hands covering my mouth, muting my shouts.

I kicked and screamed, screamed and kicked. He was going to kill me.

When I opened my eyes, I was on the floor, covering my face with the book in my grip, shaking from fear, shaking from memories. I hated that part of me—the one that sometimes slipped back into the past. I hated how it shook me, how it still had a hold on me at times, but mostly, I hated when others noticed. Most of my panic attacks I'd been able to keep hidden. Most of the panics were a secret of mine.

He laughed at my reaction. "What a fucking nutjob. I'm out of here."

He hurried down the stairs and slammed the front door on his exit.

With haste, I stood up and rushed to Cheryl's side. I bent down, reaching my hand out to help her up. She swatted it away.

"God, Maggie. Why don't you just get a life of your own and butt out of mine?" she grumbled, standing up and rubbing her cheek. "You're so embarrassing."

She hurried to her bedroom and slammed her door shut.

I rushed over to my bedroom, grabbed my notebook and a marker, and ran back to Cheryl's door, knocking.

She opened it and rolled her eyes. "What do you want?"

I scribbled on the paper. *You didn't sleep with Hank.*

She ran her fingers through her hair and shifted on her feet. "Go away, Maggie."

You were shopping with Mama yesterday. You didn't sleep with Hank.

"It's none of your business."

Jordan hit you.

"I provoked him."

He hurt you.

"I pushed him, Maggie. I pushed him."

I gotta tell Mama and Dad that he hit you.

"Will you just shut up, Maggie?" she whisper-shouted as she reached for the page in my notebook and crumpled it up, tossing it into her room. "You don't understand anything about relationships or boys, even. That's just how Jordan gets sometimes. I push him, and he pushes back. Stop making a big deal out of things. Not everyone is as traumatized and damaged as you, okay? And just because you're a freak and don't have a life of your own doesn't mean you can meddle in mine."

I stepped back.

Ouch.

For a second, Cheryl's upper lip twitched and her eyes glassed over; perhaps she was feeling regret for hurting my feelings? She shook her head back and forth, shaking off the feeling. "I'm not going to apologize, all right? You pushed me, Maggie, so I pushed back. Anyway, Jordan and I aren't even together anymore, so it doesn't matter. I'm on to bigger and better things now. So if you don't mind…" She took her hand and waved me off. "Bye."

I sighed and walked off to my room, back to my quiet corner of the world, and picked up my book once more.

Sometimes I wondered what it'd be like to leave the house, but if there were people like Jordan outside those doors, I was better off staying at home.

I couldn't concentrate.

I'd been sitting on my bed with my book open to page two hundred and nine for several minutes, yet I hadn't been able to read. My mind kept replaying Jordan hitting my sister. The shocked expression on Cheryl's face as his hand made contact. The loud gasp that fell from her lips.

I shut my eyes.

Shh…

"You okay this evening, Magnet?" Brooks said, standing in my bedroom doorway later that night with a backpack hanging on his shoulder. My eyes opened and I took a breath of relief. He never knew how perfect his timing was, but he always showed up when I needed him.

I closed the book in my grip and sat cross-legged on my bed, looking up at him. His shaggy brown hair was getting long—his rock star style—and was touching the bottom of his eyebrows. Every now and then, he'd slightly flick his head back to move the hair from his eyes. Sometimes he'd pucker his lips together and puff hard to move the strands, but never—and I mean never—did he use his fingers to guide his hair. He always smiled so wide whenever he looked at me, which in turn brought smiles to my lips. I didn't always feel like smiling, but Brooks? He made me feel as if smiling was all I ever wanted to do.

"Can I come in?" he asked.

The answer was yes. The answer was always yes.

He sat down on my bed. I reached for the notebook and pen on my nightstand, opening it up to the first free page. Beside my bed was a trash can filled with balled up pieces of paper from the nights before when Brooks came to visit. It was the way we communicated the best. In the mornings, we just listened to music, but in the afternoons, he'd speak and I'd write. I'd tried the same form of communication with Mrs. Boone, but she had told me she wasn't going to aid me in killing trees. Plus, she said I had a voice and should be able to use it.

"I hear Mrs. Boone and you had a fight," he said. I rolled my eyes and he snickered. "She means no harm, you know that, right? I went over to her place to drop Muffins back off, and she told me everything she said to you. I'm not saying her delivery was right, but her heart was in the right..." His words faded off as he saw my annoyed glare.

"She was right." He snickered. "You are grumpy."

I started writing on the paper. *She called me Jessica.*

He frowned. "Yeah." He shifted his body slightly and looked up.

I cocked an eyebrow.

He pretended not to notice by looking higher up. My fingers nudged his shoulder. "I'm not supposed to say anything, Maggie."

I nudged him again.

He sighed. "Okay, but you have to promise not to tell anyone, all right?"

I scrunched my nose. *Who would I tell?*

He laughed and tapped my nose twice. "I forgot I'm talking to the one girl who's perfect at keeping a secret. So, my mom said Mrs.

Boone's been struggling with her memory. She found her wandering around last weekend, and Mrs. Boone was confused about her whereabouts. Mom said she thought it was maybe the early stages of Alzheimer's, and she wanted Mrs. Boone to get checked out, just in case."

Did she?

He frowned. "You know Mrs. B, a bit stubborn, to say the least. She said she was fine and didn't need anyone meddling in her affairs."

A worrisome feeling grew in my gut as I imagined something seriously being wrong with Mrs. Boone. Even though I hated her, I loved her so much. The idea of anything happening to her made me nauseous.

As I went to write a few more words to Brooks, he blocked my hand from the paper. "Wait, I got something for you. For us." He took off his backpack, unzipped it, and pulled out a huge dry-erase board with a new pack of markers. "I figured this is an easier way to write and not waste all that paper. Plus, if we ever have to tell secrets, I don't have to speak out loud, and then we can just erase the evidence."

I smiled.

He smiled.

I took a marker and began writing, but before I could write anything, he spoke.

"I broke up with Lacey today." My marker dragged across the board as my mouth dropped open. He laughed nervously and shrugged. "Yeah, I know." Lacey and Brooks had been dating for about nine months—nine months, two weeks, and four days to be exact—not that I'd been counting.

Why?

"Well, she kind of broke up with me, I guess. She said she couldn't handle being the third choice in my life."

Third?

"Music…and, well…" He gave me a grin that was more of a grimace. "You."

My chest tightened and I sat up straighter. He continued speaking. "She thinks I spend too much time with you, seeing you every day. She's a bit jealous and has this crazy idea that you and I have something going on."

Did we? Was there something going on between us?

He rolled his eyes. "Which of course, we don't. I told her you and I are just friends, because we are."

Right. Of course. We had nothing going on. I held the anchor necklace I wore around my neck each day in the palm of my hand and squeezed it lightly.

Brooks and I were just friends; why did that feel like a punch to my gut?

"Anyway, I thought I'd tell you before anyone else did. It kind of sucks because I spent all that money on my tuxedo for prom tomorrow. Whatever, no big deal."

I knew it was a big deal to him, though, because whenever Brooks was hurt, he chewed on his right thumb.

I'm so sorry, Brooks. I'm sorry you're hurting.

"Yeah, me too. I liked her, you know? Lacey was great. But…" He frowned at the words on the dry-erase board, then took the palm of his hand and erased them. "See? With one swipe of the hand, the hurting is gone."

He stood up and started walking around my room, running his fingers across the spines of all of my novels. I knew the hurting wasn't gone, because another thing Brooks did when he was sad was pace and thumb through my books.

The tiny bookshelf I'd had since I was a small kid was now stacked high with novels, and those that didn't fit on the shelves were standing up around the perimeter of my bedroom.

Unlike most people, my books were not grouped together by genre or author name. My books were placed together based on the color of their binding. All reds sat beside one another, while all the purples stayed close together. So, when one walked into my bedroom, they saw a rainbow border wrapping around the space.

"What's this?" he asked, picking up a small notebook with leather binding.

I shot up from the bed and hurried over to him.

He smirked wickedly. "Oh my...could this be Magnet's diary?"

I leaped for it, and he held it over his head. I leaped again, and he moved it behind his back. My arms were wild, trying to rip it away from him.

"What kind of stuff do you write in here, huh? Your dirty little secrets? I can't help but wonder..." He smiled wider and his grin made me happy, and mad, and excited, and scared all at once. The more he leaped up to avoid me getting the journal from him, the more I leaped up to try to snatch it. Every time our skin brushed against one another, I wanted to move in closer. Every time he touched me, I wanted more. He kept laughing and laughing. "I'm sorry, Maggie. I know you'll never forgive me, but I gotta. I just gotta read one page to see what kind of thoughts go through your—"

He opened to the first page.

He stopped moving.

He stopped talking.

He stopped laughing, too.

"Maggie's to-do list?" he asked.

My cheeks felt warm, my stomach knotted. I walked back to my bed and sat down.

He followed, sat, and handed me the journal.

It was reading's fault.

Reading was both a gift and a curse for me. Those books made me able to escape into a world I'd never experienced, but at the same time, they reminded me of all the things I'd been missing.

So, I made a list.

A list so that if somehow, someway, I became able to step outside that front door of mine, I'd have things to do, to see, to explore.

Wishful thinking, maybe, but if books had taught me anything, it was that dreaming was always a worthy cause to take part in.

My list grew each day, too. Every time something exciting happened in one of my novels, I added it to my notebook, along with the name of the novel where I got the idea. Horseback riding, thanks to *National Velvet*. Going to a ball and dramatically running away, due to *Cinderella*. Standing in two places at once, because of *A Walk to Remember*.

There were hundreds of items on my to-do list, and some days I wondered if I'd ever get to cross even one thing off.

"It's a list of things you want to do?" he asked knowingly.

I nodded.

"You can do them all, you know."

Maybe.

Then, I erased the word.

He wrote: **Definitely.**

Then, he erased the word, but it stayed in my mind.

We sat quietly for a moment, both staring at the blank board.

"What do you want to be when you grow up, Maggie?"

I'd thought about it a lot, that question. What did I want to be? What *could* I be? An author, maybe. I could publish books through the Internet, and I'd never have to leave my house. Or maybe an artist, and Daddy could take my artwork to fairs to sell it. Or maybe...

I picked up my marker and wrote down exactly what I wanted to be.

Happy.

Brooks picked up a marker of his own and wrote what he wanted to be, too.

Happy.

His fingers wiped away our words, and he leaped from my bed, went over to my desk, and began to scramble through my pens and pencils. When he found the one he wanted, he headed back over to me and began writing on the board.

Someday you're going to wake up and leave your house, Magnet, and you're going to discover the world. Someday you're going to see the whole wide world, Maggie May, and on that day, when you step outside and breathe in your first breath, I want you to find me. No matter what, find me, because I'm going to be the one to show it to you. I'm going to help you cross things off your to-do list. I'm gonna show you the whole wide world.

Just like that, I was his, and he'd never even know it.

Promise? I wrote.

Promise, he replied.

I went to erase the words, and when my hand glided over them, only my promise disappeared. He smiled and showed me his Sharpie marker. "It's not coming off. I want you to keep the board just like this. Keep it as my promise to you. I'll get you a new board tomorrow for random conversations."

My lips parted as if I were going to speak, yet no words came out.

He smiled knowingly. "You're welcome. Music now?"

I nodded, and we both lay down on my mattress as he pulled out his iPod.

"Waterfall" by The Fresh & Onlys.

"The way the electric guitar climbs in this song is fucking amazing. It feels like you're in the middle of nothing and everything at the same time. If you listen, you can hear how perfect the bass player is, too. The way they scale up the fretboard is..." He sighed, slamming his hand against his chest. "Gold."

I hardly ever knew what he was talking about when he spoke about music, but I liked the way it brought him to life.

"Brooks." Calvin poked his head in my doorway and cocked an eyebrow at his best friend. "We're practicing in five. Come on. We need to go over the letter we're sending off with the demo tapes," Calvin said.

Brooks and Calvin were famous...well, *kind of* famous—the kind of famous only I knew existed. They were the lead singers in their band and were extremely well trained in performing in our garage. Even though they were undiscovered, I knew someday, they'd be something big.

They were too good to not be noticed.

"You're coming to tape us, right, Magnet?" Brooks asked, standing up from my bed, seemingly chipper as ever.

Of course I was coming. I reached for my camcorder, picked it up, and then stood to my feet. In my other hand, I grabbed my current read. I never missed band practice; it was the highlight of my day. I always sat and recorded them from the kitchen, too. Mama and Daddy had gotten me a camcorder a few years back because a therapist said he thought I might open up and speak to the camera or something. It turned out to be hours of me staring at myself, blinking, so instead of wasting the camcorder, I used it to record my brother's band.

Before heading downstairs, I moved over to my bedroom window, which faced the street and looked across the road to Mrs. Boone's front porch, where she rocked back and forth in her wicker chair while Muffins slept beside her.

Her lips moved as if she was holding a conversation with the invisible man sitting in the stationary wicker chair beside her. *Her Stanley.*

My fingers touched the chilled glass and her lips curved up into a smile. She chuckled at something she said then touched the empty chair beside her and made it move in harmony with her rocking.

Mrs. Boone's life was slowing down, and for many days she lived in her memories. When she wasn't living in her memories, she was telling me how I should've been making my own. It may have seemed sad to many the way she lived nowadays, but to me, Mrs. Boone seemed so lucky. She might've been lonely, but in her mind she was never truly alone.

My memories were sparse, and some of them—maybe most—I was sure I had stolen from storybooks. Parts of me were angry about the way she pushed me, but another part knew I needed to be shoved. She was part of the reason I had a to-do list at all. Even when she was rude, she still believed in me having a future.

Those who believed in you when you didn't believe in yourself were the ones to hold close.

Maggie

"One, two, one, two, three, go!" Calvin chanted in the garage before rocking out on his bass guitar with Brooks and their band. I sat on the kitchen floor, recording them from the garage door, and whenever they'd break to talk, I'd go back to reading my novel.

When I was younger, reading hadn't been my strong suit, but as the years went by, it became the voice I had lost. It was almost as if the characters lived inside my head and shared their thoughts with me and vice versa.

In the past ten years, I'd read over eight hundred books. I'd lived over eight hundred once upon a times. I'd fallen in love about six hundred and ninety times, fallen in lust maybe twenty times, and fallen in hate about ten billion times. Through those pages, I'd smoked pot, been skydiving, and gone skinny dipping. I've been stabbed in the back by friends—both physically and emotionally—and mourned the loss of loved ones.

I'd lived the lives of each character within the walls of my bedroom.

My father brought me a new book—or five—every two weeks on his payday. I assumed he spent twenty percent of his life in bookstores, searching for my next read.

My favorite time of each day was when the boys came home from school and played their music in the garage while I sat reading and listening in the kitchen. I'd always take a break from reading when the boys started fighting over lyrics, or chords, or Owen's drum playing.

"I'm just saying, Rudolph, you're two counts off beat," Oliver, the keyboard player, said with a groan. Oliver was a bigger guy who sweated more than he breathed. Every shirt he wore had sweat stains to the max. When he stood from his drum stool, the butt sweat stains were intense, and the guys always mocked him about it. Plus, Oliver was hungry—all the time. If he wasn't eating, he was talking about eating. He was a regular meatatarian who loved any kind of meat more than anyone I'd ever met. Besides his excessive sweating and love for steaks, Oliver was also the biggest teddy bear in the group and never fought over anything with anyone, except when it came to Owen, also known as Rudolph. The two fought over anything and everything each day. That day, the fight started because Rudolph was two counts off; he was always two counts off.

"You don't know what the heck you're talking about, Oli. You're playing too fast. You need to pull back." Rudolph was the complete opposite of Oliver—a vegetarian, stick-thin, and always layered with clothes because no matter the temperature, he was freezing. He always had a red nose, thus the nickname.

"Dude, are you kidding me? You know nothing about nothing. You need—" Oliver started.

Rudolph cut in. "No, you need—"

"TO CLEAN OUT YOUR EARS!" Oliver and Rudolph both hollered in unison. It only took seconds before they were standing face to face, pushing and poking each other while screaming. Oliver wrapped his arm around Rudolph's neck and forced his head under Oliver's armpit.

"Argh! Gross. Come on, Oli! No one deserves this!" Rudolph shouted, his face turning the same color as his nose. "Let me go!"

"Say it! Say it!" Oliver ordered. "Say I'm the best at the keys!"

"You're the best at the keys, okay, dickhead?"

"And say Mom loves me best because I was born first!" Oliver mocked.

"Screw you, Oli…" Oliver pushed Rudolph's head deeper under his arm, making Rudolph whimper like a sad puppy. "Okay! Mom loves you best! She loves you best, you freaking meatball."

Oliver dropped his hold on his younger brother—younger by seventeen minutes—and clapped his hands together with a wide smirk. The two were fraternal twins and fought like it, too. It was always entertaining to watch.

As I watched the guys continue to fight, Brooks and Calvin stood in a corner, looking at a notebook where they scribbled lyrics and any ideas they had for the band. Most of the time, Brooks and my brother were complete dorks like the twins, except for when they were rehearsing. They were driven, focused, and determined to be the diamonds in the rough from Harper County, Wisconsin, that made it to Hollywood.

Mama came walking into the kitchen with four pizzas in her hand and hollered, "Boys! Food!"

That was enough to get all of them inside the house. The only thing better than Hollywood was pepperoni pizza.

I sat at the table with the guys as they went over their plans of buying huge mansions, Ferraris, yachts, and monkeys once they hit it big time.

"Don't you think we should come up with a band name if we are going to be huge?" Rudolph asked, stuffing his face with his gluten-free cheese pizza.

"Wait, so Parrots Without Parents is a no go?" Brooks asked, wiping his saucy face with the back of his hand.

"I thought that was kind of awesome," Oliver offered.

"I thought it was ridiculous!" Rudolph disagreed. "We should do something involving ninjas!"

"No, pirates!"

"Ninja pirates!" Calvin shouted. The boys all started talking over one another, and I sat quietly, nibbling at my pizza, taking in their actions. Most of the time I felt like a fly on the wall whenever I was around people, somewhat eavesdropping on their lives, because for the most part, they forgot I existed due to my silence.

But every now and then...

"What do you think, Magnet?"

Brooks nudged me gently in the side, and with the small touch from him, everything inside me warmed up. His eyes smiled my way and my heartbeat increased. I loved that about him. I loved how he could see me when the rest of the world forgot I existed. I gave him a small smile and shrugged.

"Come on," he said, flipping open his notebook to a blank page and handing me his pen. As I took the pen from his grip, I allowed my fingers to linger against his hand. He watched my every move, and I made sure to make every move count.

Did he feel it? My heat? My want? My need?

As I began to write, he smiled, studying the curve of my hand as it ran across the paper. When I finished, I pushed the notebook toward him.

"Crooks," he said out loud, holding the notebook in his hand.

"Crooks?" Rudolph bellowed, bewildered.

"*Crooks?*" Oliver echoed, a pitch higher than Owen.

"C is for Calvin, O is for Owen, the other O is Oliver, and then well, Brooks is the rest," he explained. "Right, Maggie?"

I nodded.

Yes. Yes.

The fact that he understood the meaning of the name without me explaining it made my heart want to explode. How could he understand the thoughts in my head that I never voiced? How could he read me so effortlessly?

"Crooks!" Calvin shouted, slamming his hand against the table.

"I love it. I fucking love it," my brother cheered. "Just think about being on stage: 'Hi, we're The Crooks, and we are here to steal your ears tonight.'"

I giggled to myself as they kept chatting.

"We're The Crooks, and we're here to steal your money tonight!" Oliver joked.

"We're The Crooks, and we're here to steal your hearts tonight!" Brooks laughed.

"Yeah! Yeah! Or how about: We're The Crooks, and…and… and…" Rudolph frowned. "Well, hell, you all took the best one-liners."

"You snooze, you lose, kid brother. Maybe if you added more protein to your diet, your brain wouldn't be so slow." Oliver chuckled.

"Yes, Oli, because you eating Bambi is what makes you smart. That's it. That's probably why you got an A in calculus, right?" Rudolph replied sarcastically. "Oh wait, you got a D minus."

The twins started arguing, and I knew there was nothing that was going to stop them until she showed up. *Cheryl.* She seemed completely over her earlier interaction with her ex-boyfriend and back to her flirty self.

"Hey, boys," Cheryl sang, swaying her hips and twisting her hair around her finger.

I taught you that move when we were kids!

"I didn't know you were all going to be over here tonight." Cheryl always did this weird voice drop thing whenever she talked to guys. She tried to sound seductive, but to me, she sounded like someone who smoked fifteen packs of cigarettes a day. Ridiculous. And of course she knew they'd be there practicing—they were always at our house.

"Oh, hey, Cheryl!" The twins perked up, and their eyes fell to her personal set of twins.

"You look good," Rudolph barked.

"No, you look great!" Oliver shouted.

"Brilliant!"

"Stunning!"

"Sexy!" the twins yelled in unison.

Cheryl batted her eyes and completely ignored them, zooming her stare in on Brooks, who wasn't giving her the time of day. Calvin's and Brooks' heads were back in their notebook, looking at their future plans. Brooks never seemed too interested in my sister, probably because he'd known her since she was wearing diapers. I could tell that bothered Cheryl, though—every girl wanted Brooks to notice her...including me.

"Hey, Brooks," she said. "How are you?"

She kept twirling her hair, and I kept rolling my eyes. Brooks glanced toward her and smiled before turning back to his notebook. "Good, Cheryl. How are you?"

She hopped up on the dining room table then pushed her boobs together, pressing her elbows against them.

"I'm doing okay. Jordan broke up with me today."

Really? He broke up with you? That's not what I heard...

"Oh yeah?" he replied politely, hardly interested. "Sorry to hear that."

"Yeah. Rumor has it, you broke up with Lacey." She frowned, dramatically of course. "Or, well, she broke up with you. That sucks."

Brooks shrugged. "It happens, I guess."

"Yeah, it's just sucky because I was supposed to go to prom with him, seeing as how he's a senior. I already bought my dress."

"I don't have a date!" Rudolph shouted.

"Me neither!" Oliver jumped in.

"But you two don't already have tuxedos. I know Calvin went with Brooks to buy theirs... Oh! I have an idea!" Cheryl shouted, clapping her hands together.

Oh no.

"How about you and me go together, Brooks? We could go as friends, ya know? It doesn't make sense for us to both miss the event, right?"

Brooks hesitated, because he was kind. He didn't want to embarrass Cheryl in front of everyone, and Cheryl knew that, too. That was probably why she'd asked him in front of the group.

"Don't you think that's a great idea, Maggie?" Cheryl said, shooting a warning glare at me before turning back to Brooks with a sugary sweet voice. "Maggie was the one who was there for me after the breakup today. She knew how big of a deal prom was to me, too. We've been talking about it for weeks."

No, we hadn't. I hadn't even known my sister was going to prom until moments before her ex-boyfriend hit her.

I shut my eyes for a beat.

Shh…

"Well…" Brooks' voice cracked and I opened my eyes. He rubbed the back of his neck and glanced my way, his eyes begging for help, but what could I say?

Nothing.

"I guess that could be cool, just going as friends."

It amazed me how a heart could shatter in a crowded room and the sound couldn't be heard by a single person.

11

Maggie

I hated everything about prom—the dresses, the slow dancing, the flowers. I hated how artificial and cliché it all appeared, how fake it seemed, but mostly I hated the fact that I'd never be able to attend a prom because I was homeschooled. I also hated the fact that Cheryl was only a junior this year and was attending her *second* senior prom.

"I mean, it's not like you could go with him anyway, and it doesn't make sense for him to go by himself, ya know?" Cheryl snapped her gum over and over again as she stood in front of my vanity, applying her fifteenth layer of candy apple red lipstick. I sat on my bed with a book against my chest, listening to my sister talk my ear off.

She wiped off the red lipstick and then applied a deep purple shade. When she finished, she smiled at herself, as if she was so proud of her beauty—as if it was her own doing and not just genetics. Her long gold dress sparkled every time she swung her hips, which she did often. "Plus"—she smirked wickedly—"I think he has a crush on me."

I snickered to myself.

No, he doesn't.

She whipped herself around to face me and pushed her lips together. "What do you think? This color? Or the red?" She frowned. "I don't even know why I'm asking. You know nothing about makeup. Maybe you'd know more if your face wasn't always in a book." She hurried over to me and sat down on the bed. I held my book closer to my chest, but she snatched it out of my hand and tossed it to the floor.

Oh my gosh. That had to be some form of abuse, didn't it? She had literally bruised and battered dozens of characters—dozens of my friends. Snatching the book from my grip was rude, but throwing it was reason enough for a termination of our family ties.

"Seriously, Maggie. You're already weird with your no talking and no leaving the house thing. Do you really want to be known as the girl who only reads? It's kind of creepy."

Your face is kind of creepy.

I simply smiled and shrugged.

She flipped her hair. "So, back to the important things. I mean, I'm pretty sure he's still sad about Lacey breaking up with him before prom. Also, I know how much you care about him, so I offered myself up to be his date, because I knew you wouldn't want him to miss out on the one thing he was looking forward to. I'm only going for you, Maggie."

How noble.

It took everything inside me to not roll my eyes in my sister's face. *Sister*—I used the term loosely that day.

"Anyway, I told Brooks how supportive you were about the idea of me going with him, so thank you for your support." She gave me a cheesy smile and flipped her curly hair over her shoulder again. "I think Calvin and Stacey are meeting Brooks and me in our backyard for photographs and stuff in about ten minutes. So yeah, which lipstick?"

I pointed to the purple one because I wanted her to look awful.

She chose the red, which made her look gorgeous.

"Perfect!" She stood up from my bed, smoothed out her stunning gown, and shimmied herself in front of my mirror one last time. "I better get heading outside. Brooks will be waiting for me." She swayed her hips left and right the whole time she walked out of my room.

The moment she was out of sight, I rushed over to my novel, picked it up, and rubbed the cover. *Sorry, friends.* The book was tucked tightly in my arms as I hurried over to the set of windows that faced the backyard and stared down at my brother and his girlfriend laughing and cuddling in their fancy prom clothing. Calvin had a way of making Stacey laugh so hard it rocketed into the sky. Her hands always rested against his chest, and his eyes always rested on her. I'd wondered what that would be like: to be seen through a pair of eyes filled with love.

My stare moved to Cheryl, who was taking selfies, while impatiently waiting for Brooks to show up and be her arm candy. He wasn't one to ever be late to anything, so I was somewhat surprised to not see him yet. My stomach filled with knots as I rushed to my other window to see if he was still across the street at his parents' house. I couldn't remember the last time I'd seen Brooks in a tuxedo, and I would've been lying if I'd said I wasn't interested in the sight. He always looked so handsome—so happy.

My heartbeats rushed through my chest, waiting for him to step out of his house, waiting for him to walk across the street to my backyard, waiting for him to fall in lust with Cheryl.

I shut my eyes and took a deep inhale. A small prayer raced through my head.

Don't do it, Brooks.

He deserved more than that. He deserved more than Cheryl's games.

He deserved to be loved by someone who knew how handsome his lopsided smiles were, how brilliant his mind was, and how good he was at communicating with no words falling from his lips.

"You okay today, Magnet?"

It was my favorite set of words. My eyes flew open and I turned to see Brooks standing in my doorway, wearing a navy blue tuxedo, a black and white polka dot tie, and matching polka dots socks. His dark brown hair was slicked back, and his dark brown eyes were smiling all on their own like they always did. In his hand was a clear box holding a wrist corsage, a beautiful array of yellow flowers and pink ribbons.

Wow, Brooks.

He looked better than my mind could've imagined and butterflies flew through my stomach as I raked my fingers through my tangled hair. I smiled. He smiled back, always out of the left side of his mouth. I wondered if he knew...? If he knew how dizzy that smile made me?

"Can I come in?" he asked, stuffing his hands into his slacks.

I nodded. *Always.*

He stepped into my room and walked over to the window to look down at the backyard, where Cheryl was texting someone, her thumbs slamming on the keys. Within seconds, Brooks' cell phone dinged. "She's already pissed at me for being late," he explained, slightly rocking back and forth. His phone dinged two more times. "That's the seventeenth message from her."

I stared down at my sister, who was going out with Brooks just to spite me. For some reason it made her feel better about herself to see how bad off I was with my no speaking or leaving the house.

"I didn't want to go with her," Brooks explained. He tilted his head toward me and frowned. "After Lacey broke things off with me, I figured I'd just stay home or something. Play some video games. Maybe come over here and play some music with you or something, but Cheryl kept telling me how much it meant to you that I'd go with her."

I cocked an eyebrow.

He snickered. "Yeah. I should've known." We stood quietly for a few moments, watching Cheryl panic, and watching Calvin and

Stacey fall deeper in love. A few birds danced past the window, and Brooks released a low sigh. "You think Calvin and Stacey know how annoyingly perfect they are?"

I nodded, and he snickered. Yeah, they knew.

"Cal and I are performing at the prom tonight. Did he tell you?"

He had. After spending years listening to them practice in my parents' garage, it would've been amazing to see them live that night. A dream come true.

"Stacey's going to record the performance and send it to you, you know, if you want to see it."

I took his hand in mine and squeezed it twice. *Yes.*

He squeezed my hand back.

Yes. Yes.

"You want to dance with me, Maggie May?"

I turned his way and his cheeks reddened. My stare met his lips, almost wondering if I had imagined the words leaving his mouth. He nervously chewed his bottom lip as a small chuckle came out. "I mean…you don't have to. Sorry. That was stupid. I just… With Lacey breaking up with me, and with Cheryl being…Cheryl, I thought it'd be nice to dance with someone I actually care about on the day of my prom."

My inhales were heavy and my grip on my novel was slipping, as my now panicked stare met his nervous eyes.

I'd never danced. I didn't know how.

I'd only read about dancing, and proms, and two people becoming one in each other's arms.

"You don't have to. Sorry." He cleared his throat and looked back at the window. He muttered the word "stupid", and I could tell he was internally beating himself up.

I placed my book against the windowsill and nodded.

He must've been watching me out of the corner of his eye, because his smile stretched without turning my way. "Yeah?" he asked.

Yeah.

I ran my fingers through my messy hair and goose bumps formed on my skin. My long white maxi dress didn't look anything like Cheryl's and nothing like Stacey's. I wore no makeup and had few curves to my ghostly pale body, but Brooks didn't seem to care. He always looked at me and made me feel like I was enough, no matter what.

He turned my way and smiled.

"Can I have your wrist?" he asked.

I held it out, and he opened the box with Cheryl's corsage then slipped it on my arm.

"Just for now, you know, to make it seem more real."

He pulled out his iPod from his pocket and flipped through his music before landing on the song of his choice. He handed one earbud to me, and he took the other, then he pressed play and placed the iPod in the front pocket of his slacks. I raised an eyebrow, unsure of the song playing.

"It's something I wrote and played acoustic a while back. It's just instrumentals. No one has heard the lyrics or anything, but I guess you can hear them now. Because, I wrote them for you."

Swoon.

I loved it already.

He walked over to me and held his hands out. I stepped forward, and he wrapped his arms around my lower back, then my arms fell around his neck as he pulled me closer. His skin smelled like shaving cream and honey—my new favorite scent. If it was a dream, I swore I'd never wake. As we swayed, he pulled me closer. And as he pulled me closer, he began to sing.

She lies against my chest as her raindrops begin to fall
She feels so weak, floating aimlessly, slamming against the walls
Praying for a moment where she won't begin to drown
Her heart's been begging for an answer to the silent hurts her soul
keeps bound.

An ache formed in my chest as I listened to his voice. His lips lingered over mine, his words falling against me. I felt the small breaths he exhaled into me and felt his shaky fingers against my spine. I felt his soul, my body pressed against his, my eyes staring at his singing lips. *Brooks...*

I'll be your anchor
I'll hold you still throughout the night
I'll be your steadiness
during the dark and lonely tides
I'll hold you close, I'll be your light, I'll promise you'll be all right
I'll be your anchor
And we'll get through this fight

He drove me crazy. His hold, his touch, his voice, his words. Everything about his soul lit me on fire, and I was proud to burn beside him.

She tries each day to escape the flooding of her mind
She loses hope when darkness locks her in a bind
She slips away from me and I try to hold on tight
I promise it will all be over by daylight

I'll be your anchor
I'll hold you still throughout the night
I'll be your steadiness
during the dark and lonely tides
I'll hold you close, I'll be your light, I'll promise you'll be all right
I'll be your anchor
And we'll get through this fight

I'll hold you close, I'll be your light, I'll promise you'll be all right
I'll hold you close, I'll be your light, baby, we'll be all right

I'll be your anchor
And we'll get through this night

"Maggie," he whispered against me, our lips not yet touching. Our bodies shook against one another and he laughed. "You're shaking."

So are you.

He smiled as if he'd read my mind, and I tried my best to read his.

"You're my best friend, Magnet, but…" His lips grew closer, and I swore I felt them brush against my own. His fingers massaged into my back in circles, and I melted each time a circle was complete. "What if she was right? What if Lacey was onto something? What if there is something more than friendship between us?" His grip on my lower back got tighter, pulling me closer. Our lips brushed together again, and my stomach knotted.

"Step back, and I'll step back, too," he told me. I moved in closer, placing my hands against his chest, feeling his heartbeat. His stare fell to my lips, and his trembles became my own. "Tell me not to kiss you, Maggie. Step back, and I won't kiss you."

I stayed still.

Of course I stayed still.

I stayed and waited, and died, and waited.

When he found his place, when his lips glided against mine, my brain went dizzy and I came back to life.

His lips pressed against mine, gently at first, and everything inside me became a part of him. His fingers wrapped around my back and he pulled me in closer, pushing his lips harder against mine, and for the first time in a long time, I felt it.

Happy.

Is it real?

Am I allowed this?

Am I allowed to be happy?

The last time I'd been kissed was by the same boy who wrapped his arms around me, who held me as if I were a promise of a dream he didn't know he had.

This kiss was different than all those years ago. This time we didn't count the seconds, but I did count the breaths he stole from me.

One...

Two...

Twenty-five...

This time the kiss felt so real, so perfect, so much like forever.

This time is forever.

"Maggie, have you seen—"

Brooks broke his hold on me and jumped backward, turning his back to the person at the door. The headphone in my ear was snatched out, making me stumble forward.

My eyes flew to Mama standing there, shocked. "Cheryl's red lipstick," she finished her sentence. An awkward silence rose, and Mama narrowed her eyes as Brooks straightened out his tie. "Brooks, I think Cheryl is waiting downstairs for photos."

"Right, of course. Thanks, Mrs. Riley. Let me just get..." He walked over to me and took the corsage from my arm, then just like that, forever was over. "I'll-uh-I'll see you later, Maggie." He hurried past Mama, keeping his head down from embarrassment.

Mama stayed there staring at me, and I could feel the disappointment in her stance. I hurried over to the dresser where Cheryl had left her lipstick, then handed it off to Mama.

She frowned. "She's your sister, Maggie May, and she's going to prom with Brooks. What do you think you're doing?"

My head lowered.

I don't know.

"I know Cheryl can be a handful at times, but...*she's your sister,*" she repeated.

She left before I could write down any kind of response. She wouldn't have read it, anyway. Mama was like Mrs. Boone in that way—she wanted actual words, not pieces of paper.

I headed over to my window and looked down at Brooks' arms wrapped around Cheryl's waist for the photos. He was giving the camera his best fake smile, and whenever he'd look up at my window, I'd step out of view.

It was a beautiful dream, he and I.

But that's all it was.

A dream from which I was forced to wake.

"You bitch!" Cheryl screamed, barging into my bedroom as I changed into my pajama pants. My arms yanked my pants up and I stumbled backward, taken aback. Her mascara raced down her face with her tears and her red lipstick was smeared. The bottom of her dress looked as if it had been dragged through grass, and her eyes were wide. "I can't believe you! I can't fucking believe you told them!" she screamed.

I blinked once, confused. *Told who what?*

"Oh, don't give me that innocent shit." She laughed hysterically, and from her laughter, I could tell she was on something; her eyes were too wild to not be. "It's actually ridiculous that anyone buys into the bullshit you push when really you're a monster! I can't believe you told Mom and Dad about what happened with Jordan yesterday!"

My lips parted, but no words came out, which pissed her off more. I hurried over to pick up a piece of paper and a pen, to write that I hadn't told our parents, but she slapped it out of my hands.

"What the hell is wrong with you? Why the hell do you open your mouth if you're not going to say anything? And what's the point of writing on paper? That's the same as talking, Maggie! Just use your fucking voice, freak!"

My body started trembling as her rage escalated. She headed for the walls of my bedroom and started knocking over all my perfectly-lined-up books. She threw them around the room, infuriated, and began ripping pages out of them. "How do you like that? Huh? How do you like someone screwing with your life, the way you screwed with mine?"

I'd never seen her so mad, so pissed off. "Dad showed up to prom and cussed Jordan out. I was fucking mortified. But that's not all—no. Before I was embarrassed in front of the whole student body, I tried to kiss Brooks, and he said he couldn't. You know why?" She laughed wickedly, picked up one of my novels and started ripping pages out. I rushed at her to try to stop her, but she was stronger than me. "Because he said he had feelings for you. For you! Can you believe that? Because I couldn't. Why would anyone ever want you? What are you going to do? Date him and never leave the house? Are you going to have romantic dinners in the living room? Travel the world on the Discovery Channel in the living room? You're not worthy of Brooks. You're not worthy of shit."

"Cheryl!" Daddy shouted, rushing upstairs. "Go to your room."

"Are you kidding me? She gets to ruin my life and I'm the one who gets in trouble?"

"Cheryl," Daddy growled. He never lost his temper. "Go to your room. *Now.* You're drunk and high, and you're going to regret what you did to your sister in the morning."

"She's not my sister," Cheryl snapped back at Daddy before dropping the remaining pages of the novel in her grip. "I wish you had stayed lost in those woods." She pushed past Daddy and hissed, "And you're not my father."

I saw it happen: a part of my father's heart shattering.

He bent down to start picking up my novels, and I placed my hand on his arm to stop him.

He felt my shaking, and I felt his.

His fingers brushed against his temple and he let out a harsh breath. "Are you all right?"

I nodded slowly.

He shook his head. "Your mom found the note crumpled in Cheryl's room. We told her that, but she was too drunk to comprehend anything. Brooks was already trying to get her to come home, but she stormed off with Jordan before we could get her to listen, and I guess she beat us home." He took off his glasses, then pinched the bridge of his nose. "I should've driven home faster, then she couldn't have taken her anger out on you, or destroyed your room like this." His eyes watered. "Your books."

I took his hand and squeezed it once. *No.* Not his fault.

"Let me help you clean up this mess."

I squeezed his hand once more. *No.*

He gave me a broken smile and pulled me into a hug. He kissed my forehead and said, "The world keeps spinning because your heartbeats exist."

I wanted to believe him, I did, but that night the world had crashed because of my heartbeats.

"Holy crap," Brooks murmured, as he stood in my doorway later that night. His tie was hanging loosely around his shoulders and his hands were stuffed in the pockets of his slacks. I'd been sitting in the middle of my floor, surrounded by my novels and the torn pages. It was impossible to find the right pieces to go to the right stories.

They were all destroyed.

My eyes locked with Brooks', and seeing the hurt in his eyes made me realize how bad everything actually looked. I was sitting in the middle of a puzzle of tales, and I hadn't a clue how to connect the pieces.

He frowned. "Are you okay, Magnet?"

I shook my head.

"Can I come in?"

I nodded.

He walked around the books, tiptoeing to avoid stepping on any of their spines. "It's not that bad."

Liar.

When he gasped, my stare fell to his hands, where he held my journal. "Oh no…" he said softly.

My emotions took over.

My to-do list—it was completely destroyed. Dozens and dozens of adventures I hoped to one day experience were ruined, and I couldn't help but to burst into tears. I knew it seemed dramatic, but those books, those characters—they were my friends, my safe haven, my protection.

That list was my promise of tomorrow.

And now I had nothing.

It only took seconds before Brooks' arms were wrapped around me tight, and I fell against his chest, sobbing. "You're gonna be okay, Maggie," he whispered. It was a promise that felt empty. "You're just tired. We'll fix this in the morning. Everything's okay."

He led me to my bed and laid me down then began scrambling around my room, digging through the piles of books. When he found one that wasn't damaged, he sat on the floor beside my bed and opened it to the first page. He bent his legs up and rested the book on his knee. Then he unbuttoned his cuffs, rolled up the sleeves of his dress shirt, and finally picked the book back up.

"The Walk Home," he said, reading the title. "Chapter One. Lauren Sue Lock wasn't having an upbeat day…"

He read to me as I cried uncontrollably. He read to me as my tears slowed. He read to me as my racing heartbeat calmed. He read to me as my eyes grew heavy. He read to me as I fell asleep.

I dreamed of his voice reading to me some more.

When I woke the next morning, he was gone. As I climbed out of my bed, parts of me wondered if he had truly been there at all, but he'd left enough evidence to tell me of our night.

Every book was placed back around the perimeter of the bedroom, going from reds to purples. Every book was carefully taped back together. On my desk was my to-do list, resting inside my journal, damaged, yet somehow more whole than before.

Resting on top of the journal was a Post-it note that read, *You're okay today, Maggie May Riley.*

I loved him.

I wasn't certain when it had happened. I wasn't certain if it was a group of moments collected over time or simply the heroic act he'd performed while I was sleeping, but it didn't matter. It didn't matter when, or why, or how it had happened. It didn't matter how many moments gathered together to form the love. It didn't matter if it was right or wrong.

Love didn't come with guidelines. It flowed into a person with only hope as its current. There wasn't a list of rules to follow, making sure you cared for it correctly. It didn't give you instructions to keep it pure. It simply showed up quietly, praying you wouldn't let it slip away.

Brooks

There was something to be said about timing. Getting the timing right in any situation was always important. Saying the right things at the right moments, making the right choices when choices had to be made. As I walked up to Maggie's room, my chest was tight. As I'd spent the time taping all the pieces of her books together, I hadn't been able to stop wondering what she'd think when she woke the next morning. I wanted to make her smile. If I could only do one thing for the rest of my life, it would be to make her smile, and it was time for her to know that, to know how I felt. How when we were together, she was always on the forefront of my mind. How when we were apart, that was where she remained.

"I wanted to return your book last night, but I really needed to see what happened to Lauren Sue Lock. Plus, I got you a new dry-erase board," I said, standing in Maggie's doorway. "You okay today, Mag—"

Before the words could leave my mouth, Maggie rushed over to me and pressed her lips against mine. I stumbled backward into the hallway, catching her in my arms. I didn't question her kiss; I fell into it. I allowed her to kiss me as I kissed her more. When she pulled back a bit, I combed her long hair behind her ears.

She blushed, and I kissed her cheeks. She lowered her stare, and my fingers went under her chin to lift it up. I kissed her cheeks again. Then her forehead. Then her nose. Then every invisible freckle that trailed across her face.

Then, her lips. "Good afternoon, Maggie May."

She smiled at me and kissed my cheeks. Then my forehead. Then my nose. Then every invisible freckle that trailed across my face.

Then, my lips.

I imagined her saying it to me, too. *Good afternoon, Brooks Tyler.*

She took my hands in hers and walked backward, leading us into her bedroom. When we were inside, I kicked the door closed.

For a while we were stupid and silly, simply staring and smiling. We kissed, too; that might've been my favorite part. Her finger danced across my shoulder blade and she studied my body, as if I were real. Her fingers moved down my arms, then down my sides, before traveling up my chest. She laid her palm against my chest, feeling my heartbeat.

"For you," I said.

She blushed some more, and I kissed her cheeks some more, too. I took my finger, moving it across her collarbone, down her sides, back up her sides, and then moving my palm to her heartbeat.

She bit her bottom lip and held up four fingers then pointed at me. *For me.*

Her heartbeats were made for me, and mine for hers.

"I like you."

She pointed to herself then held up two fingers. *Me too.*

"Date me?" I asked.

She stepped backward, almost shocked by my words. She shook her head.

I stepped toward her. "Date me?" I asked again.

She stepped backward again, shaking her head.

"Stop saying no, please? It's kind of a punch to my confidence."

She shrugged her shoulders and moved to her desk where she picked up a notebook and started writing.

How?

"How? How what? How do we date?"

Yes.

"Well, like anyone dates, I guess."

How do you date other people? How did you date your ex-girlfriends?

"I don't know, hung out with them a lot. Some liked to go shopping, to the movies, to…" My words trailed off. She frowned. The way I had dated in the past wasn't the way I could date Maggie. "Oh. I get it, but I'm not trying to date them. I'm trying to date you. However that works, I want to do it. I want to be around you. I want to kiss you. I want to hold you. I want to see you smile. Plus"—I held up her journal—"dating is on your list."

She shook her head.

"Maggie, I taped this book together piece by piece for over five hours. I think I know what's in your journal." I flipped through the pages and held it out toward her when I found it. "Number fifty-six: date Brooks Tyler Griffin, from The Book of Brooks."

A sly smile found her. *I didn't write that.*

I shrugged. "Listen, you don't have to be embarrassed. I'm flattered. Even though I didn't create the list, I'm here to make you follow it. Heck, if I'd known you were so madly infatuated with me, I would've started dating you years ago."

She cocked an eyebrow and slammed her hands on her hips, and I knew exactly what she was thinking.

"Okay, to be fair, when we were ten and you planned our wedding, I was at the age where I hated girls. You can't hold that against me."

She quietly chuckled and rolled her eyes. I loved that. I loved when she laughed, even though it was so quiet. It was the closest thing I had to her voice.

"See that? We have this thing where I know what you're thinking without you even talking. You're my best friend, Maggie. If dating you means spending every night in this house with you, then I'd be the luckiest guy in the world." I combed her hair behind her ear. "So I'm going to ask you one more time: will you be my girlfriend?"

She shook her head, laughing, but then started nodding and shrugged. I could hear the words she didn't speak so clearly. *I mean, whatever, Brooks. I guess I'll date you.*

Message fully received.

We moved over to her bed, fell on it backward, and I pulled out my iPod for our first official couple song. "Fever Dreaming" by No Age. The song was loud and fast-paced, everything a dating song shouldn't have been. I was going to switch it, but Maggie started tapping her fingers against the bed. Then her foot started tapping against the floor, and my fingers and feet followed her direction as the drums kicked in. Seconds later, we were standing, jumping up and down, rocking out to the music. My heart was racing as we stood so close to one another and jammed out to the song. When it was over, our breaths were heavy. Maggie reached for her marker and wrote on her board.

Again?

I played the song again, and again. We danced, and danced until our heart rates were high and our breaths were short.

Our timing was so great that night.

Our timing was finally right.

Every day that passed with Maggie felt right.

Every hand hold felt warm.

Every kiss felt real.

Every hug was perfect, except for when they weren't.

It wasn't often that things weren't perfect between Maggie and me, but if I was being honest, some days were tough.

Dating Maggie was one of the best decisions I'd ever made, but that didn't mean it was always easy. Even so, it was still always right.

The more time I spent with her, the more I noticed the small things no one else noticed about her—like how the sound of running water made her flinch, or how when someone touched her when her back was turned, she'd jump out of her skin. Or how when more than two people were in a room, she melted into the corners, or how sometimes when we'd sit and watch movies, tears fell down her cheeks.

"Why are you crying?" I asked.

Her fingers grazed her eyes and she seemed surprised by the tears. Wiping them away, she gave me a tight smile and held her anchor necklace in her hand.

Then, there were her panic attacks.

In all my years of knowing Maggie, I'd never known about the panics.

She kept them hidden, and to herself. The only reason I knew they existed was because some nights I'd sneak into her room for a sleepover. Sometimes she'd fall asleep, and she'd twist and turn so much I swore her nightmares were going to give her a heart attack. When I woke her, her eyes were wide, horrified, as if she didn't know who I was when I touched her.

She crawled into a ball and covered her ears as if she were hearing voices that didn't exist. Her body was covered in sweat, her hands trembled, and her breaths were heavy. Sometimes her fingers wrapped around her throat and her breaths were short and erratic.

Whenever I tried to dive deeper into her mind, she pushed me away. We'd have fights where I was the only one shouting. Fighting with someone who didn't fight back was worse than fighting with someone who threw chairs. You felt hopeless, as if screaming at a stone wall. "Say something!" I begged. "React!" But she always stayed calm, which only pissed me off more.

It drove me mad, trying to discover what was still eating at her all these years later.

It drove me mad that I couldn't fix her hurts.

I'd dated quite a few girls before her, and it had always seemed easy. I figured if I had things to talk about with them, that meant we were a match. If we liked the same hobbies, we were supposed to be together. I never struggled with not knowing what to say in my past relationships; we always talked, sometimes for hours. When it came to silence, it always felt off. I was always searching for the next thing to say, the next conversation.

It wasn't that way with Maggie. She didn't respond to words.

During her most recent panic attack, I figured out how to help her. Before, when I screamed at her, demanding for her to let me into her head, it never worked. When I begged for understanding, she pushed further away.

Music would help. Music could help. I knew it could. Music was the one thing that always helped me. As she sat on her bed crying, I shut off her bedroom light and turned on my iPod, playing "To Be Alone With You" by Sufjan Stevens.

It didn't help her the first time it played, or the second, but I sat quietly, waiting for her breathing to come back to normal.

"You're okay, Magnet," I'd say every now and then, unsure if she could even hear me, but hoping she did.

When she finally came around, the song was on its eleventh loop.

She wiped her eyes and went to grab a piece of paper, but I shook my head and patted a spot on the floor beside me.

She didn't have to offer me any words.

Sometimes words were more empty than silence.

She sat across from me with her legs crossed. I shut off my music. "Five minutes," I whispered, holding my hands out to her. "Just five minutes."

She placed her hands in mine, and we sat completely still and quiet, staring into each other's eyes for five minutes. The first minute we did it we couldn't stop laughing. It felt a bit ridiculous. The second minute, we snickered some more. By minute three, Maggie started to cry. By four, we cried together, because nothing hurt more than seeing her eyes so sad. By the fifth minute, we smiled.

She released a breath she'd been holding, and I let go of mine.

It was freeing to feel so much with someone who felt it too. It was during those moments that I felt I learned the most about her. It was in those moments that she learned the most about me.

I hadn't known you could hear someone's voice so clearly in the silent moments.

13

Maggie

Brooks never asked me about my panic attacks again, and I was happy about that. It was something I wasn't ready to talk about yet, and Brooks understood. I knew, though, if there was a day I was ready, he'd be willing to listen, and that meant more to me than he'd ever know.

Instead of filling our summer with serious topics, we filled it with kisses. When we weren't kissing, we created our own to-do list for a future together. I liked the way he believed in me someday leaving the house.

I liked the idea of me seeing the world with him by my side.

"It's gonna be great, Maggie. Plus, since I'm going to college one town over, I can come see you every afternoon after school is out. It's gonna be easy," Brooks often said. His hope in us made me more hopeful than ever.

Then, we'd go back to kissing. Kissing, and kissing only.

I wasn't good at the good stuff.

It wasn't a surprise I wasn't good at the good stuff, because I'd never had a boyfriend to practice any of the things people did when they were in relationships. Whenever Brooks came over and his hands started to wander, I tensed up—not because he touched me—I wanted him to—but because I wasn't sure how I was supposed to touch him back.

It was embarrassing. I hated it. I felt as if I've read enough books with enough sex references to be able to know how to touch my boyfriend, but it was far from the truth.

"It's fine, really." Brooks smiled, standing up from one of our kissing sessions that always led to more kissing. "We don't have to rush."

I didn't feel rushed, though. I felt stupid. *Where do I put my hands? Would that feel good to him? How do I know if he really likes it?*

"I better get downstairs for band practice." He straightened out the crotch area of his jeans, which made me feel even worse. I was such an accidental tease. "I'll see you downstairs, all right?"

I nodded. He leaned in and kissed my forehead before hurrying away.

The moment he was out of sight, I grabbed my pillow, placed it over my face, and silently screamed into it. My legs kicked back and forth in frustration. *Ugh!*

When I heard quiet whimpering, I looked up from my pillow to see Cheryl walking down the hallway, holding her cheek. She hurried into her bedroom and slammed the door.

I was there two seconds later, knocking.

"Go away!" she shouted.

I knocked once. *No.*

I listened to her groan. "Please just go, Maggie. I know it's you."

Turning the knob, I slowly opened her bedroom door to see her standing in front of her mirror, touching a slice under her eye that was dripping blood down her cheek.

"Goddammit, Maggie! Don't you know how to listen?"

Walking closer, I made her face me and examined her cut. Tilting my head, I gave her a questioning stare.

She grimaced. "Jordan thought since I had him drive me back from prom weeks ago, it meant we were back together. And seeing

118

how I hated being alone, I went back to him. But it turned out, he didn't fully forgive me, and as the weeks went on, he became more and more mean. So, when I told him I didn't want to be with him anymore…he got a bit…upset."

My chest tightened.

"Don't freak out, okay?" she warned as she slowly turned her back to me and lifted up her t-shirt. My hands flew over my mouth as I stared at her red skin, where it looked like Jordan beat her.

Cheryl…

Snickering, she said, "If you think that's bad, you should see him."

I frowned.

She frowned, too.

He had probably walked away without a hair out of place, leaving my sister with scars not only on her body, but also on her mind.

I walked off and went to the bathroom to get a wet washcloth and a bandage. When I came back, I led her to her bed, pulled her desk chair over, and sat down. As I started cleaning her cut, her body trembled the whole time.

"I'm not pressing charges, Maggie," she asserted. "I know that's probably something you'd want me to do, but I'm not. He's over eighteen. He'd be charged as an adult, and I can't ruin his life like that…"

I kept cleaning her face, not reacting to her words at all.

"I mean, it's my fault. I shouldn't have left with him on prom night. I sent confusing signals."

I tapped her leg once. *No.*

She was blaming herself. I'd been there before, too. Sometimes my mind still put fault on me. *I shouldn't have been in those woods. Mama told me not to wander off. I put myself in a dangerous situation. It was my fault.*

But when I took a bath and slipped beneath the water, I cleared all of those thoughts.

Sometimes our minds acted as a form of kryptonite, and we had a responsibility to our own self-worth to aggressively tell it to fuck off with its lies.

I was not to blame.

And neither was Cheryl.

A tear fell down her cheek and she wiped it away. "What's your deal, anyway? Why are you helping me? I trashed your room. I said some shitty things to you, and still you're helping me. Why?"

My shoulders rose and fell.

She reached over, cringing from the pain in her back, and grabbed a pencil and paper. "Why, Maggie?"

You're my family.

More tears fell from her eyes, and she didn't even try to hide them. "I really am sorry, ya know, for what I did to your room, to you. I just..." She tossed her hands up in frustration. Her voice filled with deep shame and loud remorse. "I don't know what I'm doing with my life."

I doubted most people did. Anyone who claimed to have their life figured out was a liar. Sometimes I wondered if there was anything to truly figure out, or if we were all walking around looking for a reason when no reason truly existed.

"I want to tell Mom and Dad what he did," she whispered, her eyes filled with sadness. "But I know they'll just freak out. They are already pissed at me for all of the other shitty mistakes I've made. I've fucked up too much for them to really care."

I tapped her leg once more. *No.*

"How do you know?"

I held up the family piece of paper one more time. After that, she built up the courage to tell our parents. The moment they hugged her and told her none of it was her fault was the moment Cheryl released the breath she'd been holding for what seemed like years.

120

"I miss him," Cheryl said, plopping down on my bed a few weeks after her 'official' breakup with Jordan. The cut on her face was healing pretty well, but I knew the damage to her mind wouldn't be healed as quickly. "I mean, I don't miss *him*. I miss the idea of him. I miss the idea of someone being by my side. Today I sat and tried to think of the last time I'd been single and I couldn't come up with an answer."

I grimaced, and she continued to speak. "What if I'm one of those girls who can't be alone? What if I'm supposed to always be with a guy? What the hell am I supposed to do with my time if there's no guy for me to talk about? I don't know if you noticed, but I'm not really the best at making friends with girls. No females ever come over to hang out with me, probably because I've stolen most of their boyfriends. What the heck am I supposed to do?"

Standing from my desk chair, I moved over to my wall of books, searching for a certain read for my sister. Grabbing *The Handmaid's Tale* by Margaret Atwood, I held it out to her.

She knit her brow as a gloomy expression overtook her face. "What am I supposed to do with this?" I cocked an eyebrow, and she raised one back. "Maggie, I don't read." The combination of those four words created the saddest sentence I'd ever heard. I pushed the book out toward her again, and this time she took it warily. "Fine. I'll try it, just because I'm so fucking bored, but I doubt I'll like it."

It took her three days to finish the book, and when she did, she came back quoting it, her eyes wide with emotion I'd never seen from her. "You want to know my favorite line? *'Don't let the bastards grind you down.'* God. So. Fucking. Good. Margaret Atwood is my spirit animal." She held the book out toward me and narrowed her eyes. "You got any more like that?"

I passed her a new book every three days. After a while, we started having Friday night girls' nights where we ate Doritos, drank too much soda, and lay on my floor with our feet propped up on my bed frame. "Freakin' A, Maggie. All this time I thought you were reading to escape the world, but now I know, you didn't read to escape it; you read to discover it."

The best night by far was when Cheryl finished *The Help* by Kathryn Stockett. Throughout her read, she had tears that sometimes turned into laughter, and vice versa. "THOSE FUCKING BITCHES!" she'd holler every now and then. "No, really, THOSE FUCKING BITCHES!"

One night as two a.m. rolled around, I was sleeping in my bed when Cheryl began poking me in the side to wake me. "Maggie," she whispered. "Sis!" When my eyes opened, she was holding the novel to her chest and had the biggest smile on her face, the kind of smile kids have when they hear the sound of an ice cream truck coming down their road and they have just enough coins in their pockets for a Bombpop. "Maggie. I think I'm that thing. I think I'm it."

I raised a tired eyebrow, waiting for her to explain what thing she was.

"I think I'm finally it." Her smile grew bigger somehow, which made me smile, too. "I think I'm a reader."

As the days and weeks passed by, Cheryl started staying home more nights. She'd spent most of her time reading books. When she came to visit my room, she wasn't telling me all the stories of her wild adventures with different guys. She started talking about her wild dreams of adventure—traveling the world, seeing some of the sights she read about in the novels. She started building her own to-do list, too.

One night when she was talking about London, I brought up sex, and her mouth hung open with bewilderment. "Oh my gosh, Maggie!" she said, ripping the paper out of my hand tearing it to pieces. "One: those are the kinds of notes you never want Dad to find, and two: are you and Brooks having sex?"

My cheeks heated up and I shook my head.

"But you are doing some stuff, right? Oh my gosh! I've dreamed of these conversations with you! Okay." She plopped down on my bed and crossed her legs. "Tell me everything you two have done." Her eyes were wide with wonderment.

Kissing.

She nodded rapidly. "Uh-huh, uh-huh! Nice! What else?"

I wrote kissing again.

"What? But you two have been dating for like, weeks now. That's a long time to just be kissing. Why haven't you done anything else? Are you not ready? Because if you're not ready, that's fine. Brooks wouldn't care."

No. I'm ready.

"Then what's the issue?"

I blushed. *I don't know how to do anything.*

"You mean…anything? Like hand jobs? Or rim jobs? Or blow jobs? Or nip-lick jobs? Or pineapple-upside-down-cake jobs?" I cocked an eyebrow, and Cheryl nodded. "I know what you're thinking, all of these seem like unpaid positions, but trust me, if you do them right, you'll be paid in full."

Ohmygod. I couldn't handle her sometimes. But still, I missed her so much.

She jumped up from her seat and hurried out of the room. When she returned, she had candy, bananas, and other random fruits, including rings of pineapples. "Okay, we'll start from the beginning." She picked up a banana. "Hand jobs 101."

"Hey, girls," Brooks said, popping his head into my bedroom.

Cheryl threw her body over the items. "We're doing nothing!" she shouted.

Good job, sis. Not suspicious at all.

Brooks arched an eyebrow. "Oookay. I was just supposed to tell you dinner is ready, and your dad told me I had to go home because I'm no longer welcome in the house where Maggie sleeps."

I smirked. *Sounds like Dad.*

"Okay, well, you can leave now," Cheryl replied, giving Brooks a tight smile.

He walked over to me and kissed my forehead. "I'll see you tomorrow."

When he left, Cheryl groaned and sat up with a banana smashed to her chest, leaving residue all over my blanket. "Sorry for the mess," she said, wiping banana off her shirt. "But trust me, if you do it right, the messy stage is completely normal."

Brooks

On a cloudy Saturday night, I headed over to Maggie's room to hang out. We spent a lot of time in her house, and I didn't mind at all. As long as she was there, I was happy. I walked up to her bedroom, and she was already standing in her doorway with a stack of papers in her hands. She looked different than normal. Her hair was curled, and was she wearing...makeup? She was still beautiful, just a different kind of beautiful.

Guess what!

I smiled wide. "What?"

She dropped the first piece of paper to reveal the next one.

My parents got me a cell phone for my graduation gift.

"No way. Seriously?"

She nodded rapidly and dropped the next piece of paper.

Seriously.

I stepped farther into her bedroom and checked the hallway once to make sure Mr. Riley wasn't looking before I closed the door. "Does this mean I can now send you inappropriate text messages?"

Her cheeks reddened. It didn't take much to make Maggie blush, and I loved whenever it happened. She flipped through her pages and reached for the right response.

Don't be a freak.

I cocked an eyebrow and moved in closer to her, wrapping my arms around her. "What about inappropriate pictures?"

She flipped through the pages again.

Don't be a freakier freak.

I laughed. She bent forward, placing her hands against my chest. As her fingers moved lower toward my crotch, she slowly slid her tongue against my lips, parting them before kissing me hard. It was a new move for her and I groaned, loving it more than she knew. "Maggie, you can't tell me to not be a freak and then do something like that."

She stepped backward and bit her bottom lip, dropping another piece of paper.

Okay, then be a freak.

I narrowed my eyes, feeling a small twitch in my jeans as I stared at her. Her long hair was wavy and still a little damp from her shower. It lay over her shoulders, brushing against the spaghetti strap dress that skimmed across her toes. She looked so simple in the most beautiful way. Her cheeks were still red, but her eyes were determined.

"You want…?"

Yes.

"What about your parents?"

She dropped another piece of paper, and I couldn't help but smirk. It was as if she knew everything I'd ask.

At my grandparents' until tomorrow.

"And Calvin?"

With Stacey.

"And Cheryl?"

She smirked and rolled her eyes, dropping her third to last piece of paper.

Who knows?

Brooks?

"Yes?" The way she swayed back and forth was killing me. She was so fucking beautiful, and I swore she had no damn clue.

She held up the last piece of paper in her grip.

Come undress me now.

I stepped closer to her, running my fingers through her hair. "Are you sure?" I asked. She nodded. My mouth moved to her neck and I licked it slowly, sucking it gently. My mouth traveled down her collarbone, kissing her every step of the way. When I came to her strap, I slid it down her arm, lightly biting into her skin. A slight gasp left her, and the sound alone made me want her even more.

"We'll go slow. We don't need to rush," I said, knowing it was her first time. I moved her other strap down her shoulder and her loose dress slid to the floor. I stepped back, studying her body. Her white lacey bra didn't match her pink cotton underwear, and somehow it was perfect. Her legs looked lean and long as her arms rested at her sides. "You're beautiful," I whispered.

She stepped toward me, took my shirt from the bottom, and slid it over my head, tossing it on top of her dress. As she unbuckled my belt, I stepped out of my shoes and socks. She unzipped my jeans and they fell to the floor.

Maggie studied my body, her eyes moving up and down as I studied hers. Her fingers ran along my chest, moving lower and lower, to the edge of my boxers. My eyes closed as her thumb brushed against my hardness, and she slowly started stroking me through my boxers.

"Mag…" I groaned, feeling her start to stroke harder. Her free hand wrapped around the edge of my boxers, and as she started pulling them down, I opened my eyes. She was lowering herself to get on her knees. Her hands were shaking against me, and my hand flew under her forearm. "Maggie, what are you doing?"

She looked at me, confused.

"I mean…" I snickered. "I know what you're doing, but you don't have to…" I pulled her up to a standing position. My fingers combed through her hair. "I know you haven't done anything before."

Embarrassment filled her eyes and as she began to turn away from me, I rotated her back, taking her hands in mine. "Who told you to do that? Cheryl?"

She squeezed my hands twice.

I hated that. I hated that she felt she had to do certain things because of what others said. "Five minutes?" I asked, taking a few steps back from her.

She closed her eyes, took a deep breath, and stepped backward. When her eyes reappeared, she smiled and unhooked her bra, dropping it to the floor. I slid my boxers off, tossing them to the left. Her panties glided down her beautiful thighs and she stepped out of them.

Her hand flew up and she nodded. Five minutes.

We stood there, staring at one another. Five minutes to erase any fears. Five minutes to remember who we were. Five minutes to find our own way, our own story.

When five minutes were up, I took Maggie's hand into mine and led her to lie down on the bed. "Maggie..." I kissed her lips. "We don't have to do what other people do..." I kissed her neck. "We're not them. We don't have to follow their guidelines." I kissed her collarbone, and she closed her eyes as I moved down her body, kissing every inch of her, tasting every piece. "You don't have to do things a certain way."

I spread her legs apart, kissing her thighs. My mouth grazed against her skin and she twisted her fingers into my hair. "And you can always pinch me or hit me if you ever want to stop."

She arched her hips up toward my mouth, demonstrating how much she wanted me to continue, silently begging me to taste her. Oh, how I wanted a taste. I glanced up at her, and her eyes were on me. She was watching my every move, and I wanted her to see it all. I wanted her to watch me explore her body, to taste her body, to love her body. She and I, we weren't following anyone else's rules, no one else's transcript. We were writing our own story.

Leaning forward, I swept my tongue against her, slid a finger deep inside, and introduced her to chapter one.

15

Maggie

"I cannot believe that! I just can't."

The next Saturday night, Mama was having her girlfriends over. The girls had gone to high school with her, and since they now lived in different states, they only came around once or twice a year, which was too much if you asked me. Whenever they were around, I did my best to stay invisible. They weren't the nicest people in the world. There were five of them, including Mama. Even though they had gone to high school together, I hadn't a clue why they all traveled to hang out with each other—they couldn't stand one another at all. Everything they talked about always seemed like a competition. If Loren's daughter walked at ten months old, Wendy's drove a car at nine months. If Hannah could run a 5k, Janice could do a 10k in less time.

Their favorite topic of all, though, was me. When it came to my silence, they were all professionals on what it meant to be mute.

I sat at the top of the stairs, listening to them discuss me that evening. I wished Brooks were over, but he and the boys were off watching some super indie underground band play at some hole-in-the-wall venue. He kept sending me videos of the space, where they were packed like sardines and it was loud as ever. Whenever the camera faced him and I saw his giddy smile, my heart fell for him just a little bit more.

I wanted to be there with him, feel him holding me in his arms, completely losing myself to the sounds. In the video, I saw Stacey swaying back and forth to the music with Calvin, and I felt selfish— selfish for not being there for Brooks, selfish for not being able to do the things normal couples did.

"She really has a boyfriend?" Loren questioned, finishing off her glass of wine before pouring some more. "How is that even... possible?"

"Who is it?" Wendy hammered.

"Brooks," Mama said nonchalantly while eating chips and salsa.

"Brooks *who*?" Wendy hammered some more.

"Griffin."

"*What*?" all four girls screeched at once.

"No way," Janice said. "But Brooks is... He's pretty popular with the ladies, isn't he? I get that he visited her every day out of the kindness of his heart, but *dating*? That can't be true."

"Is that even healthy?" Loren questioned. "You know, with Maggie's...condition?"

"Her condition?" Mama asked.

"You know, her...trauma. I'm just saying. I read an article once—" Loren started.

"You're always reading articles once," Hannah cut in, her tone a bit feisty.

"Yeah, but this one had actual scientific statistics. It said individuals who suffer traumatic incidents as children struggle with relapses in their healing when placed in relationships."

"Loren," Hannah scolded.

I liked Hannah. Mama should've stayed friends with her and ditched the others.

"What! It's true. Her being with Brooks could trigger some kind of relapse, and really, what are they going to do? Date in Katie's house forever? All I'm saying is this doesn't seem like a good idea. It could really backtrack any progress, no matter how small, that Maggie has made. Plus, it doesn't seem like a fair trade for Brooks. What does he get out of the equation?"

Shut up, Loren. He gets me.

I didn't want to hear anymore, but I couldn't walk away.

"You know what? I say que sera, sera," Hannah chimed in. "They're kids, let them live a little."

Right on, Hannah! Hannah was the least dramatic of the group. If anything, she only showed up for the pizza and wine. I couldn't fault her—Mama always ordered pizza from Marco's, which was the best in town.

"That's stupid thinking, Hannah. 'Live a little.' That's the kind of thought that got you married three times and divorced three times."

"I'm going for my fourth in both arenas, too." Hannah poured herself some more wine, smiled, and started singing, "Que sera, sera."

"You know how your mother feels about you eavesdropping," Daddy whispered, walking up the staircase to sit beside me. He had a bag of peanut M&Ms in his hand and handed me a few. "Plus, these women are vipers. You don't need to be brainwashed by their crazy."

I smiled at him and rested my head on his shoulder.

"Are they talking about you again?"

I nodded.

He frowned. "I told your mother to change the subject, or to stop inviting the four horsemen to our house. It's really not a big enough property to be the headquarters of the apocalypse. Don't let them get to you, Maggie, all right?"

I wasn't worried about them getting to me. It had been made clear to me a long time ago that those women were insane. What I worried about most was how their words affected Mama. Even when she tried to fight against their opinions, they still slipped through the cracks into her unconscious mind. Sometimes when Mama reacted to situations, she wouldn't react like herself, instead saying things the four horsemen would say. Daddy always said to watch out for groups, that they sometimes turned you into a person you'd never otherwise become.

"I'm just saying, she's never going to get better if you allow this to go on." Loren started again. "There's no way that she should be allowed—"

"Oh, Loren, shut it!" Mama shouted, stunning both Daddy and me. She even stumbled back a bit, shocked by her own sounds. "That's enough. Yes, my daughter has her issues, but there's no reason for you to sit here belittling her for an hour straight. I'd never do that to you about your child, and I'd expect the same kind of respect about mine. As far as if my daughter dates, and who my daughter dates, that's up to her father and me to decide. Now, I respect your opinion—but that's all it is. An opinion. You're welcome to have it, but if you could keep it from me, that would be grand."

"Wow," Daddy whispered, a small smirk on his lips. "There she is," he said. "There's the woman I married."

The subject changed, and Loren even muttered an apology.

"Joke?" Daddy asked.

Of course.

"Why did the run-on sentence think it was pregnant? Because its period was late." He laughed, slapping his knee, and I rolled my eyes so hard.

God.

I loved my father.

It was past one in the morning when the horsemen rode off to their hotels. Brooks hadn't texted me in a while, and I figured he was just having the time of his life at the show. A couple hours later, I woke up to my door slowly opening.

"Magnet?" Brooks whispered. "Sleeping?"

I sat up in my bed.

He smiled and entered my room, shutting the door behind him. He walked over to my desk and turned on my lamp, lighting up the room enough for a three a.m. wake-up call.

"Sorry I stopped texting. My phone died mid-show. Then when the show was supposed to be over, it went into this crazy encore! God! The energy of the room, Maggie. I swear, you could feel the walls vibrating from the energy alone. And the artists!" He kept going, waving his arms around with excitement, telling me everything about the band, the guitars they used, the keys, the drums, how Rudolph got hit in the face with a drum stick, how Oliver was the one who hit him in the face.

He was bursting from his seams with joy. The way music transformed him—the way music freed him from any of life's restraints—I loved it.

I loved his joy.

"I got you this!" he said, reaching into his pocket and pulling out a pin from the show. "They were the band tonight: Jungle Treehouse. Gosh, Maggie, you would've loved it. I know you would've. I wish you could've been there. On the way back to your place, I charged my phone in the car and downloaded a few of their tracks onto my phone if you want to listen."

I did.

We lay down on my bed with his earbuds in, and our hearts on our sleeves, listening to the music as the dim light glowed in the corner. He tilted his head in my direction, and I tilted mine is his direction, too. He clasped his fingers with mine and placed his hand over his chest. I felt his heartbeat racing through his chest as the music vibrated from my soul to his.

"I love you, Maggie May," he whispered, looking into my eyes. "I mean, I keep staring at you, and I can't help but think, 'Wow. I'm really loving this girl right now.' You know? Everything about you,

I love. The easy days and the hard ones, too. Maybe I love you even more on the hard days. I'm not sure if I'm supposed to say it yet, because I don't know if you're ready, but that's okay. You take all the time you need, but I wanted to let you know, because when you love someone, I think you gotta scream it, otherwise the love in your chest becomes a bit heavy. It weighs you down, and you start wondering if the other person loves you, too. I'm not worried about that, though. I'm just sitting here, next to you, looking at the small freckles on your face that most people miss, thinkin' about how much I love you in this moment."

I snuggled closer to him, resting my head on his chest, as his arms wrapped around me. He closed his eyes and held me against him as his chest rose and fell with each inhale and exhale, falling asleep after a few minutes. I pressed my lips against his neck, kissing him softly. I grazed my mouth against his, and he stirred a bit. I took his bottom lip between my teeth and nibbled it gently. His eyes awakened, sleepy and dazed, but he smiled. He always smiled when he looked my way.

I kissed him once and then met his stare. I kissed him again, and he pulled my body on top of him.

"Yeah?" he whispered.

I nodded.

I loved him.

I loved him, and he knew it. Even if I couldn't say the words, he felt them in the way I touched him, the way I kissed him, the way I held him.

And wasn't the best kind of love the kind one felt?

"I love you, too," he said softly, his lips resting against mine. "I love you, too," he said once more.

We started undressing one another, slowly, with ease, with care. That night we made love for the first time. With each touch, I fell more for his spirit. With each kiss, I tasted a part of his soul.

In my mind, I whispered back to him, time and time again. With every tear and every heartbeat, I spoke to him. So quiet, yet so loud.

I love you, too. I love you, too. I love you, too…

"Are you ready?" Brooks asked, walking into my room with his acoustic guitar on his back a few days later.

Don't you have band practice?

He nodded. "Yeah, but not with The Crooks tonight. Tonight I'm starting a new band called BAM."

Oh?

He bit his bottom lip and walked over to me, kissing my forehead. There was always a tenderness that he had whenever he touched me. I loved that feeling. "Yeah. It stands for Brooks and Maggie."

What?

"It's on your to-do list—play in a band. I figured why not start crossing things off your list right away? No reason to wait when we can do some of the things now. Now come on. I'll teach you how to play Bettie."

Bettie?

"Named after my grandma."

Swoon.

He placed his guitar in my hands and as I went to strum, he stopped me. "Whoa, whoa, whoa. You can't play her like she's just here to be used, Maggie. You need to introduce yourself. You need to learn about her, her parts, like her beautiful headstock, and her neck, which is home to the fretboard." He went on explaining the different parts of the guitar for a good thirty minutes, and I listened selfishly. I loved how much he loved music. I loved how he wanted to introduce me to his world. When it came time, he had me practice fretting the strings, then later on, we went over the first position chords.

Whenever I messed up, he still cheered me on. "That's good, Magnet! You're literally one hundred times better than me when I started playing."

After a few hours of playing, Daddy came and told Brooks he was never allowed back into our house after he caught us kissing. "I better get going anyway, seeing as how you're yawning."

As he stood, I grabbed his arm, making him pause. Rushing over to my books, I picked up one of my favorite books.

"*The Kite Runner*?" he questioned, taking the book from my hands. Khaled Hosseini's novel was one of my favorite reads that Daddy had given me, and I wanted Brooks to know that part of me—the same way he wanted me to know music. The book was marked with small pink tabs, indicating my favorite sections. "It's one of your favorites?"

Yes.

"Then I'll read it twice," he replied, kissing my temple. As he leaned in, he whispered against my ear. "I'll sneak back into your room tonight after your dad's asleep for a sleepover."

"GO HOME, BROOKS!" Daddy hollered, making us both chuckle.

16

Brooks

"Um, Earth to Brooks. You still there, dude?" Rudolph asked, tapping me on the shoulder as I sat on Oliver's stool in the garage. Rudolph kept waving his hand in front of the book I held with an apple in his grip. "Normally when we are on a break from rehearsing, you're strumming a guitar, but now you're like…"

"Reading!" Oliver said, walking out of Calvin's house with two apples in his hand. He bit into both at the same time and chewed loudly. "I didn't even know you knew how to read. Are you sure the book isn't upside down?"

I shushed them, waving my hands at them as I flipped the page. My forearm was filled with small yellow tabs I was using to write notes back to Maggie. The twins kept trying to get my attention, but I was too far deep into the book.

Calvin came into the room, holding three apples in his hand and biting out of all three. Dramatic. My friends were dramatic. "Dude, don't bother. He's too much in love to focus on anything else."

"Ugh. Not more of this love shit," Oliver whined. "First we had to deal with Calvin wanting to write the name Stacey into every song we make, and now we have Brooks reading. READING!"

"For the first time in my life, I agree with my brother," Rudolph said.

Oliver thanked him by giving him a wet willy.

"God! I take it back. You're disgusting."

I went back to ignoring them. It was interesting to see where Maggie put her tabs, and if any of mine overlapped them. I loved discovering the parts that made her laugh and cry, the parts that made her angry and happy. It was the best feeling.

"So, my dad was thinking of getting rid of his boat," Calvin said. "He wants to sell it in a few weeks, and wanted to see if we want to have a farewell dudes' trip and go fishing before we all head off to college in the fall."

"He's selling the boat?" I choked out, looking up from the book. "But, that's like…our boat." We'd spent so much of our youth sitting out on the lake. I knew we hadn't done it in years, but the idea of Mr. Riley selling it made me pretty sad.

"Is this the same boat you two chicks are always reminiscing about?" Rudolph asked.

"The same boat you wrote a song about?" Oliver jumped in.

"Yup. That's the boat."

"Well, hell. I'm in. If this boat had the power to make Brooks stop reading, then it must be something worth experiencing." Oliver tossed his apple cores into the trash can, and Rudolph rushed over, picking up the cores with a paper towel and putting them into a paper bag.

I cocked an eyebrow at my weird friend, and he shrugged. "What? I'm helping my mom make a compost in our backyard. Apple cores are primetime for it. Anyway, if we can get organic fruit and I don't have to physically harm a fish, then count me in."

"The apple you ate isn't organic, brother. Mom told me not to tell you—which is why I'm telling you." Oliver smirked as Rudolph's face turned red.

It was mere minutes before they started hollering again.

So I went back to reading my book.

A few weeks later, Mr. Riley took the guys, including my dad and my brother, Jamie, out on the boat for one last ride. It was the perfect day. We ate a crap ton of junk food—except Rudolph, who brought organic grapes and homemade organic banana bread he'd made with his mom. Surprisingly, when he offered it around, everyone chose chips instead.

"You're missing out on the huge health benefits of flax seed and chia seed, but okay, by all means, eat your genetically modified corn chips," Rudolph said.

Oliver took a handful of Fritos and shoved them into his mouth. "Don't mind if I do."

We sat out there for hours, talking about our future and how even with college approaching, we were still going to keep band practice as a priority in our lives. Just because we were going to school didn't mean the dream had to die; it simply meant the dream had to shift a bit with the changes of life.

"Brooks, can you grab me a beer from under the deck?" Mr. Riley asked from across the boat.

I hopped up and did as he said. "Here you go, Mr. R."

He thanked me and then invited me to sit next to him. I sat.

He opened his beer and took a few sips. "So you and Maggie, huh?"

I swallowed hard, knowing that it was about to happen—the girlfriend's father conversation. "Yes, sir." Sir? In all my years of knowing Mr. Riley, I'd never called him sir. Heck, I'd never called any person *sir*.

He pulled in his fishing line and then cast it farther out into the water. "I wasn't sure how I felt about that, if I'm honest. Maggie's my little girl. She's always going to be my little girl."

"I get that completely."

"And Maggie is unlike other girls, so you can understand my reluctance on the subject of her being in a relationship. I've actually gone back and forth on the subject with Katie. Part of me was going to come out here on the boat today and ask you to break things off with her—because of Katie. She truly thinks it's an awful idea."

How could I reply to that? Knowing Maggie's own mother didn't support our relationship felt like a punch in the gut, but before I could reply, Mr. Riley spoke again.

"But as I was getting my fishing rods from the upstairs storage closet, I heard you two. What I mean is, I heard her. She laughs with you. She actually laughs out loud, and I can't for the life of me think of the last time I heard that sound from her. So, as long as you keep my little girl laughing, you'll have my blessing."

I swallowed hard. "Thank you, sir."

"No problem." He chugged the rest of his beer. "But the moment she stops laughing with you, we're going to have a serious talk. If you ever hurt my daughter"—he looked me dead in the eyes and crushed the can in his hand—"well, let's just say, don't hurt my daughter."

My eyes widened with fear. "I won't hurt her, and you were right about what you said—Maggie's not like other girls."

He released the threatening stare from his eyes, and his old happy-go-lucky smile was back. He patted me on the back. "Now go have a good time."

"Thanks, sir."

"Brooks?"

"Yes?"

"Call me sir one more time and we'll have to have another talk that won't have such a happy ending."

After the boating trip, Calvin and I convinced Mr. Riley to let us come with him when it was time to sell old faithful. We pulled up to the coastline, where James' Boat Shop was located right off of Harper Lake. Even though it was the same lake that we fished on, it was still a good twenty-minute drive around the coast, seeing how the lake was that large. James' Boat Shop had a big wooden sign out front that read: We buy, sell, rent, and trade.

140

On the front porch was a dog that barked and barked as the three of us walked up the steps to meet up with James.

"You're a loud pup, huh?" Mr. Riley smiled at the dog who still howled, but wagged his tail.

The screen door opened, and a tall, buff man stepped outside, wearing jeans and a shirt that looked too small. "Quiet, Wilson! Shh!" The man smiled at us. "Don't mind Wilson, he's all bark and no bite. I've been trying everything to get that mutt to shut up for the past eight years, but I haven't had any luck."

"No worries," Mr. Riley replied. "I've been trying to get these two kids to shut up for the past few years, too, with no luck."

The guy smiled and held out his hand. "I'm James Bateman. I'm guessing you're Eric from our phone conversation. So that must be your baby," he said, gesturing toward the boat hooked up to Mr. Riley's truck. He walked over to the boat and started rubbing it down. "You sure you don't want to do a trade maybe? I could get you something real nice for this girl."

Mr. Riley grimaced. "No, thanks. We could really use the extra cash—at least that's what the wife told me."

"Ah, it's best to always listen to your wife." He laughed.

Mr. Riley chuckled. "The great struggles of marriage."

"I know the struggle too well. That's why I'll probably never do it again after my wife left me."

"I thought the same thing after my first wife left, but here I am again." Mr. Riley smiled, looking down at his wedding band.

"No regrets?" James asked.

"Never," Mr. Riley replied. "Even on the hard days."

James snickered, nodding. He patted Mr. Riley on the back. "You give me hope that maybe someday my situation will change. So, how about we head inside and talk numbers?" He turned toward his shop and shouted, "Michael! Michael, get out here for a second."

A young guy came outside. He looked to be in his early twenties. "Yeah?"

"Can you show these two boys some of our top of the line boats while I work with a customer? Boys," James redirected his words to Calvin and me. "My son will take care of you and keep you entertained. Michael, how about you show them around Jenna for a few?"

"Sure thing." Michael smiled and waved us over to him. "So, interested in seeing the best yacht that no one in Harper County can actually afford to buy?" he asked.

"Heck yeah," Calvin replied. "Is it the kind of yacht Leonardo DiCarpio would party on?"

"Sure is. My dad and I actually went out of our way to get a boat like Jenna. She's not for sale because she's our pride and joy, but a few people from the north side of town rent her out every now and then for weddings, or retirement parties." The north side of town was where all of Harper County's money was located. A person had to have a nice sized wallet to live on that side of town.

When we walked around the corner there were dozens of boats docked up. There were workers running around caring for the boats. I'd never been in a place with so many different sized water vehicles, and I wanted to take them all home with me. My top three favorite things in the world were Maggie, music, and being out on the water. Someday I planned to have all three of those things happening at the same time.

"Holy crap," I muttered, staring at Jenna. It had to be Jenna. She was the biggest and most beautiful boat out there. Maggie would've probably slapped me for staring the way I did.

"She's something else, huh?" Michael asked.

"Oh, she's more than something." I rubbed her side as we walked over to her.

"Wait until you climb aboard." Michael laughed.

When we were on the yacht, I felt as if I were Leonardo—rich and cool as hell.

"So, this babe comes with all kinds of water sports equipment. We have a Yamaha WaveRunner Jet Ski, a Kawasaki Ultra 250 Jet

Ski, and one Kawasaki Super Jet stand up Jet Ski. There's snorkeling gear, fishing supplies, and all that jazz, too. As far as entertainment." Michael walked us below deck and smiled before opening a set of doors. "We only have the best. We have this area, the main saloon with a sixty-five-inch plasma television. Over here we have the sky lounge with two full bars. Then there are the master stateroom, the VIP cabin, and the three guest cabins which all hold fifty-inch plasma televisions and the most comfortable beds you'll ever sleep on. What do you guys think?" he asked.

Calvin's eyes were bugged out the same way mine were.

"So, this is what royalty feels like." Calvin sighed. "I love royalty."

"We'll take it," I bellowed.

Michael took us to the top deck, and we stood at the nose of the boat.

"So, Michael, you and your dad just run this business together?"

"Yeah. He took on the business from my grandpa. I plan to do the same someday. There's nothing I love more than this, the boats, the water."

"There's nothing else you'd ever want to do?" Calvin asked.

Michael's eyebrows grew closer as he thought on it. "No. Nothing else. After my mom ran off with another man Dad had a hard time moving on. He went into a deep depression. I was fourteen and remember there being days when I had to force him to eat. He blamed himself for her leaving."

"Why did he blame himself?"

"I really don't know. He worked long hours, and I knew it bothered her, but that wasn't a reason to leave him. Yeah, they fought, but they laughed more. Yet sometimes people aren't always who you believe them to be, and it turned out we were better off without her. He'll never say that, though. He still keeps a picture of the three of us on his office desk. Some days I feel as if he's waiting for her to come back. The only thing that helped him heal was being out on the water. It cleansed him, I think. If it weren't for this place, I probably would've lost my father, too. This place is home to me. What about you guys? What do you want to do?"

"Music," we said in unison.

Michael laughed. "Well, don't stop until you make it. Then, you come rent out Jenna from me and my pops."

"I apologize ahead of time for my childish actions that are about to take place, but I have to do it," my best friend stated. Calvin jumped up onto the railings and held his arms out.

I laughed. "I always knew you'd be Kate Winslet and I'd be Leo in this situation."

"Shut up and hug me!" Calvin said mockingly.

I hopped up behind him and wrapped my arms around his waist. "I'll never let go, Cal!" I shouted as he held his arms out.

Michael chuckled. "I wish I could tell you the amount of Titanic bromances I've witnessed on that railing."

"Bromance?" Calvin questioned. "Oh no, we're in a committed relationship."

Michael's eyes widened with guilt. "Oh, I'm so sorry. I didn't..."

"Don't mind Calvin, he's a liar. I'm actually banging his sister." I smirked, watching Calvin grimace as he shoved me away from him, forcing me to hop down.

He jumped down, too. "If I ever hear words about my sister being banged again from you, there's a good chance you won't be alive shortly after."

"Touché." I would've been lying if I said I didn't like getting under his skin like that. He hated all conversations that included talk of his sister being kissed by me—so banging was really crossing the line. That's why I always made them.

17

Maggie

Every time Brooks delivered a book back to me, I raced through it to see his added tabs with his notes and thoughts included. We started doing this regularly, and each time a book returned to my bookshelf with more Post-its than before, I felt as if Brooks was becoming more and more a part of my world. He must've felt the same every time I played a chord right. I had recently played "Mary Had a Little Lamb" using one finger at a time to strum, and he'd just about cried with excitement.

After being with him, my idea of what love was changed.

I'd fallen in love with hundreds of different men from hundreds of different books. I had thought I knew what love looked like based on the words within those pages. Love was togetherness, strength, and something worth living for.

What I didn't expect were the fears true love brought with it. The fear that I'd never be enough for him. The fear that he'd find another. The fear that sometimes love was worth dying for. The fear that love wasn't always enough. Loving someone meant being vulnerable to the chance that someday they might leave, and all I ever wanted was for Brooks to stay.

I tapped him gently on the shoulder, and he stirred from his sleep. *Sleeping?* I wrote once he seemed awake enough to read.

"Sleeping," he replied with a tiny smirk. "Overthinking?"

He knew me so well. My lips brushed against his ear before I moved to kiss his neck.

Do you promise me the same type of love I've read about in my books?

He shook his head, yawning. His arms wrapped around me, pulling me closer as I became engulfed by his warmth. "No, Maggie May. I promise you so much more."

18

Maggie

"You're actually drinking your tea," Mrs. Boone said, flabbergasted on a Monday afternoon at lunchtime. "You never drink your tea."

What could I say? Love makes us do ridiculous things.

"It's that boy, isn't it?" she asked with an arched eyebrow. "Is he the reason you've been acting like a giddy schoolgirl each time I come to visit?"

I kept sipping my tea.

She smirked knowingly and continued eating her sandwich.

"*Oh my gosh!* I know what I want to do with my life!" Cheryl hollered, running into the dining room and jumping up and down with her hands waving wildly while holding a book. "I know what I want to be after I graduate school next year!"

"Well, out with it," Mrs. Boone ordered.

Cheryl paused her erratic movements and stood up straight, holding her novel to her chest. "I want to be an activist."

Mrs. Boone and I raised our eyebrows in wonderment, waiting for Cheryl to finish her sentence. "An activist of…?" Mrs. Boone asked.

Cheryl blinked once. "What do you mean?"

"You have to be an activist of something. Environmental issues, or politics, human rights, or perhaps animal cruelty. Anything. You can't just be an activist."

Cheryl poked out her bottom lip. "Seriously? I can't just be an activist?"

We shook our heads. "Well, fuck—err—I mean frick. Sorry Mrs. Boone. I guess I'll go try to find out what kind of activist I want to be. Ugh. It just sounds like more work than I wanted to do, though." She glided from the room significantly less enthusiastic than when she'd entered, making both Mrs. Boone and me laugh.

"I swear, your parents must've fed you kids stupidity for breakfast each day. It blows my mind how idiotic you all are." She picked up her sandwich and was a second away from biting into it when she said, "Wait, was Cheryl holding a book?"

I nodded.

She dropped her sandwich, shaking her head back and forth. "I knew the end of the world was coming. I just didn't know it would be so soon."

I giggled to myself and kept drinking my tea.

It didn't taste so bad that afternoon.

"You're not listening to me, Eric, I just want to make sure we're doing the right thing," Mama said to Daddy later that night as he paced the living room. She held a glass of wine in her hand and sipped at it while speaking to him. I sat at the top of the stairs with Cheryl beside me. "Maggie dating Brooks might not be the best thing for anyone. Loren said—"

Daddy snickered sarcastically. "'Loren said'. Jesus, of course. You know, for a second I believed they didn't get to you when they came to visit, but it seems I was wrong. I should've known this had something to do with those women."

"Those women are my friends."

"Those women couldn't care less about you, Katie. You think they come here to hang out with you because they care? They come here to mock you, to tell you to think about moving, knowing you can't. To see how your life is so fucking depressing compared to their perfect lives, which is fine, but when they sit all night talking about our daughter—"

"They meant no harm. They were giving me information on how to help her."

"They were belittling her!" he shouted. Cheryl and I both jumped out of fright. Daddy never shouted. I'd never seen his face so red in my life. "They were belittling her, insulting her as if she were deaf and couldn't hear them. I don't know what's worse, the fact that you let those women into our house to gossip about your own daughter, or the fact you that you stood up for Maggie just to take it back a few days later. You're sitting here worrying about her having a boyfriend when she's the happiest I've seen her in years. You'd see it too if you actually looked at her."

"I look at her."

"You look, but you don't see, Katie, and then you invite those trolls to our house, and they talk about Maggie as if she's nothing."

"She is something. Don't you see? This is why I want to try the therapist Wendy—"

"She's happy, Katie!"

"She's sick!"

"She's getting better right in front of us, and it's like you secretly don't want her to. Don't you want her to leave? To live?"

Mama hesitated before saying, "But Loren—"

"Enough!" he hollered, swinging his hands in annoyance and accidentally knocking the wine from Mama's hand, sending her glass to the carpet where it shattered.

The room went quiet.

Daddy took off his glasses and rubbed the palms of his hands against his eyes before placing his hands on his waist. The two stared at the red stain on the carpet, the same type of accidental spill that used to happen before, when they were happier together, before I began to break their love apart.

Without any more words, they went their separate ways.

"What just happened?" Cheryl whispered, her body shaking slightly.

I took her shaky hand into mine to try to calm her nerves.

In that moment, I was happy I didn't speak, because otherwise I would've had to tell Cheryl the truth. I knew what was happening to our parents: they were falling out of love right in front of my sister and me.

Falling out of love meant you couldn't laugh at mistakes.

Falling out of love meant you screamed your irritations.

Falling out of love meant going your separate ways.

"A box of goodies for Maggie May," Brooks said later that night, standing in my doorway.

I smiled his way, uncertain of what he had in mind. He walked into my room and sat on the floor, placing the box in front of him. He patted the floor, inviting me to join him.

What did he have planned?

"It's a taste test," he explained as I sat down. "Since you can't speak, I want to at least know everything else about you—the way you react to certain things, your expressions—so we are doing a blind food taste test. In this box are random foods—some sweet, some mushy, some sour as hell—and you are going to taste them. Then, we are going to switch."

I smiled, not sure how I could love this boy any more than I already did. He held up a blindfold and leaned forward, tying it around my eyes. "Okay. Can you see me?" he asked. I shook my head. "Okay, good. Now part your lips."

I opened wide, and he dropped a piece of food into my mouth. My lips relaxed around it. *Mmm…chocolate.*

I loved chocolate as much as any wise person.

"A look of pleasure, perfect. Up next…"

My face wrinkled up with the next food—Sour Patch Kids.

He couldn't stop laughing. "Oh my God, I wish you could see your scrunched up nose right now."

The next items included grapes, spaghetti sauce, lemon slices, and cheese—which I was certain was old.

When I took my blindfold off, I couldn't have been more excited, because it was my turn to torture him. I tied it around his eyes, and he smirked, biting his bottom lip. "Kinky."

I rolled my eyes. First, I placed cold mashed potatoes into his mouth, and he liked it more than he should've. Next came spaghetti sauce with hot sauce—he didn't love that one—bananas, and more. Lastly I took a piece of chocolate, rolled it in ketchup, and squeezed some lemon juice on top of it. He instantly tried to spit it out, but I covered his mouth with my hand, snickering as he wiggled his body around, trying to swallow it.

"That's just evil, Maggie. Evil." He laughed, wiping his hands against his mouth. I leaned in and kissed him, and he took my bottom lip between his teeth and gently bit it.

Mmm…I like that.

Before we could kiss again, Calvin, Rudolph, and Oliver came bursting through the bedroom door.

"Holy shit!" Calvin screamed.

I cocked an eyebrow, and Brooks appeared as confused as me.

"Oh my God, oh my God!" Rudolph said, walking in circles, his hands shaking nonstop. He was hyperventilating, but that wasn't uncommon for Rudolph. It didn't take much for him to get worked up in a frenzy.

What freaked me out the most was watching Oliver jump up and down. Oliver wasn't one to jump up and down: he was much more into sitting down than anything else. I'd never seen him so excited.

"What? What is it?" Brooks exclaimed, bewildered.

Calvin paused. "Are you…wearing a blindfold?"

The twins whistled in unison. "Kinky."

Brooks tossed off the blindfold. "Never mind that. What's going on?"

The three boys stayed quiet for a moment before returning to their previous levels of excitement.

Calvin ran over to Brooks, placed his hands on his shoulders, and started shaking his body. "Holy shit! Holy shit! Holy…!" Calvin shoved his cell phone into Brooks' hand.

Brooks' eyes narrowed as he read the words. I raced behind him so I could read along. Each word hit me harder in my gut. "SHIT!" Brooks hollered, his hands shaking.

I took the phone from him to reread it.

"How is that even possible?"

"They saw our cover of their song on YouTube, then checked out our originals, then tweeted about us!"

"It was retweeted over forty thousand times in the past two hours," Rudolph shouted, his nose redder than normal from his excitement.

"More than fifty thousand times, you noob," Oliver corrected.

I tapped Brooks on the shoulder and handed the phone back to him, pointing. *Oh. My. God.*

"One hundred and sixty thousand retweets!" Brooks said.

All at once the boys screamed, their throats probably burning. "AH!"

"I didn't even know you put us on YouTube, Cal!" Brooks shouted; shouting was the only thing any of them could do. The guys were so anti-mainstream because they always said they were indie and cool, until mainstream knocked on their door and they lost their minds.

"I didn't!"

"Was it you, Rudolph? Oli?" Brooks asked.

"No," the twins said in unison.

"Then who…" He slowly turned my way, and I gave him a small smile. The guys all turned at the same time and stared at me with knowing eyes. "You did it? The videos you recorded of us?"

I nodded slowly and within seconds, everyone's arms were wrapped tightly around me, jumping up and down.

"You're so fucking amazing, Maggie!" Oliver said, giving me a noogie.

"Holy crap, Mags, you have no clue how much you've just changed our lives," Calvin said.

"Dude!" Oliver started waving his arms at Calvin. "Read them the direct message."

"There's a direct message?" Brooks asked.

"Oh." Calvin nodded ecstatically, scrolling through his phone. "There's a direct message." He cleared his throat and the twins cleared theirs, too, having it fully memorized.

"Dear Calvin, I'm Mark, the manager of The Present Yesterdays. We came across your videos a few days ago and haven't stopped watching. Your sound is clean, crisp, and something the industry is missing. If you're interested, I'd love to set up a meeting with you guys to chat about your future plans in music. Peace!" The three quoted it in perfect unison, and my heart pretty much jumped from my chest.

The Present Yesterdays was the greatest pop-rock band of our time. The guys had introduced me to their music, and I'd been in love with them before the world even knew they existed. How was any of this possible?

Brooks turned to his bandmates with the widest eyes, and I saw it take over them, too—the realization that dreams really did come true, even for boys who rehearsed in garages in small-town Wisconsin. The wave of emotion took over us all as we began to jump around the room and celebrate.

I'd never been so happy to see others' dreams start to come to life. "This is all because of you, Magnet," Brooks said, pulling me into his chest. "It's because you used your voice for us to be heard."

He reminded me that night that I had a voice, even though no words ever left my mouth.

I still had a voice.

The next evening my hour-long bath lasted longer than normal. I had the same type of routine as before: I'd read, I'd wash up, and then I'd slide under the water and remember what had happened in those woods, reminding myself that it wasn't my fault. My mind was still so good at holding onto those images, but recently the visions were being blurred by more current memories.

Whenever I tried to envision the devil's face, I'd see Cheryl laughing with a book in her hand. Whenever I was running in the woods, I'd see myself running into Brooks' arms. Whenever I'd trip, I'd see Mrs. Boone scolding me.

They weren't gone, the bad memories. I knew my mind still held the image of the devil, but I was becoming better at keeping him locked inside the closet. I wasn't certain if that was thanks to Brooks, Cheryl, or time, but either way, I was thankful.

After I'd remember, I'd come up for air, take a deep breath, and go back under to dream.

I'd dream of a future. I'd dream of me exploring the world, climbing mountains, seeing Italy, trying snails in France. Watching Brooks and my brother perform live in a huge arena. Having a family. Discovering what it means to be alive. The water cleansed me of the darkness that was trying so hard to hold on to me. I was slowly becoming renewed. I was beginning my life for the first time…

"Maggie—I got you some fresh… Oh my gosh!" Mama screeched, running into the bathroom and pulling me up from beneath the water. Her rapid movement forced me to open my mouth, making me inhale water. I started coughing, my throat burning as I spit up. What was happening? Mama's hands were shaking and she started screaming, holding me in her arms. My ears were filled with water and I tried to shake it out as she hollered for Daddy.

"Eric! Eric!" she cried, her voice more panicked than it needed to be. What was she doing? Why was she freaking out? Did she think...

Oh my God, no.

No, Mama. I wasn't trying to drown. I wasn't trying to drown myself. Tears flooded my eyes as I saw the panic she was experiencing. She pulled me from the tub, wrapping me in towels. As she cried, still screaming Daddy's name, he came running into the bathroom.

The water in my ears made it hard to listen. I tried to stand, but Mama was holding me so tight.

So tight.

"She tried to drown herself, Eric!" Mama said. Daddy's eyes grew heavy and he asked her to repeat herself. "I told you. I told you this was all too much for her."

I shook my head. *No, Daddy.* My hands were ghostly pale. *I wouldn't do that. I wouldn't kill myself. I'm happy. Remember? I'm happy.*

I needed paper. I needed to write to them. I needed to let them know.

I wasn't trying to kill myself. They were both crying now, and Daddy could hardly breathe as his stare met mine. He looked away from me. He needed to know Mama was wrong. She'd made a mistake. She didn't know all the facts. She had pulled me up for air, not knowing I could breathe best beneath the water.

They were fighting again.

Cheryl and I sat at the top of the steps, once again watching. My hair was still soaked from my bath, and Cheryl brushed it as we listened.

"You still don't believe me?" Mama cried, stunned.

"You're overreacting," Daddy said to Mama. "She said she wasn't trying to—"

"She didn't say anything, Eric. She doesn't talk, but her actions were loud and clear tonight."

"She was taking a dip under the water when you crashed in! She was holding her breath! Jesus, Katie! This is Loren talking, not you."

"Don't put this on her. Don't put this on my friend. I know what I saw. Your daughter was drowning herself."

"My daughter?" Daddy huffed, blowing out a low whistle. "Wow."

I felt it too, Daddy—the punch to the gut.

"You know what I mean."

"No, I don't think I do. Lately I have a hard time understanding anything you say."

Mama rolled her eyes and walked off, coming back with a glass of wine. "She's sick."

"She's getting better."

"She's getting worse, and I know it has to do with Brooks. I know it does…"

I studied Mama.

I studied every single movement she made. Daddy didn't see it, because he only heard her paranoid chorus, and he was too busy spitting out his angered verses. He didn't see her fidgeting fingers, her trembling legs, and the tiny twitch in her bottom lip. She was scared. Horrified. The level of fear in her body was more than a reaction from that afternoon. The fear in her movements had been in place for years, it seemed.

But what was she so afraid of?

Daddy tossed his hands on the back of his neck. "We're running on a hamster wheel, here, Katie. What is it that you have against Brooks and Maggie being together? Because you didn't seem to have an issue until the fantastic four came to visit. I swear, you talk so much crap about Maggie not talking, you can't even find a voice of your own. You run off to your friends for their bullshit opinions on our family, and then you drink a bottle of wine each night. Tell me, Katie: who's the one who needs help?"

Mama's eyes widened, shocked by his words. Daddy seemed just as flabbergasted by his own sounds. She stormed toward their bedroom, and Daddy called after her to apologize, but she was already charging back toward him with pillows and blankets.

"You can stay out here until I get the help I need," she snapped. "And by the way, when she ends up in the same shape as Jessica, know that you did it. Know that you caused it to happen."

Who's Jessica?

She left and didn't return. Daddy stormed out of the front door. Why did everything feel like it was falling apart when for the first time in my life I felt as if I was finally falling back together?

"I know I used to never be home at night but…did they always fight like this?" Cheryl whispered. I shook my head. She kept brushing my hair. "It's almost like they're strangers."

That was heartbreaking.

"Maggie?" Cheryl whispered, her voice cracking. "Did you, though? Did you try to…"

I flipped around so I was facing her, took the hairbrush from her hands, and placed both of her palms against my cheeks. I started shaking my head back and forth, staring her dead in the eye. *No. No. No. No.*

She left out a breath. "I believe you. Mom would, too, if she actually took the time to look you in the eyes."

I couldn't stop the thoughts of how my parents were falling apart all because of me. I wasn't sure what to do. Did I leave Brooks to make them whole again? Did I stay for my own selfish happiness? What was I supposed to do? What were the right choices? How could I fix it all?

I didn't mean to make my parents fight. It was an accident. *I swear it was an accident…*

I blinked once, and I saw him.

The devil—he'd come back to visit.

No…

I tried to blink him away. I was getting better. I was becoming whole.

"Shh," *he whispered. My eyes were wide with fear.* "Please, don't yell. It was an accident." *He moved his lips to my forehead and pressed his mouth against my skin.* "Shh," *he said again. His lips traveled to my earlobe and I felt his lips touching me before he hissed one last time.* "Shh…"

He was there in my mind. I could feel his presence.

Shh… Shh… Shh…

Brooks

Maggie told me she hadn't been feeling well the past few days and refused to see me. I tried my best to talk her into having me visit, but whenever I showed up, her mom sent me away, saying she needed more time to heal.

After band practice one afternoon, I didn't give her much of a choice.

"You're not really sick, are you?" I asked, catching her walking out of the bathroom before she got back to her room. Her eyes widened as she stared my way, and I saw a tinge of panic. "Are you mad at me?" I swallowed hard, growing nervous. Had I done something wrong? "Is it because I told you I loved you? Was it too soon? Did I freak you out? I'm sorry, I just…"

She shook her head back and forth and rushed over to me, taking my hands into hers. She squeezed once. *No.*

"Then what is it?"

She looked up into my eyes and hers started watering over. She began to sob, and I didn't know what else to do, so I held her. I held her close to my chest, and she fell apart in my arms as I collected all of her pieces.

"Music?" I asked her.

She nodded, and we walked to her bedroom, closing the door behind us. She started calming down as we listened to the music playing. We lay on the bed, and it wasn't long after she fell asleep in my arms that her nightmares began. When she woke, she was so close to me, yet felt a million miles away.

"Maggie, you can talk to me," I swore, pacing her room as she awakened from a dream that had pushed her to sobbing tears. She sat up in a ball on her bed, rocking back and forth, not looking my way.

When I moved closer to her, she flinched, almost as if she feared my touch, almost as if she thought I'd hurt her. "Maggie," I begged, my voice and heart cracking. "What's going on?"

She didn't say anything.

"We can do five minutes," I said, bending down in front of her. "Magnet, we can do five minutes. Focus, all right? You can come back to me. It's okay."

She kept swallowing hard with her hands clenched to her neck. Her eyes were wild, and I knew she was too far gone to hear me.

"Mr. Riley!" I shouted through the house. "Mr. Riley!" I shouted again, running through the house. When he came out of his bedroom, he looked at me with his eyes wide and full of concern.

"What is it?" he asked.

"Maggie. She's in her bedroom. I don't know what's happening. She's just…"

He didn't wait for me to reply. He launched up the stairs to where his daughter was having a meltdown. Mrs. Riley was there, too, a few seconds later.

"Mags," he said, his approach slow and cautious. "You're okay," Mr. Riley assured her. The closer he grew, the more she tensed up, but he didn't stop moving in on her. He held his hands up, showing he wouldn't hurt her, and when he was close enough, he wrapped her in his arms and held her against his chest. She clung to his t-shirt and pulled him close, sobbing into his arms.

What happened to you?

My mind was racing as I watched her fall apart against her father. My gut was in knots, hating the fact that I wasn't able to protect her. Why couldn't I fix her? Why couldn't I take her pain and make it my own? He carried her downstairs, and I followed.

Calvin and Stacey walked into the front door laughing together, their arms wrapped tight around each other. When they saw the commotion, their laughter came to a halt.

"What's going on?" Calvin asked.

Mr. Riley didn't respond. He just carried Maggie to his bedroom. Mrs. Riley followed closely behind him.

I couldn't move. I couldn't stop shaking.

Calvin walked over to me, placing a hand on my shoulder. His eyes were narrowed and confused. "Brooks? What's happening?"

"I don't know," I said. My throat was dry and my chest was on fire. "She woke up and…freaked out. I didn't know what to do. I couldn't stop it. I couldn't stop her from…" My eyes watered over, and I pressed the palms of my hands against my face. I couldn't talk anymore. Calvin didn't push me to say anything. He and Stacey simply walked over to me, wrapped their arms around my body, and held me up.

I hated the comfort they were giving me, though, because Maggie needed it more.

She needed someone to fall into her memories and erase the dark waters she swam in each day.

I sat on the staircase, waiting for Maggie's parents to come out of their room. Cheryl, Calvin, and Stacey joined me.

We didn't say a word. I kept flipping through my iPod, searching for some kind of music that could make her feel better. Music always made her smile.

When the bedroom door opened, we all shot up. Mr. and Mrs. Riley frowned our way.

"She's sleeping again," Mr. Riley said.

"Can I see her?" I asked. I held up my iPod toward Mr. Riley. "I just think some music might help. It always helps her."

His lips parted, but Mrs. Riley cut in. "I think everyone should call it a night." She ran her fingers through her hair, and Mr. Riley shut his mouth.

I started to argue, but Mrs. Riley gave me a tired expression, so I nodded my head. "Well, if you could just give it to her, Mr. R, just in case it can help her? I don't need it right now." I handed my iPod to him, and he gave me a forced smile.

Everyone headed into their own rooms, and I was forced to leave. I hated the feeling in my gut, I hated not know how she was doing. How was I supposed to walk away without knowing if she was okay?

"Brooks, can I speak with you for a second?" Mrs. Riley asked as I walked toward the front door. Her arms were crossed and her eyes heavy.

"Yeah, what's going on?"

She glanced around the room, making sure everyone had departed, then stepped closer to me. "I want you to know…Maggie's sick. She might not look it, but her mind…" She frowned. "Whatever happened to her all those years ago, it affected her. Even on the days she seems okay, there's a big part of her that's missing. I know you like her, but being in a relationship with her… I don't think that's smart. She's broken."

I would've been lying if I'd said I wasn't taken aback by her words. She spoke about her daughter as if she were a freak, an outcast. Yeah, Maggie had a few bad days, but who didn't? Glancing around the corner, I saw Maggie peeking out of her parents' bedroom, listening in. I gave her a smile, and she gave me a frown. Before that moment I hadn't known a frown could be more beautiful than a smile. "Not all broken things need to be fixed. Sometimes they just need to be loved. It would be a shame if only people who were whole were deserving of love."

"Brooks." She sighed, as if my words were pointless. "You're young, and you have your whole life ahead of you. I can't help but think you'll hold yourself back trying to have Maggie feel included. You're going off to Los Angeles next week for your music career, where you're going to have all these new experiences—"

"Maggie and I have new experiences every day."

"Yeah, but you're going to have new opportunities, bigger opportunities."

"So will she."

Mrs. Riley sighed, rubbing the back of her neck. "You're not getting it, Brooks. Maggie's not leaving this house. Ever. I know you're trying to be hopeful, but now's the time to be logical. You should break things off with her before you do more damage."

"She'll leave. I know she will. We've spoken about it, you know. She has dreams, too, just like you and me. She has dreams."

"Look. Brooks…I get that she's your friend, and I get that you like to share your music with her, but that's not going to help her. A relationship needs more than music to exist. It needs meat, not just bones. Maggie can't give you what you'll need for a real relationship."

"You don't know what I need."

"With all due respect, I know what you don't need. You're young and in love, I get it, but Maggie's not the best fit for you."

My chest was tight, and I knew if I stayed a second longer, I'd say something I'd regret. I glanced up at where Maggie was standing, but she was gone, so I opened the front door and stepped onto the porch, turning my back to Mrs. Riley.

"I'm sorry, Brooks, but this is for the best."

Turning to face her one more time, I snapped. "With all due respect, Mrs. Riley, I think you're wrong about her. Maggie's smart. She's so smart, kind, and expressive, even without words. She says so much when you can't hear her. Yeah, her mind is busy, but it's deeper than any ocean. She sees things in different ways than most, but why is that a bad thing? And you're wrong about music, too.

If you think for a second music can't heal people, then you're not listening closely enough."

I started on my way, my heart racing.

"She tried to kill herself," Mrs. Riley shouted, making me pause my steps.

I turned back, denial running through my mind. "No."

"Yes, she did. I know I probably seem like the big bad wolf, but she's not okay. You were right, her mind is deeper than any ocean, but one day the tides are going to rise so high, she'll have no choice but to drown."

She tried to kill herself.

I couldn't breathe.

She tried to kill herself.

She wouldn't.

I couldn't fucking breathe.

I walked around the neighborhood, lap after lap after lap. I kept thinking maybe I'd done something wrong. Maybe the way I had held her or touched her had sparked a flashback. Maybe I'd said something wrong.

"It's hard, isn't it?" Mrs. Boone asked me from her porch as I did another lap around the neighborhood, trying to clear my head. I stopped in front of her house as Muffins rolled back and forth in the grass. "When she has her meltdowns."

"How did you know?"

She smiled and glided back and forth in her wicker rocking chair. "I know Maggie, and I know the look on people's faces when she falls apart. I've seen it on her parents' faces more than I'd like to admit. Now come on up here. Take a break. Come inside and I'll make you some tea."

I arched an eyebrow. *Inside?* I hadn't ever seen Mrs. Boone invite someone into her house. Half of me thought if I walked in she might kill me, but the other half was way too curious about what it'd be like inside her home.

Her screen door squeaked as she opened it. She held it wide for me to walk inside, following closely behind me. "You can wait here in the living room. I'll go heat up some water," she said, walking toward her kitchen.

I paced around the living room, looking at her home. Her house was a museum; every piece of artwork looked like it was from the 1800s, and every statue sat behind a glass casing. Everything was polished and clean, and seemed to be in its rightful place.

"Are you sure you don't need help?" I asked.

"I've been making tea for years and never needed help."

I wiped my hand across her fireplace mantel, my fingers collecting dust, and I frowned. I wiped my hand against my jeans. Her fireplace was the only place in the room with dust. It was almost as if she collected every inch of filth and dropped it on the mantel. *Strange.* I lifted up one of the dust-covered frames and stared at Mrs. Boone with a man I assumed was her husband. She sat in his lap, smiling up at him as he smiled at her. I'd never seen Mrs. Boone smile the way she smiled in the photograph.

I picked up another photo, one where the couple stood on a boating dock with a child in front of them, who was laughing in the picture. The transition of the girl growing in the photos was hard to watch. She went from a smiling kid to someone who frowned, to someone who displayed no emotion at all. Her eyes looked so empty. There had to be over thirty frames packed on the fireplace, each picture showing different moments from Mrs. Boone's past.

"Who's the girl? In the photos?" I asked.

She peeked into the room before stepping back into the kitchen. "Jessica. My daughter."

"I didn't know you had a daughter."

"Did you ever ask?"

"No."

"That's why you didn't know. You stupid kids never ask questions. All you do is talk, talk, talk, and no one ever listens." She walked back into the living room, fidgeting with her fingers before sitting on her couch. "The water is heating."

I picked up a dust-covered record and blew off some of the grime. *"Sittin' On The Dock Of The Bay,* by Otis Redding?" I asked.

She nodded. "My husband and I had a cabin up north on the lake. I still own it…I should sell it, but I can't bring myself to do it. It's the last place my family was at our happiest," she said, remembering. "Each evening Stanley and I would sit at the end of the dock, looking out at the sunset while that record played and Jessica ran around in the grass, trying to catch dragonflies."

I sat down in the chair across from her and smiled her way.

She didn't smile back, but I didn't mind. Mrs. Boone was known for not smiling.

"So…" I cleared my throat, feeling awkward in the silence. "Does your daughter ever come by to visit?"

Her eyebrows lowered, and her hands fidgeted against her legs. "It's my fault, you know," she said, her voice somber.

"What's your fault?"

"The night of the accident… What happened to Maggie, it was my fault."

I sat up straighter in my chair. "How so?"

Her eyes grew gloomy. "She stopped by my yard that night. She asked if she could pick flowers from my yard for her wedding. I yelled at her and sent her off, telling her to not come back." Mrs. Boone studied her shaky hands, still tapping her fingers against her legs. "If I hadn't been so mean—so harsh—she could've spent more time in my yard. She wouldn't have wandered off to the woods. She could've been safe from whatever it was that took away part of her mind that night."

Tears started falling from her eyes, and I could feel her hurt. I understood her guilt, because I had felt it too all those years ago.

"I thought the same thing, Mrs. Boone. I was supposed to meet her that night in the woods, and I was late. If I hadn't taken all that time picking out a tie, I could've been there to protect Maggie. I could've saved her."

She looked up and wiped her eyes, shaking her head. "It wasn't your fault." She said it so quickly, obviously afraid of me placing that kind of blame on myself. It was sad, how quick she was to take the blame, and how quick she was to make sure I wouldn't.

I shrugged. "It wasn't your fault, either."

She stood up and walked to her mantel, staring at the photographs. "She was just like Maggie as a child, my daughter. Talkative—a bit too talkative. Wild, free. She wasn't afraid of anyone, either. She saw the best in the most damaged kind of people. Her smile..." Mrs. Boone chuckled, picking up one of the frames that showed Jessica grinning wide. "Her smile healed. She could walk into a room, tell the worst of jokes, and make the grumpiest person in the room laugh so hard their stomach danced."

"What happened to her?"

She placed the photo down and picked up another, where Jessica's smile was gone. "My brother came to visit. He was going through a divorce and needed to get away, so he came and stayed with us. One night, we were having a cookout, and Henry was drinking too much, growing angrier and angrier. He started an argument with my husband, Stanley, and they were seconds away from fighting. Then came sweet, silly Jessica with her bad jokes, which made everyone laugh, even drunken Henry. Later that night, Stanley went to check on Jessica. He found Henry in her room with an empty bottle of alcohol in his hand. Henry was passed out, naked and drunk on top of my daughter, who was frozen in her fear."

"Oh my God. I'm so sorry." I said the words, and when they left my mouth, I knew they weren't enough. No words could express the feeling in my gut. I'd lived on the same block as Mrs. Boone all my life and never knew of the storms she'd sailed through.

"Jessica didn't speak after that. I quit my teaching job and stayed with Jessica to homeschool her, but her light was stolen away. She wasn't the same after what Henry did. She stopped speaking and never smiled again. I didn't blame her, though. How could you speak when a person you were meant to trust stole your voice away? Jessica always walked around as if there were voices in her head, demons trying to make her crack. When she turned twenty, she finally did. She left a note saying she loved Stanley and me, and that it wasn't our fault."

My eyes shut, remembering Mrs. Riley's words.

She tried to kill herself.

She turned my way and frowned when she saw my look of despair. "Oh, dear. I was supposed to have you over to take your mind off your own issues, and I just made you feel worse."

"No, no. I'm just so unbelievably sorry. I don't know what to even say to any of this."

"No worries. I wouldn't know either." Her teapot started whistling in the kitchen, and she shouted, "Stanley, can you get that?"

I narrowed my eyes at Mrs. Boone, and she paused. Moments later, she realized her mistake and hurried into the kitchen, then came back with the tea. We sat there and sipped the disgusting tea in silence. When it was time for me to leave, I stood and thanked Mrs. Boone for inviting me in, not only into her home, but into her history.

As she held the front door open, I asked her one last question.

"Is that why you offered to visit Maggie? Because she reminded you of your daughter?"

"Yes and no. Maggie has a lot in common with my Jessica, but there are big differences."

"What's that?"

"Jessica gave up on life. Maggie every so often has these flashes of hope. I see it more and more often with her. She's going to be okay. I know she is. I have to believe she is going to be okay. You know the biggest difference between the two?"

"What?"

"Jessica had no one. She shut us all out. But Maggie? She has friends. Maggie has you."

"Thanks, Mrs. Boone."

"You're welcome. Now stop blaming yourself, all right?"

I smiled. "Same to you."

She nodded. "Yes, yes, I know. Deep inside of me I know it wasn't my fault, but sometimes when sitting by your lonesome, your thoughts wander to places they shouldn't. Sometimes we are our own worst enemies. One must learn to be discerning with one's own thoughts. We must be able to decipher the truth versus the lies of our minds. Otherwise, we become enslaved to the shackles of struggle we place on our own ankles."

20

Maggie

I hadn't spoken to him in five days, and it had felt like the longest five days of my life.

"What are you reading now?" Mrs. Boone asked me, sitting across from me at the dining room table. When I'd asked Daddy to pass on the word to Mrs. Boone that I wasn't feeling well, she'd called me a ridiculous child who needed some tea. She also blamed my fake illness on me always leaving my hair wet after a shower.

I held my book to my chest and shrugged my shoulders, then I flipped it over for her to see the title.

"Hmm. *Before I Fall* by Lauren Oliver. What is it about?"

I narrowed my eyes at her. She always did that. She always asked me questions she knew I couldn't answer. Seeing as how she never allowed me to write on paper, it felt like nothing less than pressure, and pressure was the last thing I needed.

I placed the book down on the table and sipped at my disgusting tea, grimacing.

"So today is a day where you hate tea again, huh?" she stated.

I shrugged again.

"Where's your boyfriend?"

I shrugged once more.

She rolled her eyes. "One more shrug and your shoulders are going to get stuck midair. So childish. He's worried about you, you know. Pushing him away isn't going to help anyone. It's actually pretty rude. He's a nice boy."

A nice boy? Never in my life had I heard Mrs. Boone say anything kind about anyone.

"Brooks, you can come in now," Mrs. Boone called toward the kitchen.

Brooks stepped out from behind the kitchen door, held his hand up, and waved shyly.

What is he doing here?

"I invited him," Mrs. Boone said, once again reading my thoughts. "Sit, Brooks."

He did as he was told.

"Now, this is the point where I talk and you both listen. You're both idiots." That sounded more like the Mrs. Boone I loved to hate. "You two like each other, right? So allow that to be enough. Stop overthinking everything all the time. Just be happy. Maggie, stop acting like you're not worthy of happiness. If only people with perfect pasts were supposed to be happy, then no love would ever exist. Now, kiss and make up, you idiots."

"What's going on here?" Mama asked, entering the dining room. She looked tired, as if she hadn't slept in days, her hair wild and untamed. Her eyes shot to Brooks, and a smudge of disappointment and shock flew across her face. "You're not supposed to be here."

Mrs. Boone sat up straight. "Now, Katie, before you yell at the kids, I want you to know this was my doing."

"You? You told him to come over here?"

"Yes. The kids were sad, so I thought—"

"I need you to leave," Mama said.

"Oh, come on, that's ridiculous. Let the boy—"

"No, I mean you, Mrs. Boone. I need you to leave. You crossed the line today, and you're not welcome back into my house."

I shot up from my chair, stunned by my mother, who seemed more like a stranger with each passing day. *No!* I pounded my hands against the table. I pounded over and over again until my hands started turning red, and then I kept pounding.

"Brooks, you leave, too. You and I already spoke, and I think I made my message pretty clear. Maggie, go to your room."

No! No!

Brooks lowered his head and left. Mrs. Boone stood up and shook her head. "This isn't right, Katie. Those kids…they are helping each other."

"No offense, Mrs. Boone, but Maggie is not your child, and I'd prefer if you'd stop treating her as if she is your responsibility. She's not Jessica and you do not get to make these choices for her. I refuse to let my daughter end up like—"

"*Like what?*" Mrs. Boone barked back, obviously deeply offended. She grabbed her purse and gripped it tightly in her hold. "Like my daughter?"

A glimpse of guilt appeared in Mama's eyes before she blinked. "From this point on, there will be no more afternoon teas. I appreciate you spending time with Maggie, Mrs. Boone, I really do, but that will be all."

As Mrs. Boone walked to the front door, Mama followed her, and I stayed right on their heels. "I get what you're trying to do, Katie. I really do. I tried to do it with my daughter, too. You think you're helping her by keeping her away from the world, from the place that hurt her, but you're not. You're suffocating her. You're drowning out the little voice she has—her freedom of choice. Her choice to love, to open herself up. You're stealing that from her."

Mama's head lowered. "Goodbye, Mrs. Boone."

She had sent my boyfriend and my best friend away from me, and I couldn't understand what I'd done to deserve it. I started pounding against the closest wall to get Mama's attention. *See me. Notice me!*

She turned, unmoved by my sounds. "Go to your room, Maggie."

No. I pounded more and more, and she charged at me, wrapping her arms around me. *No!*

"Stop it," she ordered. "You think about the kind of life you'd give Brooks. Do you really want him to give up his dreams to stay here with you? How do you think you could be in a relationship with him when he's traveling the world, making a life for himself? Why would you do that to him? This isn't right for you, or him. He deserves more than dates in this house. You deserve to be alone so you can get fixed."

Get fixed?

What if I wasn't broken? What if this was just me?

Where was Daddy? I needed him to come home. I needed him to try to make sense of Mama's mind. I needed him to fix this. I kept struggling in her hold as she dragged me up the stairs. "This is for your own good, Maggie. I'm sorry, but this is for your own good."

I resisted, but she wouldn't let me go. She wouldn't let me free. I blinked my eyes and saw him. The devil.

He apologized for hurting me, apologized for pushing a few fingers into the side of my neck, making it harder and harder for me to find my next breaths.

"Mom! Let her go!" Calvin said, coming out of his room. He tried to get Mama off of me, but she shoved him away.

"Stay out of this, Calvin. Your sister is fine."

No, I'm not. You're hurting me.

Cheryl came out, and I saw the fear in her eyes. I was certain she saw it in my stare too.

Help me.

"Mom," she started, but Mama shut her up quick, too.

She dragged me to my room and shoved me inside. With haste, she shut the door, then held it closed from the outside. "You'll see, Maggie. I'm doing this for you. I'm protecting you."

What was wrong with her? Why was she acting so insane? I pounded on the door, trying my best to open it, but it wouldn't budge. I shoved my body against it, over and over again. *Let me out!* *Let me out!* My hands wrapped around my neck, and I could feel him there with me. He was choking me; he was going to kill me. *Let me out, let me out!*

I couldn't breathe. I couldn't breathe...I didn't know what other option I had.

I didn't know what else I could do, so I did the only thing that came to mind.

I fell to the floor.

I lay face down on the carpet.

I opened my mouth.

And I screamed.

21

Maggie

I blinked.

The door flew open and Daddy charged toward me. I was tucked in the corner of my room, my hands slammed against my earlobes.

I blinked.

Mama followed in after him, and he flew around, screaming at her, telling her to leave.

Blink.

Mama cried and tried to get near me, but Calvin and Cheryl held her back.

Blink.

Daddy bent down, staring me in the eyes, checking if I was okay. "Maggie?" he whispered. He choked on air. "Maggie."

Blink.

He combed through my hair, lifted me up.

"Let me near her," Mama begged.

Daddy laid me in my bed and then ushered Mama out of the room.

Blink.

I could feel him. It felt so real. He was choking me again. He was taking my air. He was back. It was real. It was real…

Blink.

Daddy left the room to go scream at Mama. All they did was scream. Calvin and Cheryl came into my room.

Blink.

The two climbed into bed with me and wrapped their arms around me. They held me tight as I shook in their grips.

Blink.

Cheryl kept telling me I was fine, and Calvin kept agreeing as I cried into my sheets, shaking, feeling broken, confused. Scared. So scared.

Shh…

Shh…

Why did Mama do that? Why did she drag me? Why did the devil do that? Why did he kill that woman? Why did he try to kill me?

Blink.

I shut my eyes. I didn't want to feel. I didn't want to be. I didn't want to blink anymore. I kept my eyes closed. I didn't want to see, but I still saw. I saw him. I felt him. I tasted him. I saw Mama, too. I saw her. I felt her. I loved her.

I hated her.

Why did she hurt me?

Why did she send away the things I loved?

Everything grew darker.

Everything became shadows.

Everything went black.

Maggie

"You okay today, Magnet?" Brooks asked, standing in my doorway. He hadn't been allowed into our house for the past week, and since Mama wasn't home, I assumed Daddy had let him in. Mama had gone to stay with her sister for a few days, a request Daddy had made. I was happy she disappeared for a while.

Seeing Brooks standing there, leaning against my doorframe, broke my heart.

How was it possible?

How could you miss someone who was only steps away from you?

He didn't ask to come into my room like usual; he stayed there with his hands stuffed into his pockets. "We fly out in the morning. We fly out to meet with the producer, to talk about our future." He smiled, but it felt more like a frown. That made me sadder than I had known I could be. Music was his dream, and his dream was coming true, yet still, he seemed so sad.

I'm so proud of you.

He snickered and looked down at the ground, sniffling. "What's going on, Maggie May? In your head?"

I don't know.

He stepped into my bedroom. "Do you love me?"

Yes.

"But you don't want to be with me?"

I hesitated to write, because I knew my words would be confusing to him. I couldn't be with Brooks, especially now. He had his dream finally coming to life, and the last thing he needed was for me to interrupt it with my issues. How could we date, with my parents falling apart? How could we be in love, with him halfway across the country? Even though I hated it, Mama was right. Brooks did deserve more than me. He deserved to be loved out loud, and my love was a whisper in the wind that obviously only he could hear.

He cleared his throat, my nonresponse seeming like all the words he was afraid to hear. "Do you love me?" he asked again.

I do.

He turned away from me for a second and wiped at his eyes. When he turned back, he gave me a tight smile and walked over to me. "Can I hold your hands?"

I held them out, and when he wrapped his fingers with mine, I felt it—the feeling of home rushing through me. A building with walls wasn't a home. Home was the place where the warmest kinds of love lived between two people. Brooks was home to me.

It took everything for me to not cry.

"You know that moment when you discover a new song? You think, no big deal, you've heard a lot of new songs, and this one's gonna be like all the rest, but when the introduction hits your ears and it rockets through you, you feel it in your bones. Then when it hits the chorus, you know. *You just know.* You know that song is going to change you forever. You'll never be able to remember your life without those rhythms, those lyrics, those chords. When the song ends, you race to replay it, and each time you hear it, it's better than you remembered. How is that possible? How could the same words mean more and more each time? You play it over and over again until it's ingrained in you, until it races through your body, becoming the flow that makes your heart beat."

My hands trembled in his, and his trembled in mine. We moved in closer, and he rested his forehead against mine.

"Maggie May, you're my favorite song."

I couldn't fight the tears, and he couldn't fight his, as our faces rested against one another. "I'm so torn right now, Maggie. A part of me wants to go to Los Angeles and chase the dream, but another part of me knows *you* are the dream. You're it. So tell me what you want. Tell me you want me. I'll stay. I swear, I'll stay."

I stepped back from him, dropping his hands.

His dream was in Los Angeles.

Mama was right.

I was no kind of life for him.

I wasn't his dream. I was his waking nightmare.

"Tell me to stay, and I'll stay," he begged. "Tell me to go, and I'll go, but don't keep me here in limbo, Maggie May. Don't let me leave, not knowing. Don't make me swim in unknown waters, because I'm certain the unknown is where I'll drown."

Go.

He read the words on my board, and I saw the switch in his eyes. He seemed shocked by my response. Hurt. Broken. The look of despair in his eyes stunned me. I rushed over to him and started trying to pull him into a hug.

"Stop, Maggie. It's fine."

No. It wasn't. He was hurting because of me. He was breaking, because I'd broken him. *Please. I need you to understand. Please.*

I held up my hand.

Five minutes.

That's all I needed. Five more minutes.

He sighed and nodded. "Okay. Five minutes."

I pulled him into a hug and forced him to hold me.

He choked out a cough. "It's not fair. It's not fair. We were happy."

I held him tighter and looked up at him. Our lips grazed against one another, and we kissed. We kissed softly first, and then harder. We kissed with our hopes and our apologies all at once. It amazed me how in the past, five minutes had felt like forever, but in that moment, five minutes was a blur.

"Maggie May," Brooks whispered, his voice cracking. "How did you do that? How did you break my heart and fix it all at once, with just one kiss?"

I felt it, too. Whenever our lips found each other, the kisses hurt and healed. We were thunderstorms and sunlight all at once. How did we do that to one another? Why did we do it? And how were we ever supposed to truly say goodbye?

He touched the anchor necklace I hadn't taken off in years before he let me go and stepped backward. "I can't stay here...I gotta go. I gotta let you go." Within seconds he walked out of my bedroom and out of my life.

After he left, Cheryl came and sat beside me on my bed. "Why did you do that, Maggie? Why did you let him go?"

I leaned against my sister and rested my head on her shoulder, unsure how to answer. It felt wrong in my chest, letting him walk away, but he had to go after his dreams without me. When you loved someone, you let them fly away, even if you weren't on the same flight.

"It's not fair," she said. "Because the way he looks at you, and the way you look at him—that's my dream. That's what I want someday."

I parted my lips to speak, but nothing came out. I gave Cheryl a sloppy smile, and she gave me a frown.

"I figured out what kind of activist I want to be," my sister told me, taking my hand into hers. "I want to fight for you, for people like you. I want to fight for those who don't have a voice, but are screaming to be heard."

Calvin and the guys were asked to stay out in Los Angeles for a few more days. They'd been offered a recording deal with Rave Records, and I could almost feel their excitement all the way from the west coast.

Brooks called me to share the news. "I know we aren't supposed to be talking...but...we did it, Magnet." His voice was so low. "We did it. We got a deal. In a few weeks, it will be official, and we'll be signing with Rave. You did this for us. You made this happen."

Tears rolled down my cheeks. I'd never wanted anything more than I wanted this amazing thing to happen for them. Those boys deserved it. They deserved everything that came to them.

"I love you, Maggie," he whispered before hanging up.

It was the last time I heard from him. Calvin called to tell the family the producer wanted them to get in the studio to record some samples while they worked on the contracts, and before I knew it, days became weeks, and weeks became months. Their lives started moving on the fast track, and I was frozen still. When September came, the band was invited to be an opening act for The Present Yesterdays on their world tour.

It seemed that in a blink of an eye, their lives were completely changed.

I tried my best to stop missing him. I read my books, I took my baths, and I listened to the iPod he'd left behind. I played his guitar, too. It turned out missing someone never became easier, it just became quieter. You learned to live with the longing pain inside you. You mourned the moments you'd shared and allowed yourself to hurt sometimes, too.

There were so many times I opened my phone and stared at his number, so many times I almost dialed him to check in. I told myself I'd only call once, just to hear his voice, but I never built up the courage to move forward. I knew deep down if I called once, I wouldn't be able to go without calling him each day to hear his voice again.

Most days I hardly left my room, afraid of running into Mama.

She and Daddy were becoming complete strangers right before my eyes. Whenever they were in the same room, one of them left. Before, when Daddy used to leave for work, he'd kiss her forehead, but those kisses were nothing more than a memory now.

The seasons came, the seasons changed, and whenever the band came back into town, Brooks was nowhere to be found. I thought maybe he had found his next adventure on the road. Perhaps our love was supposed to only be a passing moment in time.

"It's on!" Mama hollered one night, running throughout the house. "It's on!" Everyone came from their rooms, and for the first time in months, my family seemed like one unit as we stood around the radio in the dining room, listening to The Crooks' first song on the radio. My chest tightened and I gripped the anchor necklace that had never left my neck as I listened to the words I knew. Our song…

She lies against my chest as her raindrops begin to fall
She feels so weak, floating aimlessly, slamming against the walls
Praying for a moment where she won't begin to drown
Her heart's been begging for an answer to the silent hurts her soul
keeps bound

I'll be your anchor
I'll hold you still throughout the night
I'll be your steadiness
during the dark and lonely tides
I'll hold you close, I'll be your light, I'll promise you'll be all right
I'll be your anchor
And we'll get through this fight

Listening to the words felt like the kiss I'd been craving. The words felt like he'd promised to come back to me. Everyone in the dining room started cheering and hugging—something we hadn't done in so long. When Mama's hands wrapped around Daddy's body, he held her close. I swore I saw it, too, the place where their love used to exist. It was gone in a flash when they separated, but still, I had seen it, which meant somewhere inside them, that love still remained.

It wasn't until the night I received a package in the mail that I allowed myself to cry over Brooks leaving.

A book.

Water for Elephants by Sara Gruen.

Inside the book were yellow Post-its marking the best parts of the book, covered with his handwriting. In the back of the novel was a note, a note I read each day, over and over again for the passing years to come. The note was proof I'd never love another boy again.

A note to the girl who pushed me away
By: Brooks Tyler Griffin
October 22nd, 2018

Maggie May,

It's been two years since I last saw your face. Twenty-four months of missing you, dreaming of you, and wanting you by my side. Everything reminds me of you, and whenever I come back into town, I stay at my brother's house, unable to face you. If I saw you again, I wouldn't be able to leave. I know I wouldn't. My life is moving fast. Some days, I doubt I can keep up. Other days, I want to quit and come home to you. On those days, I remember how you pushed me away. This is what you wanted, and I have to honor your request.

Years before I knew what it meant to love you, I lay in your bedroom, holding your hand, and made you a promise.

I gave you an anchor necklace and promised I'd be your friend, no matter what. I've done a lot of thinking, wondering how I could still be a friend while also respecting your space. This is the best way that came to mind. I'll keep sending you novels with my thoughts; I hope this helps you remember that you're never alone. If you ever feel lonely, read the notes in the books.

If there's ever a day you call for me, I'll be there.

I love you, Magnet, both as a lover and a friend. Those are two things that will never change, even when my heart needs a break.

Always yours,
Brooks Tyler

P.S. I'm always around to listen to your silence.

A note to the boy who's on television
By: Maggie May Riley
August 1st, 2019

Brooks,

I saw you on *Good Morning America* today. Your hair is longer, isn't it? Plus, is that a tattoo on your right arm? I couldn't get a close enough look, but I could've sworn it was a tattoo. What is it of? I'm sending back my comments on *American Gods* by Neil Gaiman. I have a confession, though: I've already read it three times before you sent it to me. Seeing your side and your thoughts made it feel like a new read, though. You can't really go wrong with any of his novels.

I finished reading *The Guernsey Literary and Potato Peel Pie Society* by Mary Ann Shaffer and Annie Barrows. I'm crossing my fingers that you'll enjoy it. I loved it, but I know you're not as into period pieces as I am. It's based around World War II, and while it highlights the effects of war, there's still such a sweet, charming feel to the story. And it's hilarious too.

Did I tell you Muffins passed away? I told Daddy to tell Mrs. Boone I was sorry for her loss. Her reply? "That damn thing lived a million years. Now I don't have to waste money on cat food."

What she really meant was she missed her more than words. I miss her, too.

Always,
-Maggie

P.S. The Crooks' new album is number one again this week—I'm not surprised. I've been listening to it on repeat for the past five weeks. You're my favorite kind of sound.

A note to the girl who rereads books for fun
By: Brooks Tyler Griffin
January 5th, 2020

Magnet,

The band is in Tokyo this week, and Rudolph accidently ate fried pig ears, thinking they were organic fried pickles. It was probably the best moment I've ever witnessed. There's this nasty cold going around, and I have fallen as the next victim to the plague. The amount of cold medicine I've been doped up on is worrisome, but still, the show must go on tonight. I'm hoping to pass the cold on to Calvin soon, just for laughs. The book: *The Passage* by Justin Cronin.

The number of Post-its: one hundred and two.

I heard Cheryl got into Boston State University and is taking up a journalism degree with a minor in women's studies. Next time you Skype with her, let her know how proud I am of her.

-Brooks

A note to a boy who can go to hell
By: Maggie May Riley
June 14th, 2021

Brooks Tyler,

Seriously? *The Fault in Our Stars*?

I just cried into a tub of mint chocolate chip ice cream. Surprisingly, the salty tears added to the flavor. With that, I take your John Green novel and raise you *A Thousand Splendid Suns* by Khaled Hosseini. Cheryl had me read it, and I haven't been the same since.

Godspeed.

-Maggie

A note to the girl I hate
By: Brooks Tyler Griffin
August 12th, 2021

M,

Fuck you, Maggie May Riley.

Fuck you very much.

I loved crying over a book in front of a sausage fest of grown men.

It really upped my cool points.

-B

P.S, You're taking online classes to become a librarian? Amazing. In your last note you wrote, "Hopefully someday I'll leave home to become a librarian."

There's no hope needed.

There are only facts.

You'll be the best librarian in the history of librarians, and I'd visit your library to read every single book.

A note to a boy with a Grammy
By: Maggie May Riley
February 28th, 2024

Brooks,

I'm so proud of you.

I'm so amazed by your talents.

I hope your world tour is beyond amazing.

The book: *Oh The Places You'll Go* by Dr. Seuss.
The Post-its: Eighteen.

-Maggie

A note to the girl I respect
By: Brooks Tyler Griffin
July 18th, 2025

Magnet,
Sorry I haven't sent anything in a while. Things have been crazy with rehearsals, meetings, and interviews. I'm tired. I'm always tired lately. I still love it all, but some days, I wish I could slow down.
I feel like I should tell you something, but I'm not sure how, so here it goes.
I met someone.
Her name is Sasha.
She's a model, and she's sweet. She's really, really sweet. She's an awful singer and a worse dancer, but she laughs, which is more than I can say for most people I've met along this journey.
I don't know why I felt the need to tell you, but I thought you should hear it from me first, instead of the tabloids.

-Brooks

P.S. I reread *The Kite Runner*. It was the first book you ever gave me, remember? I don't remember crying the first time I read it, but maybe time changes the way we view stories. Maybe as we grow, life experiences shift the meanings of the books. Maybe I'm not the same person I was those years ago when I read it.

Or maybe I'm just homesick.

Part Three

23

Maggie

Each night, Mama, Daddy, and I ate dinner together at the dining room table. Mama and Daddy hardly ever looked at each other. They walked past one another like strangers.

Daddy hardly made any jokes anymore, and when he did come to my bedroom he complained more about Mama's drinking.

It was hard to believe they had ever been in love. It was hard to imagine how they used to dance.

Still, we ate dinner together each night, even if it was always uncomfortable for everyone. Fridays were my favorite nights, though, because after dinner, Cheryl always called me for a Skype date.

I'd clear my plate and hurry up to my room, eagerly opening my computer. Ever since Cheryl had graduated college, she'd been on a quest to discover the world. She had started backpacking around Europe and Asia, and hadn't stopped moving since. She'd visited all kinds of places, discovered all kinds of cultures, and witnessed more struggle than she could've ever imagined in remote parts of the world that went mostly unnoticed.

She was in Bangkok, Thailand, when she Skyped me that night.

"Hey, sister!" she said, her service not as clear as it had been a week before, but seeing her face at all still made me happy. "You're looking good."

I smiled and typed back to her. *Ditto.*

"So, today I went to see Phra Phuttha Maha Suwana Patimakon. I bet I pronounced that wrong, because when I said it earlier my tour guide told me I totally butchered the pronunciation, but oh well. It's that big Golden Buddha, ya know? It was amazing, too. Oh!" She shifted around her small hostel room and pulled out a book. "And I got you your first book from Thailand! I don't know what it says per se, but I think it's a solid one if you know how to read Thai."

I smiled at my dorky sister. I missed her so much.

Cheryl arched an eyebrow. "So since I've been gone have you started talking and cursing like your sailor-mouthed sister?"

I shook my head.

"One day I want you to spread your arms out and shout the loudest *fuck* that could ever be shouted. It will be refreshing, I think."

I don't think so.

She frowned. "It would be better if you were a bit more messed up. Less perfect, you know? I mean, I know you've got that mute thing, and the can't-leave-home issue, but those seem small compared to my being a single female and running around the dangerous world alone. You really make it hard to be your sibling."

I smirked. *Sorry.*

She snickered. "No you're not. Anyway, how are classes going?"

I'd been taking online classes at the University of Wisconsin-Milwaukee, where I'd received an undergraduate degree in English. After that, I applied to many different schools that held online Master degrees, yet I wasn't accepted to any. My rocking résumé probably wasn't the best, seeing how I hadn't done much of anything with my life.

It was a year ago when I was ready to give up, but Daddy convinced me to apply at UW-Milwaukee for their Master of Library & Information Science. When I was accepted to their online program, I cried.

Mama said it was a waste of time and money. Daddy said it was a step closer to my happy ending.

School is going well. The semester is almost over, which is good.

"Do you like, flirt with any of your classmates on the discussion boards?" Cheryl asked, her voice heightened.

I rolled my eyes, even though she was quite serious. Cheryl once tried to convince me to fall in love online. She even signed me up on a few dating sites.

"I'm just saying, Maggie. You're educated. You're beautiful. And—"

And I live with my parents.

"Yeah, but not in the *basement*. You live *upstairs*. That's different."

There's also the issue with me being mute and never leaving home.

"Are you kidding me? Men adore it when women shut up. Plus, if you never leave home, it means you're a super cheap date. Men love not spending money! You should add those things under your strong characteristics on a dating site." She winked.

I smirked, and she kept pushing the subject until I asked if she'd spoken to Calvin.

"I Skyped with him earlier, and he was telling me how he stumbled across a band on YouTube called Romeo's Quest. Total indie underground brilliant vibe. He sent me a link to their music, and I literally fell backward, so I'm passing it on now because I *know* it was made for *you*. I'll link it below. And get this: all their songs are based on Shakespeare plays!"

You don't know anything about Shakespeare.

"I know, Maggie, but that's not the point! The point is that it's different and raw and..." She paused. *"To be or not to be, that is the question!* See! I know some Shakespeare! I'm a college graduate, missy."

What play is that from?

"Ohmygosh, what is this? Twenty questions? Get off my invisible dick, sister! Anyway, after our call listen to their music. I think Calvin is trying to set something up for the band—some kind of pay-it-forward deal, seeing how they were discovered online."

Very cool.

"I spoke to Brooks, too," Cheryl said, making me tilt my head. I tried to ignore the flipping in my stomach.

Is he well?

"Yeah. He looks really good. Happy, ya know? Just tired. He has this crazy facial hair thing going on, as if he hasn't shaved in years, or something. It turns out it's only been a few months, but it looks good on him. He looks grown up."

And happy?

She nodded. "And happy."

Good. Good. I wanted him to be happy. He deserved to be happy.

After I'd found out he was with Sasha, I couldn't keep writing him. It hurt too much to know that when he received my books, she could've been sitting right beside him. And that wouldn't have been fair to her, either.

I closed my eyes, trying to envision his new look. The last time I'd seen him was when I watched the Grammys and the band won the Album of the Year award. He looked happy there, too, almost as if his dreams were fully unlocked and achieved.

"Are you happy, Maggie?" my sister asked.

I smiled and nodded, yet she didn't notice me knock once on my leg beneath the table.

Happiness was hard to find alone in my bedroom, especially when the one you loved was out loving someone else.

As Cheryl and I spoke, Mama started shouting. "I didn't break it, Eric! I was trying to fix it. You said you would weeks ago and never got around to it."

"I told you not to mess with it. Now you screwed it up more," Daddy barked back.

Cheryl frowned. "What is it they are fighting about this time?"

The dishwasher.

She didn't ask any more questions. Mama and Daddy only had two versions of their relationship: the silent version, and the angered version.

If they weren't mute, they were screaming.

If they weren't screaming, they passed one another like ghosts.

Cheryl and I spoke for a bit more before she started yawning and headed to bed.

After we ended the call, I started playing Romeo's Quest's videos on YouTube. I tapped my fingers against my stomach, listening to the instrumentals wash over me. Cheryl understood my head and my soul, and when the lead singer started singing, I felt it—an arrow to my heart.

I listened to every video they had online, over and over again. My favorite song was "Broken Nightmares" because it was sad, but somehow hopeful.

Find me in the dark because that's where I live
Open up your heart and let the shadows in

I blinked my eyes a few times, trying to envision what the band had been feeling when they wrote those lyrics, those words. Music was one of the best reminders that I was never alone in this world. It was that powerful moment when I heard the sounds and the lyrics. It seemed as if the artist crawled into my lonely head and created the song solely for me, reminding me that somewhere out there, there was someone feeling exactly as I was feeling.

I was sure Brooks would've loved them.

Brooks

"Birmingham, you have been amazing tonight! We are The Crooks, and we thank you for allowing us to steal your hearts tonight," Calvin shouted into the microphone at our second sold-out show in Birmingham, England—over sixteen thousand tickets sold, over sixteen thousand fans screaming our names and singing our lyrics.

I was sure it would never get old, standing in front of people who allowed you to live your dream out loud.

The four of us had been living our dreams for the past ten years, starting as an opening act for our favorite band, and now as the main event. Our lives were far from normal.

"Also, shooting a happy birthday to my partner in crime who turned twenty-eight today. Happy birthday, Calvin! The world's a bit drunker because your voice exists." The crowd cheered, screaming for an encore, which we weren't allowed to do because time was money, and money was something management hated to waste.

We all rushed offstage and I crashed into my dressing room, just to have Michelle, my personal assistant, immediately coming at me with a list of radio and television appearances scheduled for the upcoming week.

"Great show tonight, Brooks," she said, smiling and juggling her iPad, iPhone, and a pack of Skittles in her hands. "So tonight, there's an after party at Urban."

"The same Urban from last year where somehow Rudolph ended up in a fist-fight over tuna being made with dolphin meat?" I questioned, walking over to my sink and grabbing a wet cloth to wash my face.

"That's the one. They're throwing Calvin's birthday party tonight."

I sighed. I hated clubs, but I loved my best friend. "Therefore I have to be there."

"You have to be there, at least for photos, then you can dip out whenever. In the morning, you gotta be at KISS 94.3 by five for the radio interview. After that we shuffle over to The Morning Blend at seven, at nine we will go to The Mix 102.3 for a live stream radio shoot, and then by twelve we are meeting at Craig Simon's talk show. Back to the arena at three for sound check, meet and greet four-thirty to six, then dinner with the opening act where there will be a photoshoot with a few reporters before the show at eight. Any questions?"

"Um, yeah, when do I get to sleep?"

She snickered and began typing on her phone. "You know my motto, Brooks—"

"We can sleep when we're six feet under," I replied, echoing her words. I sat down in my chair and lifted up the package I had put together that afternoon before the show. "Can you find a post office to mail this off tomorrow?"

Michelle scowled. "When am I supposed to find time to do that?"

I smirked. "You know my motto: why not find a reason to visit a post office each day?"

"That's not your motto, but I'll do it." She snatched the book from my hand, and narrowed her eyes at me. "Does it bother you?"

"Does what bother me?"

"That she never sends books back anymore?"

Maggie hadn't sent me a book since the year before when I told her I was seeing Sasha. Did it bother me? Every single day. Did I miss the pink Post-its? Every single day. Would I ever let on that it hurt? Never. "Nah. I'm not really expecting any kind of reply anymore."

"You must've done something awful to make her stop."

"What makes you think it was my fault?"

She smiled. "The penis in your pants." She started walking off toward the door to leave. "I really hope whoever this book girl is has a huge *Beauty and The Beast*-style library, because she'll need it with all the books you've sent her way lately. You've got twenty minutes to shower and wash up before we head over to Urban." With that, she was gone.

I sat in front of my mirror and breathed in all my changes. I had bags under my eyes at the age of twenty-eight, not small bags, very noticeable bags that our makeup artist was so good at hiding. My arms were inked up from my younger days of drunken tattoos while doing concerts around the U.S., and my constantly growing beard was longer than it should've been, but my manager, Dave, told me beards were in and he therefore refused to let me shave.

I wondered what Maggie would've thought of my hairy face.

I wondered what Maggie would've thought about me.

I wondered if I ever crossed her mind the way she always seemed to cross mine.

"Hey, hairy monster," a voice said, breaking me from my thoughts. The moment I swung around in my chair to see Sasha, I felt guilt. I hated when my mind wandered to Maggie May when Sasha was around. It didn't seem fair to anyone.

Sasha walked over to me and sat in my lap. "Tonight was amazing. You're amazing," she whispered, kissing my nose. The guilt was fast to fade whenever Sasha came near me. She was beautiful, not only in her looks, but in her kindness. You didn't find many people as gentle as her in the realm of fame.

200

"Thanks," I replied, kissing her chin. "We have to make an appearance at Urban tonight."

She groaned, hating clubs as much as I did. "Seriously? I was hoping we could go back to the hotel, turn on the whirlpool, and order room service."

"Oh, don't tempt me."

Her lips glided against mine. She tasted like red wine, her favorite drink of choice backstage whenever she was able to fly out to catch one of our shows.

"I fly out in the morning. I have a photoshoot in Los Angeles, then a runway show in New York."

"You *just* got here a few days ago," I complained. Since the tour had started, Sasha and I had only seen each other a handful of times, but we always found a few minutes to FaceTime each night. She'd flown to Birmingham four days before, and even though we were in the same city, I still had to run around all the time. It wasn't fair to our relationship, but Sasha knew what it was like. I'd flown out to see her during my breaks, but she'd been working on her career just as hard as I had been on mine.

"I know. I miss you. I miss you even when you're right here."

I pulled her closer in my lap and rested my head on her forehead. "How about this? How about we make a quick stop at Urban, for an hour or so, then go back to the hotel and pull an all-nighter eating room service in the whirlpool?"

Her body stiffened up and a pleasant smile formed on her lips. "Don't you have a busy day tomorrow? When will you sleep?"

"I can sleep when I'm six feet under," I joked, mocking Michelle. "But seriously. I'd rather be tired because I got to spend time with you than fully rested any day."

Her hands fell against my cheeks, and she bent forward to kiss me. "I'm wild about you, Mr. Griffin. Now come on, you go shower and get ready for tonight."

We made our way to Urban and stayed an hour and thirty minutes—longer than we thought we had planned to stay, but it was worth it. Calvin had the time of his life, and it was the best feeling in the world, seeing him happy. Stacey was right there on his arm, too, the same place she'd been since eighth grade.

There was something about Sasha and me when we went out together—people noticed us. We were the life of every event; we laughed, we drank, we danced. Our mouths were always moving nonstop, chatting it up with people, and we had a way of finishing each other's sentences. Being social with Sasha Riggs was effortless. We gelled together so well it was impossible for anyone to doubt we had been destined to meet one another over a year ago.

The 'it' pair, magazines called us.

The next Brad and Angelina.

America's next royal couple.

It was a lot to live up to, but we did it with our charm. There was no one else I knew who could keep up with my words—with my voice.

By the time Sasha and I headed back to the hotel, we were both pretty drunk. Whenever she was wasted, she got the hiccups, and it was the cutest fucking thing in the world. We kissed the whole way up to our room, and when we made it inside, she kicked off her high heels, hurried over to the whirlpool, and turned it on.

"Grab the room service menu and order anything you want plus French fries. Lots of French fries."

I moved toward the telephone to order the food and paused when I saw *The Kite Runner* sitting on the end table.

My chest tightened as I started flipping through the book and reading Maggie's tabs.

"I'm gonna put bubbles in it. I don't know if I'm supposed to, but I'm gonna," Sasha shouted.

I didn't reply; I just kept flipping.

"Tonight was actually a lot of fun, wasn't it? I loved the crowd. There was a lot of…"

She kept speaking, but I stopped listening. The guilt started coming back to me as I read Maggie's notes. I shouldn't have felt the way I did. I shouldn't have missed her. I shouldn't have been pulled back to her every time I opened one of the old novels she sent.

"Did you order?" Sasha asked, walking my way. I opened the drawer on the nightstand and shoved the book in, closing it fast.

"Hm?"

"Did you order the food?"

"Oh, yeah, not yet."

She raised a questioning eyebrow. "What's going on? Is everything okay?"

No. "Come here," I said, sitting on the king-sized bed. She sat down on the bed, facing me. I took her hands into mine. "Can we try something?"

"You're scaring me…"

"Sorry, I just want to try five minutes."

"What does that mean?"

"I want us to stare at each other for five minutes."

She grimaced. "Why?"

"Please, Sasha? I just…I need you to try."

She nodded. "Okay." During the first minute, we struggled to make eye contact. During the second minute, she commented on how weird being quiet was. At minute three, she dropped my hands. "I don't get it, Brooks. I don't get what's going on with you. I mean, we had such a good night, and then we get back to the hotel, and you're all weird."

"I know, sorry."

She narrowed her eyes. "Is this about the book girl?"

"Who?"

She bit her bottom lip. "You know, the book girl. You think I don't notice your hands are always either on your guitar or in a book leaving notes you never leave me? Sometimes when you're reading, I could be naked in front of you doing the hula and you wouldn't even notice."

She took a deep breath. "I love you, Brooks," she said, her eyes filled with hope and a bit of worry.

My lips parted, and as I was about to speak, no words came out. All I could think of was, "Thank you."

Sasha shifted her body and stood up from the bed. "Wow. Okay. I'm gonna go."

"Sasha, wait!"

"Wait? Wait for what? Brooks, I just told you I *loved* you for the first time, and you said *thank you*. Jesus! You're such an asshole!" she hollered. "It's really hard being third, but I did it because I thought maybe somewhere along the line you'd bump me up."

"Third?"

"Third in your life. You've got your music, your book girl, and then the rest of the world, and no matter how hard the rest of the world tries to keep up with your attention, you're never fully there."

I *was* an asshole. A true asshole. "I'm sorry, Sasha."

"We're good together. Everyone can see it. We're good. We make sense."

I nodded. She wasn't wrong. She and I made sense to the whole world. I only wished we made sense to my heart, too.

She bit her bottom lip. "We're breaking up, aren't we?"

"Yeah, I think we are."

"You love her?" she whispered, a few tears falling from her eyes.

My thumbs wiped away the evidence of her sadness, but only seconds later more showed up. "I tried not to. I wanted this to work. I wanted us to work."

She shrugged. "I deserve better, you know."

I nodded. I knew.

"And just to be clear, I'm the one breaking up here, not the other way around. I'm dumping *you*. Because I'm a catch, Brooks. I deserve someone who's smart, and funny, and charming. Someone who's not distant when we're in the same room. Someone who sees me and loves me wholly, fully."

"You do. You really do."

She wiped away her tears and stood tall, grabbing her purse before leaving. "But what I deserve most—what everyone deserves most—is someone who looks at me the same way you look at those books."

Maggie

For the past few years, I'd stare out my window at Mrs. Boone's house where she'd sit and drink her tea. Mama never did soften her stance on Mrs. Boone. When Daddy told her she was always welcome in the house, Mrs. Boone declined, saying she didn't want to cause any more trouble. Still, we drank our tea. She'd always look up at me at noon and smile as I held a cup of tea in my hands. It was my favorite hour of the day, the thing I looked forward to the most.

Lately, she'd been missing.

The first few days, I didn't think anything of it. Her car was gone from the driveway, and I figured perhaps she had taken a trip, even though trips weren't something Mrs. Boone ever partook in. The next week, I started to worry when she hadn't returned.

The more days that passed, the more nervous I became. Daddy went on a search, pulling in a few others from the neighborhood, and reported her as missing to the police, but they were certain there wasn't anything they could do to help.

It was five in the morning when Daddy woke me with the news. "There was an accident, Maggie. Mrs. Boone was in a car accident and has been rushed to Mercy Hospital. She…"

He kept talking, but I couldn't hear hi. The words went in and out of my ears. I didn't cry. I was too shocked to cry. She was unconscious and in pretty bad shape. Daddy said she had been driving a bit wild, and an eyewitness said she had seemed confused and lost.

When he left my room, the more real it became. I had to go see her. She had no one to check on her. She had no family. I was all she had.

So I had to leave.

"Are you sure, Maggie?" Daddy asked while he stood in the front foyer with me, ready to drive me to the hospital.

I nodded.

Mama's head tilted up, gazing at me standing in the doorway. Her narrowed eyes had an intense focus, almost as if she was waiting for me to fail. Almost as if she *wanted* me to fail. "She's not going to do it," Mama said, a sharp tone to her voice. "She's not ready. She's not going anywhere."

"No," Daddy said sternly. "She's going." He locked eyes with me, his stare filled with hope and compassion. "She told me she was going, and she's going. Right, Maggie?"

I knocked on the door twice, and he smiled.

Mama shifted around in her shoes and crossed her arms. Her nerves were loud and clear while Daddy once again missed them. "That's a lie. Watch her. Watch her run back to her bedroom. It's okay, Maggie. You can go back upstairs. Don't let your father pressure you."

"Katie, knock it off," Daddy scolded.

She grimaced and remained silent, but I could feel her stare on me.

My hands were clammy, and my heart pounded against my ribcage.

Daddy smiled up at me. "Don't worry, Mags. You got this. You can do it," he cheered me on.

Shh…

I stepped backward once, and he noticed, stepping toward me. He rushed to me and shook his head. "No, no, no. Maggie, you can do this. Here." He extended one hand out toward me and used his other to knock on the door twice. "Yes? Remember? You said yes. You're coming."

My eyes darted to his shaky hand and when I looked back at his eyes the hope he once held was swallowed whole by confusion and worry.

"Maggie?" he whispered, extending his hand more.

I stepped backward, and hit the end table in the foyer, shaking my head back and forth.

"Come on, Maggie. We have to get going," he said.

I knocked on the table once. *No.*

What was wrong with me? I was too old to be so afraid. I was too old to be broken. I saw it in Daddy's eyes, something he spent years trying to hide from me—his exhaustion. His hairs were almost all gray, the bags beneath his eyes were deep, and his smile resembled a frown all the time. When had he stopped smiling fully? He was tired. Tired of worrying. Tired of waiting. Tired of me.

His heavy stare grew grim. "No..." He ran his fingers through his hair. "No. Don't do this. Please."

My throat tightened and I felt the devil's fingers wrapping around me again. He was cutting off my air supply. He suffocated me. My fingers wrapped around my neck, and I gasped for help. Mama studied my movements and raised an eyebrow, watching my panic, seeing my shadows of the past start to emerge. She and Daddy started talking—*shouting*. They began shouting again. Their lips were moving in a hurried fashion, but I couldn't comprehend what they were saying, because the devil was loud in my ear, drowning me once again. My hands slammed against my ears, and I shut my eyes tightly. *Go away, go away, go away...*

"Leave it alone, Eric!" Mama finally screamed, wrapping her arms around my shoulders. I couldn't remember the last time she held me in a protective manner. "She doesn't have to leave. Leave it alone."

Daddy's eyebrows dropped, and he took off his glasses, rubbing the palms of his hands against his eyes. "I'm sorry. I didn't mean to pressure you. I just thought..." He released a weighted sigh. "I don't know what I thought." As he left, he closed the front door behind him, and I closed my eyes, hearing his footsteps grow farther and farther away.

A terrifying realization flashed before my eyes: I'd never be able to leave those four walls.

When did it happen?

When did my safe haven turn into my own personal hell?

Mrs. Boone was alone, she wasn't waking up, and I wasn't strong enough to go see her. I fell apart in my bedroom. That night I sat on my floor and I did the only thing I knew could make everything better.

I called him.

"Maggie?" Brooks yawned. I hadn't thought about what time it was in Europe; it was almost eight in the evening at my house, so it had to be pretty late for him. "What's up? What's going on?"

My lips parted and I began crying into my hand. I cried for how lost I felt, and how the sound of his voice was so quick to remind me of home.

"Okay," he whispered, unsure of what was happening, but positive that I needed him. "I'll be there."

He was back in town thirteen hours later, and he didn't come alone; the whole band came back with him. Brooks didn't come to my house, though, and I wasn't certain why. I wasn't sure what hurt more—knowing he was so close, or still feeling as if he was so far away. Rudolph, Oliver, and Calvin came straight to my room and sat with me the whole time, though. They hadn't left my side since they'd landed in town.

"We're a team, ya know, Maggie? And if it weren't for you, we wouldn't be where we are today," Rudolph said, sitting on the edge of my bed.

"When Brooks said he was leaving, it was pretty much impossible to stop him. Plus, The Crooks are a unit. We couldn't perform without him. Plus, *plus,* family first, right?" Oliver said.

"We're always here for you, sis, even if we're over there. I mean, I'm pretty sure management is going to disown us for a while, but I'm not too worried." Calvin smiled and nudged me in the arm.

We sat there quietly. They didn't even know that their silence was helping me breathe easier.

"He still loves you," Calvin told me. "You know that, right?"

I shrugged. I'd hoped that was true for a long time, but based on his Twitter posts and the way his fans hung all over him, I wasn't certain if love was enough. The saddest fact in the world was that you could meet a person who changed your life forever, and they weren't the one you ended up with. The people who taught you to love weren't always the ones who stayed.

Why isn't he here?

Calvin read my words. "After we spoke to Dad and he told us what was happening, Brooks knew where you needed him most. When we got to the airport, he had a taxi take him directly to the hospital to be with Mrs. Boone."

My hand covered my mouth, and in that moment I loved him more than I ever had in my life. It was amazing to me how he could make me fall more in love with him without being anywhere near me.

I love him.

Calvin nodded. "I know. If there are any two people worthy of being in love, it's you two. I just wish life would stop getting in your way."

I closed my eyes and lay backward on my bed with my feet hanging off the edge, and Calvin lay beside me. The twins went to the floor to lie down, and Rudolph played music on his phone. We stayed silent, letting the music take us over as we waited for Brooks to find his way home to me.

Brooks

I'd been sitting in the same chair, in the same room, for the past twelve hours staring at Mrs. Boone, tubes running through her, the IVs pumping fluids into her system. Her body was bruised all over, but she wasn't broken. I couldn't imagine what she had gone through being alone, driving, and crashing. What thoughts had raced through her mind? What kinds of things did a person experience when going through that kind of panic? Had she thought of her loved ones? Had she forgotten all things within that moment? Had she been so lost in the moment that memories were hard to grasp?

"I'm sorry, Mr. Griffin, visiting hours are up," a young nurse said as she stepped into the room. "And I know this might sound super inappropriate, but do you think maybe I could get a picture with you?" she asked, her voice filled with hope.

Before I could reply, another nurse, Sarah, stepped into the room. "You're right, Paula. That *is* super inappropriate. I'm glad you noticed how inappropriate it was and decided to leave the room." Without another word, an embarrassed Paula left the room.

"Sorry about that," Sarah said. "These girls are literally going gaga over the fact that you are here. Which doesn't make sense. I listened to your music during my break today and it's awful." She winked. She'd been the main nurse stopping by all day to check in on Mrs. Boone and to check in on me. She was an older woman, in her sixties, who had a tender softness to her voice that was healing all by itself—even when she insulted you. "So, I hate to be the wicked witch, but visiting hours are ending…"

"No worries, thank you. Do you think I could have one more minute?"

She nodded. "Sure, that's fine."

"Also, I have a question, and it might sound stupid."

"Shoot it my way, son."

"Can she, like, hear me?" I asked, stuffing my hands into my pockets. "I mean, if I were to speak to her, could she hear what I was saying?"

"Some say no, others say yes. Between you and me?" she said, stepping closer to me. "Sometimes we speak for ourselves, to get our feelings out into the world. It's best to always say the words instead of holding them inside us, and if our loved ones can hear us, too… well, that's all the better."

I smiled and thanked her.

As Sarah turned to walk away, she paused. "Music, too. People say music helps. But I'm sure you already knew that."

Truer words were never spoken.

When she left, I pulled a chair closer to Mrs. Boone's bedside and took her hand into mine. "I have a selfish request, Mrs. Boone. So, I'm assuming this is the moment where you'd normally call me an idiot or something, but I gotta ask you to do this. Come back. You have to wake up, not for me, not for yourself, but for Maggie. She needs a break; she needs a win in life. She's been through so much bullshit, *so much*. Therefore, I forbid you to do this. I forbid you to stay in this shape. I don't know if you know this, but you're her best friend. You're the only thing she really has going for her, and I can't have you check out on her, because I think she'd check out, too, and I selfishly can't have that. I need you girls to get better. I need you girls to get healed. So do this for me. I'll give you an IOU, okay? Just come back to us, Mrs. B. Just come back."

I sniffled and pulled my chair even closer, remembering Sarah's last words. I leaned in toward her ear and softly began to sing "Sittin' On The Dock Of The Bay" by Otis Redding, the song that was hers with Stanley.

I silently prayed she could hear me.

I hadn't a clue why I was so terrified to see Maggie. After an eighteen-hour flight, and twelve hours in a hospital, I had thought I'd be mentally prepared to stand near her, but the moment I walked up to her porch, my hands started shaking. I rang the doorbell and when Mrs. Riley answered, she frowned at me. We hadn't spoken in years, since she'd forbidden me from her house, but this time she stepped aside and let me in.

"Thank you, Mrs. Riley," I said.

She gave me a small smile in response then disappeared back into the house.

I walked up to Maggie's room, where her door was wide open, but she was missing. I stepped inside when I saw the stack of books I sent to her—the ones she never sent back. I opened them each, flipping through, seeing her pink tabs in every single one. She replied to all of my notes, but I didn't understand. Why hadn't she sent them back?

As I turned around with a book in my hands, reading her handwriting, I paused, looking up from the book.

Maggie.

She looked beautiful.

So fucking beautiful.

A book was in her grip, and her arms wrapped around the book, which pushed against her chest. We stood still, staring at one another.

My stomach knotted as I stepped back, placing the book in my hand back to her desk. "Sorry," I murmured.

She blinked a few times and pulled on the ends of her wet hair, still staring. That was all I could say to her? *Sorry?* I hadn't seen her in years. *Years!* I had flown across an ocean for her. I hadn't stood that close to her in so long, and now, the first word out of my mouth was 'sorry'.

"How are you?" I asked, causing her to tilt her head as she stared.

There were a few things I noticed about Maggie that were different than when I'd left. Her hair was shorter, but still, past her shoulders. She gave tiny smiles, but never showed her teeth. Her lips pressed together and the corners of her mouth curved up, but it was never a full grin. It was very petite, like her figure. Her blue eyes looked lonely, too. That was the hardest part for me, staring into her eyes. She hardly blinked, but when she did, it was quicker than most, as if she didn't want to miss a second of sight.

"How are you?" I asked again. No kind of reply. "You okay today, Maggie May?" I whispered.

Her body tightened up and she shrugged.

She was still as beautiful as before, but now it was a haunting kind of beauty, the kind of beauty that made you want to laugh and cry all at once.

I stepped forward, wanting to place my hand on her arm, to remember what she felt like, but when I moved, she edged away.

"Sorry," I murmured. "I'll let you be."

She frowned. I'd forgotten that a frown could be more stunning than a smile. I stepped past her, and our arms brushed against one another, and I felt her shake. Or maybe I shook. It was hard to tell the difference between the two of us. Right as I was about to leave, I paused.

"I miss you," I blurted out, a little hurt, a little honest, a little confused. "I miss you and I don't know why, because you made it clear that you wanted me to go to Los Angeles all those years ago.

I miss you, because you stopped sending me the books. I miss you, and I don't know why, because you're right here. You're standing steps away from me, yet I feel as if there is some kind of giant wall standing between us. How can I miss you when you're so damn close to me?"

She kept her back to me as I watched her bend down and place the book on the floor in front of her. As she rose slowly, she turned toward me, and then leaped into my arms.

She literally leaped. She flew to me, and I caught her, wrapping my arms so tight around her.

God.

That felt good.

It felt so good to have her in my arms. To hold her close to me. To smell her hair, which always smelled like honey and flowers. To feel her lips graze against my shoulder. To hold her.

My Maggie May…

"Don't let go," I whispered into her hair. "Please don't let go."

She held on tighter.

That night we lay on her bed, listening to music on her iPhone, each with one of the earbuds, and it was amazing how natural it felt being there in that room beside her. They said time changed people, and it was true. We weren't the same two people we used to be, but somehow we evolved as one. Even with hundreds of miles between us.

But what I loved most about that night was how some things never seemed to change.

I loved that my favorite moments stayed the same.

Tilting my head in her direction, I asked her a question. "Why didn't you send the books back to me?"

She pushed herself up, narrowed her eyes, and seemed somewhat confused. When she reached over for her board, I waited somewhat patiently for her reply.

Sasha.

216

"What about her?" I asked.

The letter you sent, telling me about her the first time, I knew I should stop replying.

"Because it hurt you?"

Maggie shook her head. *Because it could've hurt her, seeing letters coming from another girl.*

And there she was again: the most thoughtful woman in the world.

"We broke up," I said.

Maggie gave me a questioning stare, and I rubbed my hairy chin.

"Well, she kind of broke up with me, I guess. She said she hated being the third choice in my life."

Third?

"Music...and well..." I gave her a sad grin, and she gave me the same kind back. *Music and you.* "It's not fair, you know, because every time I tried to move on your love kept pulling me back."

She moved over to me, and her lips locked with mine. When we began to kiss we hadn't any plans to stop. It was easily the best thing I'd done in the past ten years—coming home to her love.

That night we slept in each other's arms, and whenever I woke, I pulled her closer. The idea of losing her again was too much for me. Before I headed back on tour, I needed her to know I'd be coming home to her. I needed her to know we'd make it work, no matter what. I needed her to know she was and always would be my biggest dream.

Maggie

When I woke up, Brooks was gone, but my board was placed beside me and read: *Went to sit with Mrs. Boone. I'll be back later tonight. I love you.*

My hands went to wipe the words clear, and all the words erased except the last three.

I didn't mind at all.

"So, rumor has it Mrs. Boone woke up about thirty minutes ago," Calvin said as he walked into my bedroom.

My eyes widened and I leaped up from my bed, rubbing the sleep from my eyes.

"The doctors said she's doing okay. They are going to run some tests to see if it is her memory slipping, Alzheimer's or dementia or something. I don't know all the details, but for now, she's okay. She's awake, Maggie."

Seriously?

"Yup. Brooks sent a group text to everyone. I'm guessing you haven't checked your phone, or I would've heard you silently celebrating." He winked.

I rolled my eyes and threw a pillow at him, which he caught and threw back, making me tumble over. Within seconds, he jumped onto my bed, bouncing up and down. The amount of comfort that raced through me was incomparable to any feeling I'd ever felt. Knowing she was okay, knowing she'd breathe in the air of another day—that alone was so beautiful.

"So, we're flying back over to the UK early Monday morning. Our management gave us a pretty big slap on the hand for missing two shows," Calvin said. "It turns out that it's kind of frowned upon to just fly home during a tour and take care of your grandma… well, that's what they were told at least, that Mrs. Boone was our grandma…which is more or less true. Management is pretty pissy about it, ya know, time is money, but oh well. We'll start back up in Birmingham next week."

Oh gosh…I'm so sorry. This is my fault.

Calvin rolled his eyes. "It's no one's fault. Life happens. You might as well happen along with it. It's been a crazy few years, so the break is really needed. Plus…I have a secret."

I arched an eyebrow, wondering what it could be.

He grinned. "I haven't told anyone. I figured I'd tell you first because you are the ultimate best at keeping secrets due to that whole"—he took his fingers to his lips and made a zipper noise—"mute thing."

I smirked.

He smiled back, reached into his back pocket, and pulled out a small box. My hands flew over my mouth. He was going to finally ask Stacey to marry him.

He opened the box and I gasped, tears filling my eyes. Calvin shoved me. "Come on, sis. Don't cry."

I ripped the box out of his hand and studied the beautiful diamond ring, overtaken by its beauty.

"Do you think she'll like it?"

I rolled my eyes dramatically, making him chuckle. *She'll love it.*

"I'm going to show Mom and Dad too, before I head over to the hotel to meet Stacey. I've never been so damn nervous in my life, ya know? I feel like my heart is going to explode out of my chest."

He took the ring back from me and stared at it, almost as if he were nervous there was a chance Stacey would say no to the proposal. There wasn't. I'd never seen two people who were more meant to be than Calvin and Stacey. Even when Calvin had caught his break years ago, it hadn't rocked their relationship; it may have even made it stronger. Heck, they'd been wearing promise bands on their ring fingers with their initials engraved on the inside since their eighth grade graduation.

Stacey and my brother were meant to have the happily-ever-after life. They were destined for it.

I squeezed his knee, and he broke his stare from the ring, turning to me. I smiled. He smiled back, though he still had a hint of fear in his eyes.

"Thanks, Maggie. I'm going to go show Mom and Dad." He hopped off my bed and left the room. A second later, he popped his head back into my doorframe. "And, Maggie? I love you. I doubt I say that enough as a brother, but I don't know. With everything that happened to Mrs. Boone, I've just been thinking. Life is unexpected, so you might as well tell the people you love how you feel, ya know?"

My brother, the sensitive musician.

I held up the board that said *I love you* and added *too*.

After he left, it only took two minutes to hear Mama holler from her bedroom. "*Oh my God*! My son's getting married!"

"Easy, Mom. I haven't asked her yet," he replied.

"Ohmygosh, ohmygosh, ohmyGOSH! There's so much to do, so much to plan!" she bellowed. "I've been waiting for this day my whole life!"

I smiled, knowing she wasn't kidding. I also smiled because it was the happiest I'd heard her sound in years.

"You okay today, Magnet?" My favorite words. Brooks stepped into my room later that night with a bag in his hand and joined me on my bed. "So, rumor has it there's going to be a wedding sometime soon. I guess a girl who loved a boy said yes to a question and accepted a ring. I went out with the group for a celebration dinner, and all I could think about was how I wished you were there. So, I left early and brought dinner to you."

I leaned in and kissed him. We began eating more French fries than anyone should've ever eaten and stuffing our faces with giant burgers.

"You ever think about getting married, Maggie May?"

Yeah.

"You ever think about getting married to someone like me?"

I took his hand and squeezed twice.

I snuggled into his body, and he held me close to his heart.

"Someday I'm going to marry you. We're going to get married and be the happiest people in the world. Then, we are going to have the chubbiest kids ever, who smile all the time because they copied our smiles. We'll have a dog named Skippy and a cat named Jam, and we'll get a big house, with a place for you in the backyard to escape and drink wine when you need a break from the kids. A she-shed. You'll work on your dream, whatever your dream becomes, and we'll be so happy, Magnet. I can see it so much in my head, our lives. We're gonna be happy forever."

I loved his words, his hope, his plans. His plans were mine, too. Everything he wanted, I may have wanted more. I believed it was all coming our way, too. We deserved it, he and I. Just like my brother and Stacey, Brooks and I deserved happily ever after. *This time is forever.*

I heard about you guys getting in trouble for missing the concerts. I'm so sorry. I didn't mean to mess up your music.

"No big deal," Brooks spoke softly, sitting beside me with his leg brushing against mine. "It's just music." Music was his life, and he put it on hold for me. "Besides, there are bigger dreams." His eyes met mine, and he said everything with his lopsided smile and with silence. I heard him loud and clear, and I hoped he could hear my voice, too.

I love you, too, Brooks.

We fell asleep that night after making love to one another. It was the middle of the night when I awakened to his touch, his hands against me, his lips locked on top of mine.

"Maggie," he whispered breathlessly, lying on top of me in the darkness. Our clothes were tossed in a pile in the corner of the room, and I could feel his hot breaths brushing against my neck as he kissed me. His mouth traveled down my body, inch by inch, making it harder for me to catch my breath, which was fine. At that point breathing seemed a waste of time. His hands wrapped around my legs, and he parted them in a slow, controlled manner. I watched attentively as he took his hand and stroked himself. With his other hand, he slipped two fingers inside of me, making me curl my fingernails into the sheets. When his fingers pulled out, he brushed himself against me before he slowly slid inside. I felt myself relax against him with every inch, every thrust, every moan.

Yes. Yes…

He leaned forward and kissed me gently against my lips. "You okay?" he asked.

I nodded. *Yes. Yes…*

He pushed himself in deeper, pulled out slowly, and reentered me over and over again, making my mouth fall open in disbelief. Fast and hard, slow and deep.

Brooks…

How? How could such simple movement feel so… *Wow…*

He made love to me as if he were apologizing for all the years we missed. With each thrust he silently promised to never love another, and with every wild kiss, I promised him the same.

222

"You don't have to speak," he whispered, running his tongue against my bottom lip, loving me hard, deep, fast, and slow. His mouth grazed against my ear before he sucked it gently. "But by all means, you're more than welcome to scream."

Maggie

"Indoor or outdoor wedding?" Mama asked Calvin and Stacey the next morning. The dining room table was completely covered with wedding magazines and planners. Mama hadn't stopped rushing around ever since she'd found out Calvin was going to propose to Stacey, and once he had called saying Stacey accepted, she'd gone into roadrunner mode. "Oh, have you thought about a destination wedding? Paris. Oh! Bora Bora! What about an autumn wedding? Maybe spring? Spring weddings are always so beautiful, and I just love the peachy blush colors. Have you two picked out colors yet?"

Stacey laughed, leaning against the countertop and flipping through a magazine. She was so effortlessly beautiful, with her caramel skin and curly honey chestnut hair. She always looked so put together with her perfect smile and stunning brown eyes that almost smiled more than her lips. I stood in the kitchen next to the refrigerator, a few steps back from the commotion, drinking my glass of orange juice. They hadn't turned around to see that I was only a few feet away from the dining room. They were too busy breathing heavily, eating powdered donuts, and staring at Stacey's ring finger.

I stood up straighter and sipped on my orange juice. Daddy walked into the kitchen with a book in his hand and smiled my way. He came over to me and handed me my next read: *Looking for Alaska* by John Green.

"A girl was reading it in class yesterday," he said quietly before picking up a powdered donut hole and popping it in his mouth. "It must be good, seeing as how she ignored my entire lecture."

I smiled and ran my fingers over the cover of the book. I turned and grinned. *Thanks, Dad.*

"You're welcome, Sport." He leaned back against the refrigerator and stared across the way at Mama and the newly engaged couple. "Wedding planning?"

I nodded.

"I was really hoping they'd elope. We're going to have a mother-of-the-groom-zilla for the next few months."

We stood back, watching said mother-of-the-groom-zilla ask more and more questions. Truth be told, it was the most excited Mama had been in a long time. Stacey remained her calm, sweet self as she tried her best to reply. "We haven't really had much time to decide anything, Katie, but it's all so exciting, isn't it?"

Mama clapped and did a jig. "It is! I've been waiting for this day forever, and I mean, this is my only true chance to have a wedding for one of my kids."

"Mom, come on," Calvin whispered as my gut tightened. "Don't say that."

"I'm just saying, it's not like your sisters are ever going to get married. Cheryl is on this feminist kick, and Maggie... All I'm saying is I'm never going to get to plan a wedding for those two." Mama turned to Stacey, took her hand in hers, and squeezed it. "But at least I have a soon-to-be daughter to do all of this with. I feel as if I'm finally getting the daughter I was promised. Lord knows I already missed out on some major moments with Cheryl, and now she's this wild child shooting around the world, so I doubt marriage will ever be on her mind. And do you know what the people in town call Maggie? 'A horror story. A mother's worst nightmare. She's a reclusive eccentric.' It's hard not to believe them. She's sick, and she's not getting better. She's probably better off never leaving home. It's safer for her here."

Ouch.

"Katie," Daddy hissed from the kitchen. All of their heads shot up to see Daddy and me standing only a few feet away. They all frowned in unison when their stares met mine.

A shade of red washed over Mama's cheeks and she grew flustered. "Maggie May, you know you're supposed to knock when you're in a room to announce that you're here. Otherwise it's eavesdropping, and that's not nice."

Nice? My mother knew all about being nice that afternoon.

I knocked on the countertop four times.

I'm here. I'm here. I'm here. I'm here.

They kept staring and frowning. I kept standing, feeling extremely uncomfortable.

So I shifted my feet and left for my bedroom.

There was a robin dancing across my bedroom windowsill, reminding me of the freedom I'd been missing. I sat reading my to-do list over and over again, until I felt as if I knew it backward. I closed my book and placed it on the windowsill, Mama's words playing over and over in my head.

I should leave. I'm going to leave.

I should've packed up a bag with a few of my things years before, and I should've left my house a long time ago. I should've gone on adventures, and found love, and gotten married in a big church where a choir sang hymns, and the priest made bad jokes. I should've been famous like my brother, or at least something more than what I was currently—nothing.

Standing from my chair, I left my room and grabbed a suitcase from the storage room. I dragged it into my bedroom, sat on the floor, and started to pack my clothes. On top of the clothes, I packed my favorite novels. On top of my novels, I packed more of my favorite novels. On top of my favorite novels, I placed my to-do list.

I'm going to leave.

I'm going to live.

My heart started racing, and I tried to allow my mind to stay clear. *Don't overthink it, just pack and go. The first step out will be the hardest, but the most rewarding. Mrs. Boone was right. I have to live now, or I never will. I have to live so Mama will be proud of me again. I have to live because of Brooks.*

When the first teardrops hit the covers of *The Hunger Games*, I did my best to stop the waterworks. My mind was trying its best to convince me to stay, telling me of the horrors outside those walls, reminding me of the silence I'd been cursed with all those years ago.

Shh...

Shh...

I shook my head and kept packing.

Be better, be stronger, Maggie May.

When my door creaked open, I jumped, startled until I saw Daddy standing there. His eyes fell to the suitcase and he grimaced before walking over to my window that faced the street.

"Come here, Maggie," he said.

I stood up and walked over to him. He allowed a few moments of silence to pass before speaking once more.

"Emily Dickinson didn't like meeting new people, you know." Of course he knew about Emily Dickinson's life. "She only left her father's home a few times, and after some time, she never left at all. She was always dressed in white, and she never spoke many words."

I stared outside, seeing kids playing catch, riding bikes, living more life than I'd lived in all my years. I wiped away another tear so he wouldn't see it.

He saw it and smiled. He always saw my tears and smiled—but it was a sad smile, a broken grin. "Just because she was different didn't make her a freak. People called her a reclusive eccentric, too, you know. People called Einstein a mentally disabled fool."

I smiled, but somehow he still saw the sadness living within me.

"Maggie May, you're good enough just the way you are."

What a typical thing for my father to say.

"I can tell you care. You care what others think of you, what your mother thinks of you, what I think of you. Which frankly, is a waste of time. Your mother and I may be older, but that doesn't make us wiser in any way, shape, or form. We're still evolving, too. It doesn't matter what names others call you—reclusive, eccentric—none of those words matter. What matters are the names you call yourself when you are in your own company."

He smiled at me once again. "If one day you choose to step outside and explore those things, then by all means, do it, but do not do it to make your mother happy, or me happy, because in turn I think you'll lose your own happiness. Leave when you're ready, not when you feel pressured. Okay?"

I nodded.

Okay, Dad.

He kissed my forehead. "The world keeps spinning because your heartbeats exist." He turned to leave my room, but before he left, he cleared his throat, scratching at his hairy chin. "Oh, and you have a surprise in the dining room."

I walked downstairs to the dining room and sitting at the table was an old woman, with two turkey sandwiches and two cups of tea. "So," she said, holding one tea cup in her hand. "It turns out my memory isn't the best that it could be." She stood up from the table and walked over to me with a walker, limping a little. There were a few small bruises on her cheeks. But still, she looked her beautiful, overdressed self. With a tiny smile to her lips, she nudged me in the shoulder. "But it could always be worse," she said playfully. "I could've been mute."

Snickering, I nudged her back.

I had never hugged someone so tight in my life.

"Sorry, am I interrupting?" Brooks said, stepping into the dining room to see Mrs. Boone and me embracing.

"No, no. Any boy who'd sing to an old lady in the hospital is allowed to interrupt."

Brooks gave her his crooked smile. "You heard me?"

"My goodness, the whole hospital heard you. After you left each night, the nurses went crazy over your voice and your facial hair, which I couldn't understand for the life of me. Your voice was decent, but you look like a hairy monster. Shaving is okay, you know. I'll buy you a razorblade if you'd like."

I walked over to Brooks and rubbed his hairy chin. I liked it, his new look. His arms were toned and muscular, as if he'd been working out for years. He looked so grown up, so manly.

Mrs. Boone groaned. "Well, of course you like it, but your opinion is bias therefore it doesn't matter. Anyway, here, Brooks." She dug into her purse and pulled out a set of keys.

"What are these for?" he asked.

"It's a thank you, for watching over me. Calvin told me you boys are here through the weekend, and he was saying how overly stressed you have been, so I figured you guys could go up to my cabin for a guys' weekend, do whatever the heck it is that you young folk do nowadays."

"Wow, that's awesome. Thank you, Mrs. Boone."

There was a knock at the front door and Daddy went to open it, revealing a woman with a kind smile. When Mrs. Boone saw her, she rolled her eyes. "Ugh, not you again."

"Hi, I'm Katelynn," the woman said. "I'm Mrs. Boone's new caregiver. It's just kind of hard to keep up with her. She's a mover and a shaker."

"The only thing I've been trying to shake is you, stalker," Mrs. Boone murmured.

I snickered. *Good luck to you, Katelynn.* She had her hands full with that old lady.

The two of them shuffled back over to Mrs. Boone's house, and Brooks jingled the keys in his hands. "We don't have to go up this weekend. I haven't had nearly enough time with you, and I want to take in every moment."

I shook my head. We had plenty of moments coming our way. The band deserved to get away from it all, to have some dude time. After some convincing, Brooks agreed to go up north. He promised to be back by Sunday afternoon to spend his last day with me.

Then he promised me more and more days in the future.

29

Brooks

Before the guys and I drove up to the cabin, we had one major stop to make. James' Boat Shop. If we were going up to Mrs. Boone's cabin on a lake, we needed a nice boat to take with us. So much had changed since Calvin and I went with his dad to sell their boat, so it was nice to see that James' Boat Shop was exactly the same. Including a much, much older Wilson who still barked loudly on the porch.

"Quiet, Wilson!" James said, walking outside. "Damn dog hasn't shut up in years." The dog howled louder, as if telling its owner to fuck off. James smiled and scratched his gray hair. "I gotta tell you, it's not every day Grammy award winning bands call me up to see if I can hook them up with a boat. It's a pleasure meeting you all." He laughed, shaking our hands.

Calvin shook James' hand and said, "You actually met Brooks and myself about ten years ago. My dad came here to sell his boat, and your son showed us that huge yacht."

"Jenna." He nodded, pride in his eyes. "That would be her. You're not here to rent her out, are you?"

I laughed. "No. I'm thinking we might need something a bit smaller. Something to just go out and fish on."

"Well, I guess I won't argue that too much. Hmm…we just got in this nice pontoon boat for renting. It's great for fishing, has the couches and the lounge chairs for extra comfort. It really has a nice luxury feel to it, but doesn't feel like too much. I think you'll love it."

"Anything…smaller?" I asked. "We kind of want that old-school fishing feeling."

James nodded. "What kind of boat did you guys use to have?"

"A center console," Calvin replied. "It wasn't anything huge, but it worked out great."

"Ah, then a center console it is if you boys ain't afraid of being close."

"Nah," Oliver said, wrapping Rudolph's head under his arm. "We like to snuggle."

"God, I hate you!" Rudolph.

"Come on, little brother. What have I told you before? You don't have to call me God. Your Majesty works just fine."

I rolled my eyes at my bandmates who never changed. James told us to come inside to his office to work out the paperwork. As he spoke, Oliver ate all of the black licorice on James' desk, making Rudolph groan.

"You know that shit is poison, right? Like, you do understand how bad it is for your body?"

Oliver tossed two more pieces into his mouth and shrugged. "This candy is my jam."

"You're disgusting," his brother said.

"I gotta be honest, Oli. Rudolph is right this time. Nobody in their right mind likes black licorice," I said, jumping into the conversation.

"Obviously this guy likes it since he's giving it out to his customers!" Oliver bellowed while eating more.

James laughed, sliding a few pieces of paperwork my way for me to sign. "Guilty as charged. It's my favorite. I eat about a pack a day, and my son hates me for it. He said it's going to kill me someday, but I just remind him that my cigarettes will probably get me before the licorice does." James winked, making us all snicker.

James hooked us up with the perfect-sized boat for our weekend and a trailer to hook up to our car. It wasn't long before we hit the road for the long trip. The cabin was a good four-hour drive, but once you got there you didn't regret a second of it.

"I can't believe Mrs. Boone has this place up here and never uses it," Calvin exclaimed as we pulled up to the log cabin. When Mrs. Boone said the cabin was on a lake, she left out the fact that the lake was the size of what some would consider an ocean. Looking out from her dock, you could hardly see the other side.

She also had a shed with a collection of six small canoes.

The cabin itself was huge and beyond amazing. There was a total of twelve rooms, including three bathrooms and five bedrooms. The living room was decked out with a giant moose head over the stone fireplace, and in the corner of the room, there was a huge jukebox that played all the good oldies music. For a nickel, a person could select five of fifty different songs.

Next to the jukebox was a record player, along with a bookshelf filled with records. It was the best corner in the house.

Each bedroom was decked out with a theme from around the world. One had all United Kingdom décor, while another was decorated as if you'd stepped into Thailand, and so on and so forth. Going from each room felt as if you were going around the world in two minutes.

It seemed Mrs. Boone had decorated the place based on all the adventures she and her late husband had experienced. Their whole life was encapsulated in the cabin walls, and it seemed like a beautiful life that they had lived.

"I can't believe she's just now telling us about it," Rudolph exclaimed, climbing out of the car with a shit-ton of homemade white sunblock lotion on his nose. "Imagine the kind of parties we could've thrown up here!"

I snickered. "That's probably why she never told us about it. We would've trashed this place."

"Stacey would love this," Calvin said, dragging his suitcase into the house.

"FOUL PLAY!" the twins shouted, pointing their fingers at my best friend. It was funny how in sync those two were, even though they were so different.

"No mention of the soon-to-be wife at home, or you take a shot," Rudolph said sternly.

"That goes for everyone," Oliver said, pointing his fingers at each person. "There will be no mention of any females by any names, or you take a shot. If you are caught talking to a girl, you will take two shots, and so help me if somehow you manage to sneak a girl onto the property, you have to drink Rudolph's piss."

"Trust me, it's probably the cleanest piss in this house. It'd actually be an honor to drink my piss."

I rolled my eyes. A dudes' weekend. No chicks or drink piss, a solid rule to follow.

***

By midday, we were all hammered and talking about music; everything felt perfect. All that was left to do was to take the rental boat out on the water.

"Fuck that," Oliver moaned, half-asleep on the couch. "I'm going to stay right here and do absolutely nothing until it's time to eat pizza tonight."

"Come on, you can do nothing on the boat. It's a perfect day outside."

"If your idea of a perfect day is clouds in the sky, be my guest, but I'm gonna sit my big butt on this sofa and not move until it's time for pizza."

I rolled my eyes. "Fine. Where's your brother?"

Three seconds later I saw Rudolph talking to a fake plant in the corner. Not only talking to a plant, but hitting on it. "So, you come here often?" he said, stroking the plastic leaves.

I glanced at my watch. "Dude, it's one in the afternoon! How are you all this wasted?"

I lifted up the empty bottle of Fireball and realized the answer to my question. "Calvin! I need a partner in crime to come on the lake with me, and pull these two fools out there. Calvin?" I shouted, walking through the house.

He was nowhere to be found.

I searched each and every room twice. It wasn't until I walked around the perimeter of the cabin that I found him, kneeling behind a bush, whispering. "Okay, babe. I gotta go, I hear someone coming. I love you, too."

"You little punk." I laughed as I watched Calvin hang up his phone quickly and jump to a standing position.

"I don't know what you're talking about," he said defensively.

"Oh, you know what I'm talking about. You were just talking to Stacey!"

"What? No way. It's a dudes' weekend. No chicks."

I narrowed my eyes. "I'll let it slide and you can avoid taking shots if you come help me set up the boat for the afternoon and get the other two out on it."

He grimaced. "I'm not really in the—"

"GUYS! CALVIN HAS BEEN TALKING TO—"

He ran at me, slamming his hand over my mouth. "Dude, okay, okay! I don't know if you noticed, but the twins pour their shots in red solo cups."

"Well, suit up, buddy! We are going fishing. Booze, dudes, and their rods."

"That sounds like a really unfortunate title for the upcoming events. I'm concerned about the upcoming events."

"Concerned?" I asked with a sly grin. "Or excited?"

Calvin started jumping up and down like a dramatic five-year-old. "So excited! So excited! I'll get the booze and the dudes. You bring that long rod of yours."

"Don't gotta tell me twice."

He started for the kitchen and paused. "Just to be clear…the rod is your fishing rod, Brooks. Not your dick."

I wiggled my eyebrows. "Call it what you wanna call it, brother. Either way, I'm bringing it. Bring your guitar, too. We can go over some chords and lyrics for the next album." His face lit up. I'd never known someone who got so excited about work—well, other than me.

An hour later we took the boat out on the water and shut off the engine in the middle of the lake. It was peaceful, not another boat around. Then, we started drinking more. Nothing better than day drinking with your boys, on a boat in Wisconsin. It was a requirement to live in the state.

"You know, I'm a bit worried about the band," Oliver said as we sat. The three of them were wasted out of their minds, and for some reason, I'd become the one to make sure they didn't kill themselves. Every time we took a shot, I had my faithful beer can beside me, which I'd used as a fake chaser where I'd spit the disgusting shot out.

"Yeah? Why's that, Oli?" I asked.

"Well, see, I never wanted to have a girl group, and it's pretty alarming that lately three-fourths of the team has been growing vaginas."

"What?"

"It's pretty pathetic, and frankly, weird as fuck. I mean, you couldn't even go twenty-four hours without calling Stacey, Calvin. Brooks, don't think I didn't notice you snapchatting to Maggie. And my twin is currently in love with a plant, though, knowing his weird love for Mother Nature, I'm not that surprised."

I glanced over at Rudolph, who was hugging the potted plant he dragged along with him. "Her name is Nicole, and she's beautiful," he slurred with pride.

"See what I mean? My friends are turning into little babies, and I fear soon enough we'll be writing songs about marriage and diapers."

I laughed. "It's not that serious, Oliver."

He waved his hands in the air. "Brooks Tyler Griffin. You were on Snapchat. Sticking your tongue out. Pretending you were a fucking dog."

I narrowed my eyes and kept fishing. "For the record, yes, I was on Snapchat, but I was snapping to our fans. You remember them? The people who support us? It's important to give them a piece of me, Oli. You should take notes. That's why the fans like me more than you."

"Ha! Doubtful. Plus, when did you start saying, 'I love you, Maggie,' in a dog voice to your fans? I get it—some people's fandoms have names. Demi Lovato has Lovatics. Justin has the Beliebers. Beyoncé has her Beyhive. But I mean, 'I love you, Maggie' just doesn't roll off of the tongue as well."

I turned to flip Oliver off, and he flipped me two of his own birds. Touché.

The sky was growing cloudy, and the water was still. The only noise around was the four of us shouting whenever we thought we caught a fish—which we never did. Looking backward, I could hardly see the huge cabin, and looking forward, I could somewhat notice the town stores. Perfect location. All we could hear was the water moving ever so slightly.

"All kidding aside, I'm really happy for you and Stacey, Cal," Oliver said, picking up Calvin's guitar and having no damn clue how to play a chord.

"You think management is gonna be pissed?" Calvin asked.

"Ha! Of course they are. One of the lead singers of The Crooks tying the knot, breaking hundreds of hearts around the word? Management is going to try their damn hardest to talk you out of it."

"Yeah, I figured. But well, they are already pissed at us for missing shows. Might as well piss them off a bit more to see how many gray hairs we can give them." Calvin snatched his guitar from Oliver's hands and walked over to me as I sat behind the steering wheel. I picked up my guitar too and started playing the intro to our song "Split Ends". He joined in, playing on his guitar. Oliver started singing the lyrics, and Rudolph just kept talking to his plant. Working with your best friends could've easily caused issues, but that wasn't the case with my band. Other than the twins arguing with one another, we worked together effortlessly. Sure, we disagreed sometimes, but it was never over something we couldn't fix.

We stayed out on the water all afternoon. As the sky got darker, we started working on new lyrics. Our creativity was almost unstoppable when we got into our happy music zone. When the first raindrop hit us, Calvin suggested we finish back at the cabin, so I started up the boat's engine to begin the voyage home.

It only took a few minutes before the sky turned black, and rain started hammering against us. Rudolph jumped on the edge of the boat and held Nicole in the air. "Yes, my darling! Drink it all up! Drink up the water of Mother Nature!"

"It's a fake plant, you idiot," Oliver bellowed over the rain. "It doesn't need water!"

"Don't listen to the lonely boy, Nicole. My brother's never been in love with anything, besides tacos."

"Tacos are life!" Oliver shouted, shaking his fists in appreciation as a flash of lightning struck over our heads. "I love you, tacos!"

"So," Calvin said, rocking back and forth beside me as we headed for home. "Want to be my best man?" he yelled over the winds.

I wiped water from my face. "I already bought my tuxedo, dude. Me being your best man was a given."

He laughed. "Yeah, but I figured it was polite to ask."

"That's because you're growing a vagina. Vaginas are much politer than dicks."

"Yeah, that's what your mom told me last night."

"That's funny, your mom didn't say much of anything last time I saw her. Then again her mouth was pretty full, so talking was probably not an option."

He reached for my 'empty' beer can to throw at me, and when he went to he paused, narrowing his eyes. "You've been drinking this for the past four hours and it's still full."

"I—"

He went to sniff the can and gasped. "FOUL PLAY! Brooks has been spitting his shots into his beer can!" The twins gasped just as he did and started chanting with one another.

"FOUL PLAY! FOUL PLAY!"

The louder they grew the louder the storm screamed. The waters were growing more and more wild as the storm grew bigger and louder. Rougher.

"Don't worry!" Rudolph stumbled with Nicole wrapped in his arms. "We still got another bottle of Fireball over here," he shouted. As he moved closer to my direction, I saw him tipping a little too much to the edge. Jumping up from my seat, I asked Calvin to take the wheel and rushed over to my drunken friend.

"Whoa there, Rudolph, careful! A little too close to the edge."

Rudolph snickered and pinched my cheek. "You're such a sweet vagina, Brooks Griffin."

I laughed out loud, soaking wet. "That's the nicest thing anyone has ever said to me."

"That's just because America's Sweetheart Maggie May doesn't speak. If she did, she'd say some poetic shit, I bet." He paused, and his eyes grew wide. "FOUL PLAY! I mentioned a girl. I need a shot! FIREBALL!" He launched toward the bottle of Fireball, and as he moved the boat rocked. His body bent over, causing him to hang from the edge of the boat. I gripped him tight, pushing him back toward the boat. As I shoved him to safety, the storm knocked our boat sideways, making me stumble over my own feet.

"Shit!" I hollered before hitting the heavy waves. The water was ice-cold as I fell under.

"Brooks!" my friends yelled, hurrying over to the edge of the boat and tossing me the life preserver ring.

"It's not an official trip until someone falls into the water, right?" I shouted, laughing as my arms wrapped around the ring. The guys chuckled with me and started pulling me in, until there wasn't a reason to laugh anymore.

I grew closer to the boat, and pain shot through me. *"Fuck!"*

It happened in a flash, in a rushed moment.

The boating propeller struck my right side.

In point-one-second laughter transformed into horror.

In point-one-second my life shifted as I began to drown.

Blood. I couldn't see it, but I knew I hurt too much to not be sliced open.

The pain shot up my right side.

My breaths were sharp; my mind was blurred.

Drowning. I splashed for help while I swallowed water.

My right hand swung over to grip my side. *Shit.* Again.

The propeller struck me again.

Panic. My hand. My shoulder. My neck.

My life...

The waves forced me backward in the wild, harsh waters.

Lightning struck.

Thunder howled.

My best friends cried out for me, but I couldn't reply.

It happened in a flash, in a rushed moment.

In point-one-second laughter transformed into horror.

In point-one-second my life shifted as I began to drown.

In point-one-second the waves tossed me as if I were nothing.

I became nothing.

Maggie

"Maggie, come on! Hurry downstairs. We have to go."

I raised an eyebrow at the calling of my name. I'd been sitting in my bedroom, playing the guitar and strumming along to The Crooks latest album. Standing up, I hurried to the top of the stairs to see a panicked Mrs. Boone.

I walked down each step and arched an eyebrow.

She was frantic, something I'd never seen her be. "Come on now, get some shoes on. Let's go."

Go? Go where?

"Maggie, please." Mrs. Boone raced her hands back and forth on the metal bars of her walker. "There was an accident up at the cabin, and Brooks, he was hurt. We have to go."

I stumbled backward, as if someone slammed me against the wall.

Brooks, he was hurt.

Those words drowned me. My mind started racing. How was he hurt? How hurt? What happened? How were the others?

Daddy came rushing out of the back room, and Mama came

rushing in from the kitchen. They both held their cell phones, probably messages from Calvin.

"They took him to St. John's hospital. He's going into surgery," Daddy said, his words fast and scared. "I'm heading up there."

"Me too," Mama claimed.

"And Maggie," Mrs. Boone ordered. "She's coming with us. Now come on," she said, waving her hands at me. "We don't have time to waste. That's a long drive from here."

"No," Mama barked, her voice stern. "No. She doesn't have to leave. She almost had a panic attack when she tried to leave to see you, Mrs. Boone."

"But that was me, and I mean it's sweet that she tried, but this is different. I'm not her person. I'm not her Brooks. Now come on."

I shut my eyes.

Mama and Mrs. Boone started arguing, their voices growing louder and louder, and Daddy started shouting trying to calm them down. My heart was racing, trying to keep up with the commotion. My mind was trying its best to keep the devil at bay, as he kept trying to come out to find me.

Shh… Shh…

"Stop!" Mrs. Boone shouted, loud enough to force my eyes open. She slammed her walker against the ground over and over again. "Stop it! This is ridiculous. For the life of me, Katie, I can't tell who's more afraid of Maggie leaving, you or her."

"You're out of line, Mrs. Boone," Mama scolded, yet still, her body shook. For a moment I wondered myself: did she want me to ever leave?

"Of course I'm out of line! I've always been out of line, ain't nothing changed. But this isn't about me. Now, Katie, I know you told me this girl right here is none of my business. You've told me that over and over again, but this is bigger than you, Katie. This is bigger than you, and Eric, and me. This is about Maggie and Brooks right now. Maggie May." Mrs. Boone turned toward me, "if you can honestly tell yourself the demons of your past are louder than the love you have for that boy, then please forgive me. That means I have overstepped my boundaries and misread every moment I remember of the two of you. But if by chance that love is the loudest...if by chance that love is beginning to drown your soul, then you must leave. You must come with us right now. Brooks is a good boy, and he's been your anchor for all these years. Now it's your turn to be his."

I rubbed my fists against my eyes as the three started arguing again.

Five minutes.

I held my hand up, and they all paused. I rushed upstairs, into the bathroom, and filled the sink up with water. I lowered my face into the water and held my breath.

I needed five minutes to slow down my mind. I needed five minutes to let go of their shouts and find my own voice.

I needed five minutes to breathe.

I saw his face—the devil. He was choking me, trying to kill me like he killed the woman. He was going to kill me.

"Shh..."

I lost myself.

He stole me from me in that moment alone.

I felt dirty.

I felt used.

I felt trapped.

It felt real. Each day, after all those years, it still felt so fresh. But as my face stayed in the water, I remembered even more.

"Maggie May! Where are you?" Brooks hollered again, his voice breaking the devil from his thoughts.

As my face stayed in the water, I remembered him. I remembered my Brooks.

"You're my best friend, Magnet, but..." His lips grew closer, and I swore I felt them brush against my own. "What if she was right? What if

Lacey was on to something? What if there was something more than friends between us?" he whispered again, his grip on my lower back getting tighter, pulling me closer. Our lips brushed against one another again, and my stomach knotted.

I pulled my head from the water, soaking wet, but knowing where I needed to be. I raced to my bedroom and grabbed my shoes.

"Maggie May, don't do this," Mama said, standing in my doorway. Her arms were crossed, and she stared at me with eyes glassed over. "Don't leave."

I narrowed my eyes, confused. She walked over to my bed and sat down, tapping the mattress for me to join her. I couldn't even remember the last time Mama stood in my room, let alone sat down to talk to me.

"I'll make sure he's okay, I'll make sure he's getting better and knows you wished you could be there, Maggie, but please...don't go."

Reaching for my board, I began to write.

Why not?

She lowered her head and stared at her fidgeting fingers. "If you go...if you finally start moving on...how can I protect you? I didn't even know you slipped out of the house all those years ago, because I was doing laundry. I was supposed to watch over you. I was supposed to keep you safe. And if you leave...if you go explore the world...how am I supposed to protect you?"

There it was: Mama's deepest secrets and fears.

Everyone had a part of themselves they chose to keep mute.

Mama's was her guilt.

Taking the marker, I began to write the most important words I'd ever written before.

It wasn't your fault.

Mama swallowed hard before she started sobbing into her hands. Her body balled up, and I wrapped my arms around her, holding her tight. She cried as long as she could before wiping the back of her hand at her nose and sitting up a bit straighter. "Look at me, I'm such a mess. I'm sorry, Maggie May. For everything I've put you through…I just worry, that's all." She sniffled, and I laid my head on her shoulder. She wrapped her hands in mine. "You're really gonna do this, aren't you?"

I squeezed her hands twice.

She sighed and sat up straight. "Okay. So here's what we're gonna do. We're gonna walk downstairs and head for the front door. When those thoughts start coming in your mind, you gotta keep walking, okay?"

I nodded. *Okay, Mama.*

"Even when you're scared, you keep walking. And when the voices grow louder, you run. You run, Maggie May Riley. You run and run until you're out."

I took a deep breath.

"You're scared?"

Two squeezes.

You're scared?

Two squeezes from her.

"Okay. So let's go."

"Close your eyes and breathe," Mama whispered, holding my hand. "Your father and I will get you to the car."

When I took the first few steps, I felt my throat tightening. I wanted to wrap my hands around my neck and try to breathe, but I couldn't, because Daddy and Mama were holding them tight. Was I okay? Could I breathe?

Daddy squeezed my hands twice. *Yes.* How could he hear the words I hadn't said?

The next steps I took were even more painful. I needed to grab my neck. I needed to get his hands from around me. I needed to breathe. *I can't breathe.*

Mama squeezed my hands twice. *Yes, you can.*

"Almost there," Daddy said, taking more steps.

The more we walked, the looser his hands became around my neck. I envisioned Brooks. His smile. His laugh. His love. The further we walked, the easier the breaths became.

I paused my steps and opened my eyes. Daddy and Mama were staring at me, nervous.

"You okay, Maggie?" Daddy asked.

I took my hands from their grips, and raised them up to my chest, resting them against my heart. With one deep inhale, I took in the world, tasting the air, feeling the wind, allowing myself to slowly start unlocking the chains from my ankles.

With one long exhale, I took Daddy's and Mama's hands back and squeezed them twice.

Yes.

I'm okay.

Now it was time to make sure he was okay.

As we drove, I noticed it all. I noticed how the fabric of the car felt, and how the engine hiccupped every few minutes. I felt every bump we hit, and I stared at every light that flashed. It was surreal, being out of the house and seeing things I'd never seen. Buildings, trees, animals. It was all so overwhelming, almost like a dream. Yet, it was real. My chest was tight the drive. I stayed curled in a tight ball in the backseat, but I couldn't for a second stop staring out of the window. There was so much to the world that I didn't even know existed. There was so much that I'd been missing.

We arrived at the hospital hours later, and Brooks was still in surgery. The outside of the hospital was surrounded with fans of The Crooks—it seemed word traveled fast. Brooks' parents and his brother, Jamie, were there, too, trying their best to not fall apart.

The lights of the hospital were bright. They hurt my eyes. I hadn't remembered ever being around lights that were so bright. It smelled weird, too. Like cleaning products on top of cleaning products. There was so much commotion everywhere—nurses bumping into one another, items being dropped, families walking the hallways.

I closed my eyes and tried to focus. It was too much, too fast. I needed to slow my thoughts down. What if the devil was there? What if he could see me? What if he could touch me again? *No.* I needed to focus on something good, something that could keep me grounded. I needed to find peace. My fingers wrapped around my necklace.

Brooks. My anchor. My strength.

"Maggie," Calvin choked out, standing from the private waiting room. "You—you're here," he stuttered, walking over to me. His arms wrapped tightly around my body. "You're here."

Within seconds the twins joined the hug, and we stood there for some time.

"He's in pretty bad shape," Calvin said, standing around Mama, Daddy, and me, filling us in on all the information. "The propeller sliced him pretty bad up his side. The doctors said he might lose two of his fingers. It also slightly hit his throat, but…I don't know. Everything happened so fast. In a blink of an eye, everything changed. We were just out on the water having a good time. Everything was fine. But now…" He pinched the bridge of his nose, like Daddy always did. "Now everything's changed, and all we can do is wait to see by how much."

Mama and Daddy wandered off to get coffee for everyone, since we had a long night ahead of us. After coffee, they drove Mrs. Boone to the closest motel for the night to rest. In the corner, Rudolph was having a fit, blaming himself for the accident. Oliver stayed by his side, telling him otherwise. I nudged Calvin with questioning eyes.

"Brooks saved Rudolph from going overboard. The storm rocked the boat, and Rudolph almost fell overboard, but Brooks managed to pull him back. After he yanked him away from the edge, the boat rocked again, sending Brooks over."

Wow…

"Rudolph is having a hard time with it—blaming himself. It was a freak accident, though. There was no one and nothing to blame except timing."

After a while, I found a chair in the corner and curled up in a ball, waiting.

As I waited, I saw and heard everything. Every person's movement, every person's voice, every object in the room. Everything felt so close, so real since I'd left home. If a nurse dropped a pen, my head would shoot up to where the sound came from.

It was harder than I'd imagined, leaving home, but it was even harder not knowing if Brooks was all right.

So whenever the devil tried to take over my mind, I closed myself and took a few breaths, remembering that our love was louder than my past moments.

"He's out of surgery," I overheard the doctor telling Brooks' parents. I sat up straighter to eavesdrop. "He's doing okay. He was very lucky that the cut to his side wasn't too deep. Any deeper and we could've lost him."

"Oh my God," Brooks' mother muttered, tears filling her eyes.

"The troubling news was with his hand." The doctor shifted around in his shoes before crossing his arms over his white coat. "I'm sorry. We tried our best to save his two fingers, but the damage to them when they hit the propeller was too great. We were hoping to salvage them both, but were unable to. We had to amputate them both in order to improve the overall hand function."

Which hand? I wondered, my stomach in knots.

"Which hand?" Jamie called out from behind his parents.

The doctor raised an eyebrow, looking over at Jamie. "I'm sorry?"

"I said which hand."

With hesitation, the doctor looked at Brooks' parents, unsure if he should say anything in front of us all. When they gave him the right to speak freely in the room, he said the left hand. The room all groaned together.

"Shit," Rudolph hissed, pounding his hand against the wall. "Shit!"

Brooks used his left hand for frets on his guitar. He'd be unable to play with his injury, and everyone in the room felt that devastation.

"I know how hard this can be, being his career, but we're really happy to have him still here with us. I fear it might be nearly impossible for him to play the guitar again. With his throat injury singing might be tough, but I believe he'll fall back into place with his vocals over time. It will be hard, but I think with the right physical therapy and vocal work, he should be able to get his voice back to normal." The doctor gave everyone a sad smile. "He'll probably be resting for a while, but when it's time to see him, I'll have the nurses come get you."

As he left, the room went silent, except for the sound of Rudolph pounding against the wall and cursing. *"Shit, shit, shit."*

When they moved Brooks to another room we were allowed to see him two people at a time. I held back, waiting to be the last one in to visit. He was asleep when I entered the room, and I was somewhat thankful. I stood in the corner of the room, watching him sleep. His breaths were heavy and seemed hard to swallow. The scar across his neck ran from his collarbone up to his jawline. His left hand was bandaged up, and he had a few bruises on his body, but he was alive. Therefore, nothing else mattered.

"You won't hurt him," a nurse told me as she checked his vitals.

I hadn't moved from the corner for the past thirty minutes I'd been allowed into the room.

She smiled. "If you hold his right hand, you won't hurt him. They gave him some sleeping pills to help him rest up a bit. He's been a bit restless while sleeping, which makes it harder for him to heal. So, he'll be asleep for some time. But, if you wanted to sit beside him…" She gestured toward the chair to Brooks' right side. "You can hold his hand."

Nodding, I moved to his side, sat down, and slowly locked his fingers with mine. *I'm here, Brooks. I'm here.*

The nurse grinned. "I'll be back to check on him in a while."

Once she left, I scooted in closer and laid my head on his arm. His chest rose and fell every few seconds, and I counted each time it happened. I moved in even closer, wanting him to feel my heat against his skin, wanting him to know I was there. *I'm here.*

I couldn't stop staring. I couldn't take my eyes off him, because if I did, I worried he'd stop breathing.

"I'm sorry, I didn't know—" a voice started, making me lift my head from Brooks' bed. I twisted around to see a woman standing there, with a vase full of flowers. "I…" Her words stumbled off her tongue, and she frowned. "They didn't say anyone was in here."

Sasha.

I'd seen her before due to me stalking her online and staring at every photograph she ever posted on Instagram. She was beautiful, and it seemed effortless. No makeup. No fancy clothes. Just her, and her flowers.

Her eyes shifted to my hand, which was still holding Brooks'.

I dropped it quickly.

"Sorry. I'll just drop these off and get going." She grimaced as she placed the vase on the countertop. As she turned to leave, she paused. "You're her, aren't you?" she asked.

I narrowed my eyes, confused.

"Oh, don't play stupid. You're the girl. The girl who sent him the books."

I stood up, feeling awkward, unable to communicate with her.

"So nothing? You have nothing to say? I'm not trying to be rude. I'm just…" She paused. "You're not the only one who really cares about him, you know."

I tapped against my throat, and she narrowed her eyes confused. "What?"

Looking around the room, I searched for something I could write on. When I looked up against the wall, I saw the nurses' white board and hurried over to it.

I don't have a voice.

Sasha crossed her arms. "Like just today or…ever?"

Ever.

She frowned. A level of guilt rocketed through her eyes. "I'm sorry, I didn't know. What's your name?"

Maggie.

"Maggie." She pushed her fingers through her chocolate brown hair, then placed her hands against her hips. "You're crazy about him, aren't you?"

I didn't know how to answer, because I felt as if anything I said might hurt her.

She smiled. "It's okay, I know. It's hard not to be. I'll get going… If you could please not tell him I stopped by? Not for him, but just for me. I'd rather him not know."

Are you sure?

"Yeah, I am. Just take care of him, all right? He's going to be a bit broken, not being able to play his guitar anymore. It's his life. Other than, well…" Her words faded, and she gave me another tight smile. "Anywho, I'm gonna go. Just don't let him on the Internet, all right? The media can love you one day and hate you the next. It's easy for a celebrity to lose themselves after something tragic happens. This time the media was shockingly quick to turn their backs on Brooks. You know how gentle his heart is…I'm not sure he could handle the backlash. Just watch after him. Even though it seems like you're never alone in the limelight, no one ever really speaks out about how lonely it truly becomes. Remind him that his worth isn't decided by the leading headline of the week."

I promised I'd look after him.

She stepped out of the room, and I erased the board. I sat back beside Brooks and took his hand in mine once more. My cheek fell against his arm, and I went back to taking in every slight movement he made.

"Oh, and, Maggie?" Sasha said, stepping back into the room. "I just want you to know that I see it." She shifted her feet and gestured toward Brooks and me. "You look at him the same way he looked at those books. Thanks for not being the monster I built you up to be in my mind. I just wish you were a bit ugly, that's all," she said with a hint of charm.

I smirked. *Ditto.*

Brooks

Mom, Dad, and Jamie told me I'd be okay. They told me how lucky I'd been to come out of the accident with only minor injuries. Minor— bad word choice from my brother, and when he said it he realized his mistake. "Sorry, I don't mean minor, I just mean…" His words faltered. "I'm just happy you're here to see another day."

My eyes darted to my hand, which was wrapped in bandages. I hadn't spoken a word. People kept coming in and out of the room, smiling at me the kind of grins they gave to kids who lost their puppies.

Pathetic.

I felt pathetic.

The band came and sat with me awhile, and the air was thick with guilt. What hurt the most, though, was how they reminded me of music. How they were a reminder of the thing I'd lost in one moment's time. When the managers came, I'd almost lost it.

"We have to come up with a plan of attack. The media is going bonkers. We need a statement," Dave ordered.

"We need a break," Calvin said, short with Dave. "You're acting like Brooks didn't just go through a major trauma."

"But he survived," Dave said with his sly smile. "Which is the message we should push. We should showcase how strong he is and how for his comeback—"

Comeback?

I huffed and grumbled.

Everyone's eyes shot to me.

Hours before, I'd been in an accident, and now they were expecting a magical comeback for me.

Dave furrowed. "You know what, let's give it a day or two. We'll give it some time."

When everyone left the room, I sighed, not even knowing where my mind was. I still felt as if I were in that water. When I closed my eyes, I swore I could feel the waves.

The door to my room opened once more, and I wished it hadn't. I was sick of seeing people, sick of hearing them talk about what a miracle my life was—how lucky I'd been.

My body rotated to the door, and I almost fell from my bed.

Maggie.

She was standing in my hospital room, staring at me, with her hands wrapped around her body. Her blue eyes were bloodshot as if she'd been crying for hours, and her hair was pulled up into a messy bun. She never wore her hair up.

Then again, she never left home.

Was it a dream?

If so, I hoped not to wake.

I parted my lips to ask her what was happening, but my throat burned. It hurt to open my mouth. It hurt to move to my left and turn to my right. It hurt to breathe.

She gave me a tight smile and walked over to my bedside. Taking my right hand, she kissed my palm, and I shut my eyes. I kept trying to clear my throat to speak, but she squeezed my hand once, ordering me not to. So we stayed there, my eyes closed, and Maggie May holding my hand.

She hardly left my hospital room for days. When they offered her a visitor room, set up like a hotel, she declined, holding my hand tighter. She'd curl up into a ball on the small sofa each night and fall asleep. Maggie smiled at me daily, but at night, when she was one with her dreams, I'd watch her twist and turn, and sometimes waking in a sweat. Her demons weren't gone simply because she left home—but she was trying her best to keep them at bay.

"All right, it's about that time to get you up and moving around, Brooks," a nurse said, walking into my hospital room one afternoon. I hated that time of the day. They forced me to walk around the hallways using a walker. Maggie always took the laps with me, and when my left side felt like giving up, and I'd start to fall, she'd leap over to help me, but the nurse ordered her not to save me. "You can come to support, but you can't help. Don't worry, I won't let him fall."

Halfway down the hall, my chest felt tight, and my breathing grew short. "Back," I coughed out, my voice hoarse. I wanted to go back to my room and lie down.

"Nope, remember? We're gonna complete a whole lap before—"

I slammed the walker up and down, my neck throbbing with pain. *Back. Back. Back.*

It was embarrassing, feeling so weak. My hand hurt. My side burned. My mind was a mess.

The nurse gave me a tight smile, before looking over at Maggie. "I think it's a good time for a nap." She winked at Maggie. Maggie frowned, and her worry was loud and clear in her stare.

I grumbled some more. We started back to the room, and after I was placed back into bed, Maggie grabbed a notepad and sat beside me.

You okay today, Brooks?

I squeezed her hand once.

Truth was, I was angry. I was angry at my management team asking what the plan was for the remainder of the tour—even though I wouldn't be able to play. They brought up all kinds of different plans that included the guys touring without me, replacing me with another performer for a while, and having me hammer out my voice in intense vocal courses.

The scars on my body were nowhere near healed, and they were already treating me as if I didn't exist anymore. To them, even after ten years of dedicating my life to them, I was nothing more than a paycheck in their eyes.

"We won't do that," Calvin argued. "We'll wait until he's better," my best friend told them over and over again.

"Yeah. Without Brooks we're literally just The Coo. And who the fuck wants to listen to The Coo?" Oliver said.

Rudolph hadn't said much of anything. He hardly looked at me. I had the feeling he blamed himself for the accident. What I hated the most was the dark corner of my brain that sort of blamed him too. Each day I was becoming less and less of myself. Each day I was a little more bitter. I hated that Maggie sat there watching it happen, too. I hated that she witnessed my destruction.

When the time came for me to leave the hospital, Maggie and I sat in my hospital room while the nurse went to get a wheelchair. My parents had plans for me to come stay with them for a while. To get a nurse to watch over me, so I could focus on healing. But that wasn't my plan.

"I'm going back to the cabin," I whispered, because everything I said came out in a low tone. My voice always sounded hoarse whenever it came out, and I hated it.

Maggie arched an eyebrow.

"I don't want to go home. I don't want to sit with people's pity. I don't want that."

No one pities you.

"Everyone does. They act like I'm deaf. I hear them. And they

256

blame me, too. At least the media does. I don't know. I just need a break to get away. To be by myself."

I know what that's like. To be in a crowded room where everyone speaks as if you're a ghost. I'll come with you.

I frowned. "No, Maggie. You have a to-do list to get started. I'm in no shape to be able to…" I sighed. *To be able to have you.* "Why does it feel like our timing's always off?"

Her head lowered to her board, and she began to write as tears fell against her words.

Please don't leave me again.

I lifted my left hand to console her and paused, looking down at my hand wrapped in a bandage. I wanted her. I wanted her so much, but I knew where my mind was. I knew about the panic attacks I had at night, remembering the accident. I knew about the panic attacks I had during the day, realizing I was the one holding back my band, disappointing my fans, losing promoters for our tour. Losing hundreds of thousands of dollars because of my idea to force myself out on a boat.

I didn't want to leave Maggie May, but I knew I had to. She had a lifetime of her own panics. The last thing she needed while she was becoming better was to deal with mine.

Maggie

"Guess who's back? Back again? Cheryl's back!" Cheryl hollered, walking into the house with two suitcases and dreadlocks. It had been a week since Brooks sent me home and gone up to the cabin without me. Everyone tried their best to convince him not to go alone, but he wouldn't have any part of it. He had his nurses who checked in on him and cared for him each day, but otherwise, he was out on his own in Messa.

Daddy, Mama, and I sat down at the dining room table eating dinner as Cheryl came charging into our house, unannounced. Last I heard she was on some island with her boyfriend.

"Cheryl," Mama said, surprised, but still happy to see her world traveler. "What are you doing here?"

"What? Can't a girl come visit her family?" She pulled the chair out beside me and sat.

"Always," Daddy replied. "But last we heard, you were deeply in love with a boy named Jason, and getting dreadlocks on some sandy beach."

She shook her head. "True, that happened."

"Where's Jason?" Mama asked.

"Well, funny story actually. The woman who did my dreads ended up also doing my boyfriend, too." Everyone's faces dropped, and Cheryl smiled. "Aw, come on, now. No sad faces. You know what I always say, when life gives you lemons, find vodka." She reached for my hand and squeezed it. "And find family, too."

Mama shifted in her seat and looked at Daddy with sad eyes. Without words, they held a conversation, until her lips parted. "Girls, now that you're both here, I think this is the best time for your father and me to tell you the news."

I sat up straighter, and Cheryl did, too. "What's going on?" she asked.

"Your mother and I...we're..." Daddy swallowed hard and gave me a tight smile. "We're separating."

What?

No.

"What are you talking about?" Cheryl questioned, confused. She laughed nervously. "Come on. You're not separating. That's ridiculous."

"Well, it's been a long time coming actually," Mama explained with a shaky voice. "And now that Maggie has been able to leave the house, we just think it's time."

"It's the best thing, really. For all of us," Daddy lied through his teeth.

I knew he was lying, too. Because if he were telling the truth, his eyes wouldn't have looked so sad.

After dinner, Cheryl came into my room, where I was lying on my bed, listening to music on my iPhone. She lay down beside me and took one of my earbuds so she could listen, too.

"I'm twenty-seven years old, and somehow I feel like I want to become my angsty teenager self again, crawl into my closet, and listen to Ashlee Simpson's *Autobiography* album over and over again, because my parents are splitting up."

I'm twenty-eight and feel the same.

"How's Brooks?" she asked, tilting her head in my direction.

I shrugged. *He said he needed space, to be alone.*

She nodded. "I get that. When you asked him for space, he gave it to you...so I understand you feeling as if you need to give him the same."

We kept listening to the music, and Cheryl chuckled. "Remember when we were kids, and I said to you. 'I don't know what I'm doing with my life,' or something?" She started giggling. "Ten years later, and the words still ring true."

Even though the thought was depressing, we couldn't stop laughing at it. Sometimes all a person needed to relax their troubled mind was their sister and some laughter.

Within seconds, we were listening to "Pieces of Me," by Ashlee Simpson, rocking our heads back and forth. We listened to the album a few times, until our minds were back in our childhood days.

Whenever the song "LaLa" came on, we'd stand up and dance with one another. Even though I was proud of Cheryl for traveling the world, I would've been lying if I said I wasn't happy she came home.

Even though Brooks asked for his space, I needed to remind him the same way he always reminded me that he wasn't alone. I'd send him a text message each morning.

Maggie: You okay today, Brooks Tyler?

Brooks: I'm okay, Maggie May.

Then, a message each night.

Maggie: You okay tonight, Brooks Tyler?

Brooks: I'm okay, Maggie May.

Even though it wasn't enough to make me stop worrying, it was enough to help me sleep sometimes.

Brooks

The town of Messa was tiny. The lake took up most of the area. There wasn't much to the place except a grocery store, a high school, one gas station, and a library, which were all lined up on the coast of the lake. It was all on the opposite side of Mrs. Boone's cabin, though, which was even nicer. It kept me feeling more alone. I'd only traveled into town for food, then I came back to the cabin.

The only other place I'd found worth visiting was right on the outskirts of Messa—a bar.

It was a hole in the wall.

No one knew it existed, which made it perfect for me. It had whiskey, and pain, and loneliness wrapped up in its quiet walls.

I hadn't stopped reading forums online about me. I hadn't stopped watching fans turn against me, tagging me as a drug addict, calling me a liar and a cheater. They believed every lie the tabloids fed to them, turning their backs on me as if I hadn't given them my all in the past ten years.

As if I were truly every negative word written about me.

I knew I should've stopped reading, but I couldn't put down my phone or the whiskey. The comments from those who claimed to once love me stung more than they should've.

Just replace the druggie. It's been done before!
My brother died from alcohol abuse. The fact that Brooks is so reckless is concerning. I hope he finds help in the rehab center.
He's a disgrace to music. Millions would kill to have his life, and he just threw it away.
Piece of shit celebrity. Just another tale of fame going to a person's head.
This is like his fifth time in rehab. Maybe it's time to start realizing nothing's going to change.
He'll be dead by thirty, just like all the other 'late and great' drug addict performers.

I reached out for more whiskey as the words became engraved in my mind. There were supportive comments, too, but for some reason those felt like lies. Why is it that negative comments from strangers seem to hurt you the most?

"I think you had enough," the bartender said sternly, a gentle undertone to his speech as he moved the bottle of whiskey farther from my reach. He had a silver, thick mustache filled with secrets, lies, and potato chip crumbs. Whenever he spoke, the mustache danced above his upper lip, and his words fell from the left corner of his mouth. Long, curly gray hair sat on his head, which he wore pulled back into a bun. An old man bun. The guy had to be over seventy, and he somehow seemed to be effortlessly cool, calm, and collected.

The complete opposite of me.

Each morning and night, I lied to Maggie when I messaged her back.

I shut my eyes and tried my best to recall the bartender's

name, which he'd told me hundreds of times during my state of drunkenness.

Kurt rhymes with hurt.

Lately Kurt was the closest thing I had to a friend. I remembered the first time I met him, two weeks ago when I walked into his bar. I'd been a mess for the past two weeks. The first time he met me, my shoulders were rounded as I sat. My arms were crossed and my forehead met my forearms where I proceeded to try to stop my memories in the corner booth of his empty bar. He didn't ask me questions. He simply brought me a bottle of whiskey and a glass of ice that night—and the following evenings to come.

"One more," I muttered, but he frowned and shook his head.

"It's one in morning, buddy. Don't you think you should get home, maybe?"

"Home?" I huffed, reaching for the bottle, which he refused to give to me. I looked up into his blue eyes and felt a tug at my heart. *Home.* "Please?" I begged. Begged—I begged him for alcohol. How pathetic. "Please, Kurt?"

"Bert," he corrected, a grimaced smile.

Dammit.

Kurt rhymes with hurt, which rhymes with Bert, which is his name.

"That's what I said."

"Not what you said. Probably what you meant, though."

"Yeah, that's what I meant, Bert. Bert. Bert." How many times could I say his name before I forgot it again?

He sat across from me in the booth and played with the handlebars of his mustache. "What are you drinking to forget?" he asked.

I swallowed hard and said no words.

"That bad, huh?"

I didn't reply, but I pushed my empty glass in his direction. When I went into the grocery store earlier that day, my face was plastered on magazine covers, speaking of a mental breakdown I hadn't known I was having. Also, it turned out I was addicted to heroin, and I stormed out of The Crooks due to my addiction.

Then, I made the mistake of signing online and read more things about me. It baffled me how many of my fans fed into the lies.

So, it was easier for me to stay drunk.

Bert pushed my glass back toward me.

"Dick move," I muttered.

Before he could reply, a group of drunken girls crashed through the front door of the bar. They were beyond wasted, loud, and all dressed in pink from head to toe. Except for one, who was in all white. Bachelorette party. *Great.* Bert stood up and headed over to the bar to help them all.

"Oh my gosh! This place is sooo adorbs." One giggled.

"I can't believe you found it!" another shouted.

They were on what appeared to be a treasure hunt, and one of their stops was a hole in the wall bar—perfect.

I melted into the corner of my booth, wanting nothing more than to be left alone.

They all hurried over to the bar, giggling.

"What can I get you, ladies?" Bert asked.

In unison, they shouted, tossing their hands into the air, "FIREBALL!"

My eyes shut, and I was back on that boat.

"That's just because America's Sweetheart Maggie May doesn't speak. If she did, she'd say some poetic shit, I bet." He paused, and his eyes grew wide. "FOUL PLAY! I mentioned a girl. I need a shot! FIREBALL!" He launched toward the bottle of Fireball, and as he moved, his body bent over, hanging from the edge of the boat, and I gripped him tight, pushing him back toward the boat.

I shook my head. *Stop.* As I was moving across the booth, with every plan to sneak out of the back door, one of the girls spotted me.

"Oh. My. God," she hissed.

I dropped my head to the table, and tried to act normal.

"Tiffany! Look, is that...?"

The blonde turned my way. "Oh my gosh! It's Brooks Griffin!" she shouted.

All of the girls started screaming and rushed over to my table. I swore there were only a few at first, but my blurred version was confusing me more than normal. They were shoving their camera phones in my face, and I tried my best to push them away. Then, their questions and comments came flooding in.

"Oh my gosh, Brooks. I'm so sorry about your accident."

"Oh my God! Did you lose your fingers?"

"Does that mean you can't play the guitar anymore?"

"Are you going to keep doing music?"

"Can we buy you a shot?"

"Can we get a picture?"

"I love you so much!"

"Is it true about the drugs?"

"No! He wouldn't…would you? I wouldn't judge."

"I smoke pot."

"My cousin was hooked on prescription pills."

"Brian?"

"No, West."

"What happened with Sasha?"

"Did she cheat?"

"Did you cheat? I read an article about you and Heidi Klum…"

"You don't know me!" I snapped, my hands forming fists. "Why the hell does everyone keep acting like they know me? On the news, the Internet, the tabloids," I shouted, my throat burning as I hollered at the kids who weren't trying to be offensive. "No one knows what it's like to be me. No one knows what it's like to not be able to do what you love. My life was music and now I can hardly talk. I can't… no one knows…" I couldn't talk anymore. I was drunk and my neck hurt. Too many words. Too many emotions. The girls went quiet, unsure what to do, what to say. "I'm sorry," I murmured. "I didn't mean…"

"It's okay," one said, her eyes filled with guilt. "We're sorry."

They left me alone after that, leaving the bar.

Bert stood near me, staring my way, not saying one word. His head tilted to the left, and then to the right, and within seconds, he sat back down at the booth across from me. His hand landed on top of mine, and he gave it one light squeeze, a squeeze that reminded me of Maggie, because everything in the world reminded me of her.

Bert picked up the bottle of whiskey and poured me another glass.

He didn't offer me his apologies; he didn't feed me bullshit words to wash away the hurt.

Instead, he gave me whiskey to drown out the memories.

As I sipped the drink, it burned down my throat. The burning sensation reminded me of the rumors, the lies, the accident, the scars. It reminded me of every single pain that lived in my chest until it managed to completely shut down my mind.

I woke up each morning out of habit. I brushed my teeth, showered, and got dressed because of my lifelong routine, but that's about all I did. I woke up, I read lies, I drank, I went to sleep.

The band tried their best to convince me to allow them to come stay with me, but I refused. It wasn't their fault what happened, it was mine. I forced us to go out on the boat when they wanted to chill inside.

Mrs. Boone's cabin was the best place to escape from the world. There weren't cameras in my face at all times, trying to figure out my future. I was able to just be alone.

The only days I changed my daily activities were on the days it rained.

During the rain, I'd go sit in the middle of the lake, in a small canoe.

I'd boat out to the middle of the water as the raindrops fell against me. As the sky was loud, I always remained quiet and still.

266

Even though I was supposed to come to the cabin to find myself, each day I became more lost. I could feel it too, the shift in me. I was becoming colder. I was becoming a stranger to myself.

I was walking a road that would never lead me home.

34

Maggie

"This will do," Daddy said, bringing in the last box from the truck outside. We'd somehow traveled back in time to when it was just him and me in a tiny apartment, dreaming of a bigger world. Only this time there was a sister with dreadlocks, who wouldn't leave our side.

That night, Cheryl went home to stay with Mama, and I slept on an air mattress in one of the bedrooms, while Daddy slept in the other on his air mattress. Around three in the morning, I woke up to hearing movement throughout the apartment. Sitting up, I tiptoed into the kitchen to see Daddy wide awake, making a pot of coffee. When he turned to see me, he almost jumped out of his skin. "Jesus, Maggie! You scared me."

I gave him an apologetic grin, and grabbed my dry-erase board before sitting on top of the countertop.

"You can't sleep?" he asked.

I heard you walking around. Are you okay?

He grimaced. "I thought that was it, you know? I thought she was forever." He poured two cups of coffee, then handed me a mug. "When I first met Katie, she was a ray of sunlight. She had this energy about her that spread through me, you know? I don't know what happened to her over the years, but she started changing. She became colder… I wondered if it was something I did, something I said, but I lost my wife a long time ago. But heck, I changed too.

"I convinced myself she was just going through some things, that what had happened to you somehow happened to her too—not directly, just a cause and effect kind of thing. But things got worse each day. The woman I knew disappeared right in front of me each day. And the man I knew myself to be went away, too."

You miss her?

He brushed his fingers against his temple. "I miss the idea of missing her. Truth is I stopped missing her even when she was in the same room as me. Over time, I wanted to leave. But, I couldn't rush you. I couldn't make you leave when you weren't ready."

My heart landed in my throat. He only stayed with her because of me. He stayed unhappy to keep me safe.

I'm sorry I made you stay.

He shook his head. "I'd do it all again in a heartbeat."

We sat up drinking the blackest of coffee and not saying a thing. Daddy and I were pretty good at being silent with each other. It always felt right. Right before I was about to head back to bed, he paused. "An English teacher asked a student to name two pronouns. What did the student ask?"

I smiled at his joke and answered it. *Who, me?*

He chuckled to himself. "Who, me." As he walked toward his bedroom, he turned back my way and told me the truth he'd been avoiding telling himself.

"I miss her."

Even through the struggles—even through the hurt—he still loved her. That was the thing about love. It didn't leave because you told it to go. It simply stayed quiet, bleeding out from the pain, still praying you wouldn't let it slip away.

"He hasn't unpacked," Cheryl said to me from the living room.

Daddy sat at the kitchen island drinking yet another cup of coffee. It'd been a week since we moved into the new apartment, but his bedroom still lived within boxes.

"Why do you think?"

He's waiting for her to tell him to come home.

Cheryl's eyes dulled, and her brows grow closer in thought. "Mom's no better. Not trying to judge, but by the greasiness of her hair, and the swarm of flies following her around, I doubt she's even showering."

I snickered at my dramatic sister.

"Love is hard, isn't it?"

Yup.

"That's why I'm just going to get a cat. Cats don't need anything from you except for food and a place to poop. That's all I want from relationships, too. Give me some tacos and a toilet for the aftermath of tacos, and I'll live happily ever after. I'm *definitely* going to get myself a cat. And maybe tacos for dinner. Will you come over and clean the litter box for me?"

No. Probably not.

"Okay then. I'm *definitely* not getting a cat."

I snickered. My cell phone started ringing, and I answered using FaceTime.

"Hey, sis!" Calvin said, smiling into his phone.

I waved, and Cheryl popped over to be seen.

"Hey, Brother!" she shouted, waving.

"Ah, two for the price of one. Digging the dreadlocks, little sister. I'm out in LA with the guys for some meetings and stuff, and I only have a few minutes before the next one starts. But I was calling to ask for your help, Maggie."

I arched an eyebrow.

"I called Brooks, and he sounded pretty wasted when he answered. He wouldn't talk to me for long, but I think he's in bad shape. I know he told you he needed space, and I know you were only giving it to him because he gave you your space in the past, but this is different. I get him needing time to collect his thoughts, but I don't think that's what he's doing. I think he's doing the complete opposite, and I was hoping you could go check on him."

The answer was yes. If Brooks was lost, I'd be there for him. In a heartbeat. Sometimes, when people thought they needed space, they really needed anything but.

Drive me up there? I asked my sister.

She nodded. "Of course." She rubbed her stomach. "Can we stop for tacos, first? Because—tacos."

Raindrops fell over the small town of Messa as Cheryl and I pulled up to the cabin. We unloaded my suitcases and went to the front porch. I'd knocked on the door a few times, receiving no reply from Brooks. My stomach was in knots, thinking the worst thoughts possible. I was thankful that Mrs. Boone gave me a spare key when she heard I was coming up to stay with Brooks for a while.

Turning the knob, the front door opened, and Brooks was nowhere to be found, which was odd, because his car was sitting parked out front.

Maybe he walked into town.

I took out my board. *You can go, Cheryl.*

She raised an eyebrow. "Are you sure? I don't want you here if he's nowhere to be found…"

I'll be fine. I promise. I'll call you if I need anything.

She was hesitating to go, but after some convincing, she drove off. I waited in the living room, sitting on the couch for Brooks to return, but he didn't. After some time, I grabbed an umbrella and headed outside to walk into town as the raindrops kept falling. When I reached the local library, I hurried inside, taking my writing board with me.

The library was huge for such a small town, and made me feel as if I were back in my bedroom, surrounded by my favorite stories. As I walked in, a woman sitting at the front desk smiled my way. She had a sweetness to her, with her chocolate eyes and short gray hair. Her nametag read Mrs. Henderson. "Hi, can I help you somehow?"

I began writing. *I'm looking for someone, and not sure if he's been seen lately.*

She snickered. "Honey, I know it's a library, but you don't have to be that quiet."

I grimaced, and tapped my throat, and shook my head back and forth.

She frowned. "Oh my, you can't speak? I'm so sorry. Okay, well, who are you looking for?"

Brooks Griffin.

She narrowed her eyes. "Now don't come up into this town playing the sweet card, and then turn out to be a stalker of that poor boy. He's been through enough already. The last thing he needs is someone coming up to bother him for an autograph or something."

I'm a friend.

"Prove it."

Reaching into my pocket, I pulled out my cell phone, and showed her pictures of Brooks and me cuddling together.

She smiled. "Seems like you both are close friends. Okay, well, it's raining so he can only be in one place. Come on, follow me. I'll show you. But if it turns out that those pictures are Photoshopped, so help me I'll call Lucas. He's not only the town cop, but he's my husband, too."

She grabbed her umbrella, then walked me out of the library and across the road to the coast of Lake Messa.

"You see him?" she asked.

I shook my head.

"There." She pointed out to the water. "That tiny speck is him. Him and his tiny canoe," Mrs. Henderson said, staring in the same exact direction in which I stared. Brooks was seated in the middle of the lake in his solo canoe. The rain was hammering against him, but he seemed unfazed by it all. "He only goes out there when it rains, never on the sunny days."

I cocked my head to Mrs. Henderson, filled with wonderment, and she shrugged before speaking again. "A lot of the townsfolk think he goes out there during the storms trying to drown."

I knew better, though. I knew the best place in the world to try to breathe was beneath the water.

Brooks

As the rain let up I started paddling back toward the cabin. It was late, around eleven at night when the rainclouds decided to move on to their next town. I tied the canoe up to the dock and ran my hands through my soaked hair, shaking off some of the excess water.

"Shit," I mumbled to myself, freezing my ass off. I wanted nothing more than to walk into the cabin, change my clothes, and crawl into bed. Yet as I dragged myself closer to the cabin, my chest tightened, seeing someone lying on the porch swing, sleeping. *Damn paparazzi.* It wouldn't be the first time they'd tried to camp out at the cabin to get information from me, but normally the town sheriff, Lucas, was good at getting them to stay away.

After hours and hours of solitude in the water, I couldn't handle some creep sitting outside the cabin, taking photos of me.

I marched over to the porch and huffed. "Listen, you asshole. Don't you have something better to do than take fucking pictures of—" My voice faltered off as a sleepy Maggie started to wake, alert and alarmed. She jumped in her seat a bit, startled, reaching for her neck. When her eyes locked with mine, her hands eased back.

"Maggie?" I choked out, almost doubting my words. My chest

tightened more. "What the hell are you doing here?" I barked, a little confused, a little mad, but happy. Mostly happy.

So damn happy to see her.

She scrambled around her back, searching for something. When she came back up, she held a board in the air, and I began reading my own hand writing.

Someday you're going to wake up and leave your house, Magnet, and you're going to discover the world. Someday you're going to see the whole wide world, Maggie May, and on that day, when you step outside and breathe in your first breath, I want you to find me. No matter what, find me, because I'm going to be the one to show it to you. I'm going to help you cross off your to-do list. I'm gonna show you the whole wide world.

She stood up and her clothes were soaking wet as if she too had stood in the rain all night long. She sneezed and started shaking from the cold.

Maggie stood there staring at me, waiting for me to say something more, anything. So many thoughts passed through me as our eyes locked, but they weren't thoughts I deserved to think. I didn't think I deserved to miss her. I didn't think I deserved to hold her. I didn't think I deserved to love her.

All I did was drink and sleep in my self-pity.

She deserved more than my sadness. How could I show her the world while I was doing my best to avoid it?

"Come inside to dry up," I said. I saw the small tinge of sadness wash over her as she nodded. It was almost as if she hoped I'd pack up my bag and join her on the journey to complete her to-do list.

It was the first time I felt as if I truly let her down.

We walked into the cabin, and I noticed suitcases in the living room. "Yours?"

She nodded.

"I'll be right back." I walked into my bedroom and darted directly toward the bathroom, where I splashed my face with water. "Jesus, Brooks. Pull yourself together."

Seeing Maggie shook me. Being reminded of something so beautiful when all I felt lately were ugly moments was a hard transition for me. Seeing her made me want to breathe, when for the past few weeks all I'd been able to do was hold my breath.

"How did you get here?" I asked, coming back out to find her drying her hair with a towel and sorting through her suitcase for pajamas.

She scribbled. *Cheryl.*

I sighed. "It's late, and I'm a bit drunk, so I can't drive you back home until tomorrow. You can stay one night, but then you have to go. I'll show you a room."

She did as I said, and I took her to the European bedroom.

"You can stay here until the morning, then I'll take you home. First thing in the morning, Maggie. There's day-old pizza in the fridge if you want it and some sodas. Night."

I kept things short. I didn't want to dive into any kind of conversation with Maggie that night, because she had a way of making things better. I didn't want to feel better.

I didn't want to feel at all.

Turning to leave, I shut my eyes as I felt her fingers fall against my forearm. "Maggie," I whispered then hesitated, but she pulled me back toward her. I met her blue eyes, and she gave me her perfect smile. "I can't do this right now," I told her, but she didn't let me go. I broke my hold from Maggie, turning away. "I can't. I'm sorry, I can't do this."

I left her room before turning back to see her reaction. Slamming my bedroom door as I entered the room, I grabbed my bottle of Jack Daniel's, and tried to forget what it felt like to feel again.

***

"Why are you cooking? We have to go," I barked at Maggie the next morning as she stood in the kitchen cooking pancakes. I didn't understand it. I was short with her the night before. I made it clear that we were leaving first thing in the morning.

She didn't turn to acknowledge me. She kept cooking.

"Maggie!" I shouted, and still, no response.

I rolled my eyes, went to the fridge, and opened it for a beer. But, there was no beer to be found. "What the..." *Fine.* I moved over to the liquor cabinet and opened it wide, to find nothing. "Are you shitting me?" I grunted. "Maggie, where's my alcohol?"

No reply. "Jesus, Maggie. You're mute not deaf!"

She turned to me, narrowed her eyes, and gave me a look of death, which somehow forced me to apologize. "Seriously, though. Where's my stuff?"

She pointed over to the emptied bottles in the sink. My gut tightened, and I drew in a sharp breath. "You need to go home, Maggie. You need to go get your suitcases so I can take you home right now."

She walked over to me and placed a comforting hand on my cheek. Then her fingers lightly grazed over the scar across my neck. I closed my eyes. Too much. Her touch gave me too much comfort.

"You're not supposed to be here," I said, my hand falling on top of hers. I cleared my throat. "I asked you for space..." I swallowed hard.

She slid her lips against mine and held up her right hand. *Five minutes.*

I shut my eyes. "I can't..."

She pulled me closer to her, resting her hands against my chest. When I opened my eyes, she was staring up at me with so much hope.

"Okay." I shifted my feet and took her hands into mine. "Five minutes."

The first minute, I had the hardest time staring her way. She reminded me of everything I always wanted and everything I'd already lost. The second minute, she reminded me of the best days of my life. The third minute, I thought of music. Maggie always reminded me of music. She was my music.

She moved in closer, and I stepped back, dropping our hold from one another.

I shook my head. "No. You can't comfort me. I'm sorry. I can't be near you. I'm sorry, Maggie. I'm going to go into town for the day, and when I get back, please be ready to leave." I turned to walk away, embarrassed by my rawness, and as my foot hit the doorway, I spoke my truth. "You can't fix me, Maggie. You gotta let me drown."

36

Maggie

I wouldn't leave, and that pissed him off.

Each day that passed I received two different versions of Brooks Tyler Griffin. The first was the silent one, who'd walk past me without saying a word. In all my time of knowing him, he'd never once made me feel invisible until I came to that cabin.

The second version of Brooks was the drunken, rude, asshole version. It was a side of him I didn't know existed. He'd stumble home sloppy drunk so many times, and come my way, telling me how pathetic I was, and how I should've moved on with my life, because we'd never be together. We'd never have a future.

"I mean, look at you. You're sitting here, waiting for me. What's the matter with you?" he slurred, stumbling side to side in my doorway at three in the morning one night. "Stop embarrassing yourself, Magnet. This isn't going to happen. Don't you have some kind of list to get to?" He snickered and fell backward against the wall. "Or are you too afraid to do anything on your own?"

It was those nights when I wanted to leave the most. It was those nights when I wanted to throw in the towel and leave Brooks in his own misery.

But then I'd hold onto my anchor necklace and remind myself of how many times he stood by my side.

At night, I'd take baths, sink under the water, and remind myself. *That's not him. That's not him. That's not my love...*

If I walked away from him when things became hard, what would that say about me? How would I ever forgive myself if his mind went so dark and he slipped away? On the days I needed him most, he always stood by me, and I owed it to him to do the same.

Being in love with someone didn't mean you only loved them during the sunbeams. It meant you stood by their side during the cloudy nights, too.

He didn't love the person staring back at him in the mirror anymore. He didn't see the fun, charming, goofy person he used to be. He didn't laugh anymore, and I struggled to remember the last time he smiled.

It was my job to remind him.

It was my job to be his anchor.

It was my job to stay and love him through it all.

On the days Brooks was at his worst, I had to walk away. I'd go into town and explore the small shops, yet I hadn't known how hard it would be on my mind. I noticed everything—every smell, every noise, every person. My mind was on constant alert, warning me of the dangers of the world. The idea of not knowing what was coming from around the corner horrified me.

When a man accidentally bumped into me, I tripped over my feet and fell to the ground, cowering with fear. He apologized over and over again and tried to help me up, but I was too embarrassed to accept his help.

Since I couldn't go back to the cabin, I'd gone to the place that most reminded me of home—the library. Each day I'd visit the Messa

Library and sit in a back corner reading to take my mind off of the world. Mrs. Henderson always came by to visit me and slid me a piece of chocolate, winking my way. "No food or drink allowed in the library, but since you're so good at almost blending in with the walls, I think we can let this slide."

Thank you, I wrote.

"You're more than welcome." She pulled out the other chair at the table and paused. "You mind a little company today?"

I gestured for her to sit. Anyone who brought me chocolate each day was allowed to sit with me.

"What are you reading?" she asked.

I showed her the cover.

"Ah, *Persuasion* by Jane Austen. It's one of my favorite pieces of her work. Second to only to *Northanger Abbey*."

I nodded in agreement, appreciating Mrs. Henderson's wise opinion of Austen's work.

She went into her pocket, pulled out a piece of chocolate, and then popped it into her mouth. "I like to think that *Persuasion* is a perfect mix of profound moments stirred with wonderful entertainment."

This woman understood what made for a wonderful story.

"So, I told you my husband was the sheriff here, yeah?"

Yes.

She smiled. "If you met Lucas, you'd think he was born from the sweetest piece of chocolate. His voice is so soothing and he has this rich personality that everyone instantly loves. He has a spark about him; when he walks into a room the energy shifts to a brighter place. He's the love of my life, and I can tell that this Brooks is the love of yours, right?"

He is.

She popped another piece of chocolate into her mouth. "Ninety-five percent of my marriage has always been filled with happiness. Being married to Lucas was the best choice of my life, but there was a point in our story where that five percent showed up. We lived in an inner city, and Lucas was working nightshifts as a police officer. He hardly talked about the kinds of things he saw out there, but I knew they affected him. He started smiling less, he hardly laughed, and everything I did was somehow wrong to him. He shouted at me and yelled about ridiculous things. The dishwasher leaking water; the delivery boy tossing the newspaper into the bushes by mistake. Those sorts of things drove him crazy, and he hollered at me about it. I placed his anger on my shoulders, though, telling myself he'd had a tough day. My sweet Lucas had a tough work life. He worked a job where death was more common than life. He walked into houses sometimes where he'd come across children who lost their lives due to getting in the crossfire of their parents arguing. He was tired, so I took on his exhaustion. I told myself I was his rock, therefore I had to hold down the fort for both of us."

I listened to her words, hardly blinking once.

"But the thing about rocks is even though they are strong, they aren't invincible. You can't allow someone to take a sledgehammer to a stone, without expecting it to begin to crack. It took a lot of work, but we came through it after I stood up for myself, reminding Lucas that I was his partner, not his punching bag." Mrs. Henderson leaned in closer to me and placed a piece of chocolate into my hand. "I see it in your eyes, sweet girl. The way you're holding his pain in your chest. The way you're breaking while trying to appear strong. I've read some of the articles about Brooks and they are beyond harsh. Brooks is a gentle soul. That's probably why all of this media attention is so hard on him. Gentle souls hurt the most when the world turn its back on them. That's why your role to him is so important. You're his truth. So, help him, but stand your ground. Don't be his punching bag, Maggie. Love him, but love yourself, too. Just because he's hurting doesn't mean he gets to hurt you," Mrs. Henderson said. "Promise me you'll take care of yourself?"

I promise.

"Good." She grinned, and we started talking about much happier topics.

"I don't think I ever asked you what you plan on doing with your life. What's your career path?" she asked me.

I'm actually enrolled in school to become a librarian.

Mrs. Henderson popped the last piece of chocolate into her mouth and gave me a wicked grin. "Well, sweetheart, I urge you to reconsider. If I can be quite frank with you, I think you talk too much to ever work inside of a library. Have you thought about becoming a politician? They talk all day even though they hardly ever have anything much to say."

I smiled. The world needed more women like her. The world needed more people who were like the book *Persuasion*: a perfect blend of profound moments stirred with dashes of entertainment.

The following Friday, Brooks didn't come home until two in the morning. It was pouring rain until around that time, and I couldn't sleep, listening to the storm rolling through. I sat in the living room, listening to Mrs. Boone's jukebox, playing song after song, waiting for the front door to open.

When it finally did, I gasped, listening to it slam.

Version two of Brooks came walking through the door, soaking wet and drunk from his time on the lake. "What the hell is this?" he hissed, looking over at the jukebox. With five large footsteps he went to the machine and unplugged it from the wall. "I don't want to hear that."

Grumpy.

Whenever I played music around him, he'd always force me to stop.

I walked over and plugged it back in.

I *did* want to hear it.

He stood up tall and puffed out his chest. "You can't do that, Maggie. You can't come here and play that shit." He unplugged it again, and I plugged it back in. "Goddammit, will you just leave? I don't want you here. What don't you get about that? I don't want you here! You're driving me insane. I'm sick and tired of this bullshit. I'm sick and tired of you trying to push yourself into my life, to make me feel better, to force me into something I'm not ready for. How fucking dare you?" he hissed, drunk and hurt. "For over twenty years I allowed you to be whatever you had to be to get through whatever you had to get through. I never pushed you, I never pressured you, but now you're doing all of that to me. When you told me to leave years ago, I left you. I gave you your space. Why can't you do that? You're smothering me, trying to save me. But don't you see? I don't need you to save me. I don't want to be saved. I'm done. I just want you to go home. Why can't you fucking leave me alone?!"

My body trembled as his words sank in, slapping me hard.

He turned away, running his fingers through his hair, annoyed, pissed off.

The angrier he grew, the more annoyed I became. He unplugged the jukebox again, and I plugged it back in.

Every time I stepped near him, the whiskey on his breath sighed against me. With one final tug of the cord, Brooks shoved the jukebox with his right hand. "Enough! Why? Why the hell won't you leave me the fuck alone when I let you be all those years ago? Screw your music, and your hope, and your list of things you want to do. If you're waiting for me, it's never going to happen, Maggie." Each word was a hit, each word knocked me back. "You're wasting your time, so just get the hell out of—"

"YOU PROMISED!" I screamed, my voice cracking as the words flew through my mouth. My hands flew over my lips, and my stomach tightened. Did I say that? Did those words come from me? Was that my voice? My sounds? My words?

His brown eyes were perplexed, confused by the sound, by my voice. I was just as confused. He lowered his stare to my lips and stepped in. "Say it again," he begged.

"You promised." I moved closer to him, unable to hide my trembling body. My stare fell to the ground before I looked up. "You promised me you'd be my anchor, and I always promised myself to be yours if you ever needed me. I'm here because of the promises we made, but right now I don't even know who you are," I whispered. "The boy I knew wouldn't yell at me. Never. The boy I knew wouldn't beat himself down so much."

"Maggie."

"Brooks."

His eyes shut tight at the sound of me saying his name. "Again?" he asked.

"Brooks," I murmured.

When he opened his eyes, I was closer. My fingers landed against his chest. "Brooks...please, don't do this. Don't keep pushing me away. I want to help you, but you keep punching me each day with your anger, your hurt, and I can't take anymore. I can't keep being your punching bag. Don't do this to yourself," I begged. "Don't make yourself drown. It's too much, and I should know. I've been drowning for years. You're sitting here killing yourself each second, as if you were alone, but you're not." I took his hands and placed them against my chest. "I'm here. I'm here for you, but you gotta stop punching me with your words. You gotta stop acting like I'm the enemy in all of this."

I dropped his hands, and he kept staring, stunned by my voice perhaps? Or maybe by the words my mouth produced.

"It's going to be hard. It's going to be really hard. I'm not backing down, but you don't get to treat me like that, Brooks. You don't get to become something you're not. You're not a monster. You're the complete opposite of a monster. You're gentle, and kind, and funny, and my best friend. You know this. So, I'm not leaving here until you find it again," I said.

"Find what?"

I placed my hands against his chest, and gave him a gentle kiss on his cheek as I whispered. "Your voice."

Brooks

You promised.

Her voice. Her first words in years, and they were directed toward me due to her frustration. The truth behind those words kept me up all night. Along with the sound of her voice. I hated the fact that her voice came out when she was angered and hurting. I hated how I was the one who pulled her to that level.

What had I become?

"Maggie," I whispered around five in the morning. I tapped her shoulder slightly as she lay asleep in bed. "Maggie, wake up."

She stirred for a moment, before yawning and rubbing the sleep from her eyes. She raised an eyebrow, puzzled.

"I know it's early, but can I show you something?"

She nodded, and I wondered if I'd imagined her sounds earlier that night. She climbed out of bed, and I led her to the back of the cabin, down the dock, where I sat down. She joined me, sitting beside me.

Tilting her head, she narrowed her eyes at me, confused.

"Number sixty-seven on your to-do list. Watch a sunrise or sunset over the water."

A small sigh escaped her lips, and she looked up at the dark sky that was slowly beginning to wake.

"You toss and turn in your sleep at night," she said.

"Yeah. I know."

"Do you wake in sweats, too? Sometimes does it feel like you're drowning in the water and even though you know it's not really happening, it feels like you're there again?"

Quick nods. "Yes. Yes. Exactly. It's hard to describe what's been happening in my head. Everyone kept telling me I'd bounce right back, but the memories, the voices in my head…"

"They're real. The voices. The flashes. The fears. All of it is real, Brooks, and no matter how often you try to describe it to a person who's never been in a trauma, they won't get it. What happened to you had to be terrifying. I know about the tossing and turning. I know about the sweats. I know how it feels as if it's happening nonstop, every second of every day."

My head lowered. "It's been like that since you were ten?"

"Uh-huh. That's why I couldn't leave you. I know what it's like to be afraid to begin again."

"I feel stupid for my actions now…selfish. You've been dealing with this all your life, and never once were you cold. You never turned against anyone. I've been so shitty to you, Magnet. I'm sorry."

She shrugged. "Everyone deals with trauma differently. Just because I reacted to my issues in a different manner doesn't mean you had to react the same way. What happened to you was traumatic, and I completely get you being afraid of music, because of what happened to you. You feel cheated. The one thing you love, you can't yet have. But you'll get there, Brooks. You'll find your way."

"I picked up my guitar the other day. It was just sitting in the corner of the room, and out of habit, I picked it up, and then remembered I couldn't play. So instead of getting sad, I just got angry. I got drunk to stop the hurt. But after the buzz faded, the hurt was still there."

"It's going to hurt. It's painful, it's hard, and it just freaking hurts.

It hurts for so long that sometimes you think the hurting will never fade. That's kind of the beautiful part in the hurting, though."

"What's that?"

"The strength you find to keep going on. Even on the mornings when you think you won't make it, by nightfall you realized that you could. That's my favorite thing about life—that no matter what, it keeps moving on."

"What's your least favorite thing about life?" I asked.

She lowered her head for a minute in thought, before looking back at the sky. "That no matter what, it keeps moving on."

My hand rested on the dock, and when her fingers found their way to me, we locked our hold together and looked up at the awakening cotton candy sky.

"I'm sorry." I cleared my throat, feeling foolish. "I'm sorry for how cold and rude I've been, Maggie. You didn't deserve any of that. I was just trying to push you away as I self-destructed. I didn't want you to be around as it happened. The water was up to my neck, and I was ready to go under. Then, your voice pulled me up. Your voice saved me. I'm still pretty broken, but I made you a promise. I promised you one day I'd show you the world, and that's what I'm going to do. I can't swear that I won't have bad days, but I promise I'll fight for the good ones. I'll fight for you, Magnet. The same way you fought for me."

"You stayed by my side for twenty years, Brooks. I think I can handle you having a few rocky days." She laughed, and I was in love with the sound. "Besides, you've seen my darkness. It's only fair that I'd be able to see yours, too."

"Your voice, Maggie...I don't think you understand what it does to me."

She laughed, and I fell more in love with her. "I wondered what I'd sound like. Do you like it?"

"Like it? I love it."

"It's not too..." She wiggled in her seat and scrunched her nose. "Squeaky? Or childish?" She deepened her voice to an unnatural volume. "I stood in the mirror last night practicing my seductive voice. Do you like it?"

I couldn't stop laughing.

"You like it, don't you?" she said, deep as hell and awkward as all get out. "You think this voice is sexy. You totally want to bang me."

"I mean, yeah, but the voice could go. You sound like you've smoked fifty packs of cigarettes a day."

She started giggling and nudged me in the arm. We laughed and talked as if the communicating back and forth without a board was normal for us. It was effortless. Truth was, if I could've sat quietly and listened to her voice for the rest of my life, I would've been happy.

She scooted closer to me as the sun started rising. "You okay today, Brooks?" she whispered, sending chills down my spine, asking me the question I'd asked her almost every single day of her life.

I squeezed her hand twice. *Yes.*

We didn't speak another word.

Five minutes before she sat on my dock, I was completely lost.

Five minutes sitting across from her, I began to remember my way home.

Maggie still tossed and turned at night, too. Not as much as she used to, but still, she had nights of darkness that came her way. One night as we slept beside one another, I awakened to the sound of her dismay. She was whispering something to herself, her body drenched in sweat. I wouldn't wake her because I knew there was nothing worse than being pulled out of one's nightmares before they were ready to leave. I waited for her to come back to me.

When she did, she gasped, opening her eyes, and I was right there to offer comfort. For a moment her hands flew to her neck, but she took deep inhales and exhales to relax herself. It seemed over the years, she was better at easing her own panics.

"You're okay," I promised. "I'm here."

Maggie sat up and combed her hair behind her ears.

"On a scale of one to ten, how bad?" I asked.

"Eight."

I kissed her forehead.

"Did I wake you?" she questioned.

"No."

She smiled. "Liar." She shifted around in the sheets and pulled her knees up to her chest, fidgeting nonstop. I could see that part of her mind was still living in her nightmare.

"Tell me what you need," I said. "Tell me what to do."

"Just hold me," she replied. Her eyes shut.

I scooted in closer and wrapped my arms around her. My chin rested against the top of her head as I held her.

I moved my lips to her forehead, giving her a gentle kiss. My lips lingered to her tears, and I softly kissed those away. My lips then moved to her mouth as I watched her inhale and exhale. My eyes shut as my lips grazed against hers. She grazed against mine. Her breaths became mine, and mine fell into hers. "You are okay tonight," I promised her. And if she wasn't she would be by morning. Either way, I wasn't leaving her side.

She pushed her lips against mine, pressing her fingers against my chest. My tongue swept against her bottom lip before I sucked gently.

"I had a nightmare, too," I told her. "I felt like I was drowning again."

"Do you want to talk about it?" she whispered.

I closed my eyes and saw the water. I felt it. It felt so real, so cold, so close. Then Maggie kissed my lips and reminded me that I didn't have to drown alone. "Yes," I replied.

"Tell me what it felt like," she said, her voice filled with care. "Tell me what it felt like in the water."

"Panic. It happened so fast, but in my head it felt like slow motion. My mind spun as I tried to get back to the boat," I said.

290

Her lips moved to the scar on my neck, and she kissed it gently, before moving down my shoulder blade.

"When the propeller struck me the first time, I was certain that was it. I knew I was going to die. That sounds dramatic for me to say now—"

Maggie cut in. "There's nothing dramatic about that."

"Now, I have the nightmares and it all feels as if it's happening again. I feel the cold water. I feel the propeller in my skin and wake up expecting to bleed." I held my arm out, staring at my injured hand.

Her lips trailed down my left arm, and I tensed up the closer she grew to my hand. "What does it feel like?" she asked, resting her kiss on my forearm.

"There's still this kind of phantom pain that happens. It feels as if someone is clamping against the finger super tight while setting a blowtorch to it. That comes and goes, though. When I get cold, my hand turns purple. I hate the scars. They are a constant reminder of what happened."

"Everyone has scars. Some people are just better at hiding them."

I smiled and kissed her forehead. "Honestly I think the anxiety and flashbacks are the worst part."

Her eyes grew heavy. "Yeah. I know what you mean." She sat up and bit her bottom lip. "Is it okay if I talk about my scars, too?"

"Of course."

Maggie's voice was timid. I saw the fear in her eyes from the idea of speaking to life what had happened in the woods all those years ago. I'd known how hard it was going to be for her, but even with her voice shaking, she still spoke.

"Her name was Julia. Sometimes my memory tried to convince me her name was Julie, but it wasn't. It was definitely Julia," she said.

"Who?"

"The woman who died in the woods."

I sat up straighter, too, more alert.

"Her name was Julia, and she was leaving her husband." She told me every piece of detail that had happened. She told me how he looked, she told me the color of Julia's hair, her panic, her cries. She recalled the scents, his touch, his voice. For over twenty years Maggie relived her horror over and over again, never forgetting a piece of it. As she kept going, her body began shaking, but she didn't stop. She continued telling me the story of the day that changed her life. I listened, growing angry, and scared, and sad for her. I couldn't imagine seeing the things she saw as a child. I couldn't imagine moving past watching someone be murdered before my eyes.

"I thought I was going to die, too, Brooks. The same way you thought your life was ending—that's what I felt. It could've easily gone that way, too. If you had fallen forward, the propeller could've taken your life. If I didn't get away from the man, he would've killed me."

"How did you get away?"

Her eyelashes fluttered, and her eyes glimmered. "You called my name, scaring him off. You saved my life."

"Well, I guess we're even, because you saved mine, too."

We stayed up until sunrise, talking about the traumas, speaking out all of the hurts and fears we both faced. Even though it was hard, it was needed for us both. It was freeing, speaking into life our troubles. Many parts of that night were tough, and sometimes we had to pause to take five minutes to remind ourselves to breathe. Yet, I was thankful for it all, the quiet moments and the painful ones, too. I was thankful for her willingness to allow me to bleed out against her. I was thankful for her bleeding out onto my soul.

"Kiss me," she ordered.

I did as she said.

We were two souls praying to be rescued, yet with each kiss we delivered, the waters grew higher. She bit my bottom lip, and I groaned into her. She wrapped her body around my waist, and I held her in my arms. Her hips pressed hard against me, as if she were trying to hold on to me even more. My right hand moved to her chest, and I grasped her breast before moving my mouth to her neck, sucking her, biting her, needing her. Her fingers dug deep into the back of me, almost as if she were clawing into my entire existence.

She pulled back from me and locked her stare with mine. Those beautiful, sad blue eyes.

God, how I hated the sadness in her eyes.

God, how I loved the sadness in her stare.

It reminded me that I wasn't alone.

Did she see my sadness too?

Could she taste the pain against my lips?

"Lie down," I ordered.

She did as I said.

She slid my boxers off, and I tossed her white tank top to the side of the room. My tongue danced across her nipple, and she gasped. The sound made me pause for a second, but when she wrapped her hands in my hair and lowered my head back to her chest, I knew I needed to taste every part of her. I needed to engulf her existence to help make the pain of life disappear for a while.

Drowning.

We were drowning. Drowning into the sadness, choking from the pain. With every touch we exchanged, the waves crashed over us. I locked my fingers around the edge of her panties, watching them slide down her beautiful thighs. My mouth kissed her stomach, and I listened to her moan once more, looking up to see her staring at me. I could tell she wanted to shut her eyes, but she couldn't. She had to watch me, study me.

Yes? I wondered in my mind, staring at her blue eyes.

She nodded once. *Yes.*

My mouth moved lower, and I kissed her left inner thigh. My tongue slowly dragged across her right inner thigh. Then, I positioned myself against her, sliding into her wetness, feeling the tightness of our fears with each thrust, feeling the waters rising above our heads.

Our ship rocked against the tidal waves, breaking and breaking as we lost ourselves.

That night I realized a few things about life. Sometimes the rain was more pleasing than the sun. Sometimes the hurt was more fulfilling than the healing. And sometimes the pieces of a puzzle were more beautiful when scattered apart.

We made love in the dark. It was messy, it was rough, it was a side of us that we didn't know existed. We surrendered ourselves to the darkness that night, losing our way, yet somehow feeling closer to home.

As dawn grew closer, our kisses shifted to something more. With each kiss, each thrust, and each moan the tides began to descend. Maggie's eyes stayed locked with mine every time I rocked deeper into her. I loved how she felt, I loved how she whispered, I loved how she loved me. I loved how I loved her. We wrapped together as we became each other's anchors, finding our way back to shore.

When the sunbeams flew through the curtains and the birds began to sing, we kept holding one another and made love in the light.

38

Maggie

Cheryl: Come home if you can? I need your help.

I stared at the text message from my sister as I stood in the bathroom wrapped in a towel after my shower. I was beyond sleepy after an all-nighter with Brooks. Talking about what had happened to me was probably the hardest thing I'd ever had to do—but it was also the best thing I'd done. It felt as if a few of the chains on my soul were released.

"Brooks," I hollered. "I think we need to go home."

No reply.

I walked throughout the house, holding my towel close to me, and I couldn't find him anywhere. When I stepped out on the porch, the sunlight kissed my skin. My eyes darted out to the lake, and not only did I see him—but I heard him. Brooks was sitting out in the middle of the lake, singing. Singing under the sun.

By the time he came back, I had already gotten dressed and packed my bags.

"Everything okay?" he asked me.

"Yeah. Cheryl just said my parents need me there. Do you think you can drive me back?" I grimaced. "I know you might not be ready to go back, but I just need to make sure everyone's okay."

"Of course. I'll go pack my stuff, too."

"You're coming back with me?"

"I just got you back, Maggie May Riley, and I'm never going to let you go again," he said, walking over and wrapping his arms around me. "Plus, I was supposed to return that boat weeks and weeks ago, so I'm pretty sure I owe more money than I want to know."

I snickered.

We packed up the car, hooked the boat trailer up, and headed back home. The whole trip back, we didn't listen to the radio. I knew Brooks wasn't ready to dive into anything dealing with music. Just as he waited for me to find my voice, I'd patiently wait for him to find his own. And he'd find it—I knew he would. Seeing him out on the boat singing was the biggest sign to me. He was slowly but surely finding his way home.

"I think I'll wait here," Brooks said, pulling up to our house. "I don't want to interfere."

I leaned forward and kissed his cheek. "Are you sure?"

"Yeah. You go help your mom. I'll be here."

I nodded and told him I wouldn't keep him too long. The second I stepped out of the car, Cheryl came rushing out to me.

"Oh my God! What took you so long? I texted you like four hours ago!" she groaned.

I snickered, walking over to my dramatic sister. "It takes four hours to drive from the cabin."

"I know, but that doesn't mean—" She paused. Her hands flew to her chest. "I'm sorry. Wait. Back that train up. Did you just…" She crossed her arms, uncrossed them, placed them on her hips, and then crossed them again. "Did you just speak?"

I nodded my head. "Yeah, it's this new thing I'm trying."

"Oh my God." Her hands flew to her mouth. She started crying and slugged me in the shoulder. "Well, I'll be damned, my sister speaks!" she screamed, taking my hands and spinning me in a circle before pulling me into a hug. "Oh my gosh, Mom's going to freak out. This is perfect. She needs a lift me up."

"What's wrong with her?"

"Oh, you know, she's crying every night and eating ice cream like it's the only food group known to mankind."

"She misses him that much?"

"Even more than you think. Plus, Dad is a hot mess, too. For the first time in a long time, you and I aren't the troubled ones in the family." She winked before she started tearing up again. "Maggie. You're talking."

We stood in the front yard hugging for quite some time before we separated and she glanced over at Brooks. "Hey, stranger, are you the one responsible for making my sister speak up?"

He shouted out of the rolled down window. "Guilty. She kind of got pissed off and exploded."

Cheryl laughed. "Thanks for pissing off my sister, Brooks."

"Anytime, Cheryl. Anytime."

When we walked inside of the house, Mama was sitting on the living room couch, watching television. "Maggie May," Mama said, surprised. She stood up and walked over to me, pulling me into a hug. Her hair was all over the place, and I swore she had chocolate on her chin. "I missed you."

"I missed you, too, Mama."

She stumbled backward after hearing my voice. I gave her a small grin. "I know. That seems to be the main reaction today from people."

"No. What. How? What?" She started hyperventilating. "Oh my gosh, Maggie May." Her arms flew around me and she wouldn't let go. "I don't get it," she said, flabbergasted. What changed?"

"Time."

"Oh my gosh." Her hands were shaking. "We have to tell Eric. We have to call him. He has to come over. Oh my God. He needs to be here for this." She started pacing the house. "I can't believe he's missing this."

"We should surprise him," Cheryl suggested. "Like have him over for dinner." Cheryl winked over at me. She was getting two birds with one stone: Daddy would hear my voice, and our parents would be in the same room together again.

"That's..." Mama narrowed her eyes. "That's actually a really good idea! I'll order Chinese food! Cheryl! You call your dad and tell him to come over because you have big news about something."

"On it!" Cheryl said, storming off to get her cell phone.

"And, Maggie, tell Brooks to come inside. He shouldn't be sitting in his car for that long. Also..." She walked over to me and placed her hands against my cheeks. A weighted sigh left her lips. "You have a beautiful, beautiful voice. You always have, and I'm sorry I went so long without listening to it." She kissed my forehead before hurrying away to set the table.

When Daddy arrived, he was confused to see Brooks and me there, but pleased. We all sat down to dinner, and Mama was too nervous to look at Daddy, and he hardly glanced over at her. Cheryl did most of the talking, which was something she was good at doing.

"Maggie May, can you pass me the egg rolls?" Daddy asked.

Mama looked up at me and nodded once.

I cleared my throat, picked up the egg rolls, and held them out in his direction. "Here you go, Daddy."

"Thank you, sweet—" His words faltered. He looked up at me, his eyes locking with mine. Disbelief filled his tone. "No."

I nodded and knocked on the table twice. "Yes."

"Oh...oh my..." His hands flew to his chest as tears began to fall. He took off his glasses then covered his mouth with his hands. As his tears fell, more rolled down Mama's cheeks. Daddy stood up, and I followed his stance. He walked over to me and combed my hair behind my ears. He rested his hands against my cheeks, the same way Mama had. "Say something else." He laughed nervously. "Anything, really. Say anything, say everything, say the word nothing. *Anything.* Just say something else."

I placed my hands against his face, holding his as he held mine, and I whispered the words I'd always wished to say to the first man who ever loved me with his all. "The world keeps spinning because your heartbeats exist."

My family sat talking late into the night, laughing, crying, and making me say every single word in the dictionary. We Skyped with Calvin, who was in New York for business, and when he saw Brooks smiling, and he saw me speaking, he too began to cry. There were so many moments throughout the night where Mama and Daddy laughed at the same moments and fell apart together, too, yet they didn't speak to each other. Even though I noticed the trembles in their lips, the stolen glances that they took, the love that still lived in their hearts.

"Well," Daddy said around one in the morning. "I better get going."

He stood up, and I glanced over at Mama, silently begging her to say something, but she didn't speak up. She watched her love walk away again.

"What was that?" I asked her. "You need to go after him!"

"What? No. We are separated. We're both exactly where we want to be," Mama said.

"Lies!" Cheryl shouted. "Lies! When was the last time you showered, Mom?"

Mama paused, really thinking about her last shower. "I shower!" she claimed.

"Yeah," Cheryl huffed. "In Ben and Jerry's."

"Your father's happy, though. He seems happy."

I gave her a knowing look. Of course he wasn't happy. Part of his heart still beat inside of her chest. How could anyone be happy with a missing piece of their soul? "You should call him."

Her eyes watered over, and she gave me a tight smile. "Oh no. No, I couldn't. I…" Her voice shook, and her hands landed on her hips. "I wouldn't even know what to say."

"Do you miss him?"

She started crying, tears free falling down her cheeks. "More than words."

"Then tell him."

"I don't know how. I don't know what to say, or how to say it."

I walked over to her and wiped her tears away. "Come on. Brooks will drive us over to Dad's apartment. I'll help you find the words to say on the way. You can have shotgun."

Her body started to tremble, and I wrapped her into a tight hug, holding her close to me. As we approached the foyer, Mama froze. "I can't."

"You can. Here's what we're going to do. We're going to walk out of the front door toward the car. When those thoughts of worry and doubt start coming in your mind, you keep walking, okay? Even when you're scared, you keep going. When the doubts get louder, you run. You run, Mama. You run until you're back in his arms."

"Why are you helping me? Maggie May, I've been awful to you. All those years I held you back from your life. Why are you being so helpful? So forgiving?"

I bit my bottom lip. "When I was younger a woman always told me that family looks out for each other no matter what, even on the hard days. *Especially* on the hard days."

She took a deep breath.

"You're scared?" I asked.

"Yes."

"Okay." I nodded. "So let's go."

Once we made it to the car, and Brooks helped Mama into the passenger seat, she let out a breath of air. "Thanks for driving, Brooks," Mama said, giving him a tiny smile.

"Anytime." Brooks smiled and took Mama's hand into his. "You okay today, Mrs. Riley?"

She squeezed his hand twice.

A quiet, but meaningful reply.

Yes.

As we drove over to Dad's apartment building, I pulled out my dry-erase board and began writing. When Brooks drove into the parking lot and parked, I hopped out of the car with the board in my hand, and Mama followed.

"Wait, Maggie. You didn't tell me what I was supposed to say to him." Her body shook with nerves, panic, worry that somehow the man she loved didn't love her anymore. "I don't know what to do."

I held the board out to her. As she read it, she stopped shaking. A wave of peace ran over her, and she took in a short inhale and released an eased exhale. "Okay," she said. "Okay."

She walked up to the front porch, dinged Daddy's apartment number, and waited for him to come downstairs. I climbed into the passenger seat of the car and shut the door. Brooks bent forward to watch the interaction between my parents. When Daddy opened the door, I could see it—the love that came with no guidelines.

He placed his glasses on top of his head and didn't say a word. Mama didn't either. When it came time, she flipped the sign around for him to see, and Dad's eyes watered over as he pounded his fist against his mouth. Tears fell from his eyes before he pulled Mama into a tight hug. As the board dropped to the ground, they hugged one another tighter and tighter. Their bodies become one. Then, they kissed. Their kiss was messy, and funny, and sad, and whole. So, so whole.

If kisses were able to fix the broken pieces of hearts, I believed my parents' hearts were slowly falling back together.

"Wow," Brooks whispered.

Yes, wow. "We can probably leave now," I said.

As he pulled off, he asked, "What did the board say?"

I glanced once more toward my parents, who were still holding on tight, and swaying back and forth. My lips parted, and I grinned at their love. "Dance with me."

We drove back to the house to fill Cheryl in on everything that was happening, and I watched her sigh with relief. "Good. Good." She thanked me for coming to help. Brooks and I headed up to my bedroom, and we lay on my bed, with our feet hanging over the edge.

"They really love each other," Brooks said, staring at the ceiling. "After everything they've been through, they still have that love."

"Yeah. It's beautiful."

"Maggie May?"

"Yes?"

"Do you think we can listen to some music?"

His question was simple, but the meaning was huge. "Yes, of course."

He stood up and grabbed the pair of earbuds from my desk, then plugged them into his iPhone. "What do you want to hear?" he asked, lying back down.

"Anything, everything." He put it on shuffle, and we listened to all kinds of sounds.

"I sang today," he said, as we listened to music going on for an hour. "Out on the lake. I went out there to sing this morning."

"Oh, yeah?" I asked, sounding surprised.

"Yeah. I mean, I have a lot of work to do, but I think my voice will be okay. Maybe the band will be okay with me only on vocals."

"Of course they'll be okay with that, Brooks. Did you see Calvin's reaction to seeing you today? All they want is for you to come back. I don't even mean back to music; I mean come back to them. They're your best friends. They just want you to be okay. You should call them."

302

He nodded. "I will. I'm just worried about the fans, you know? A lot of them are buying into the rumors. They think I'm some deadbeat."

"Brooks, come on. Anyone who knows you, and really sees you, knows those rumors aren't true. For every negative comment, there are thousands of positive ones just wishing for you to recover and return to them. Trust me. I've been reading the comment sections, too."

He smiled and kissed me. "Thank you."

"I'm happy you sang today."

"Yeah, it was hard without the guitar. I think once I get back with the guys, and they can play for me, I'll be able to feel my way through it more."

I sat up and shook my head. "You don't have to wait. I can do it." I rushed over to the guitar in my corner and picked it up. "I've been playing along with you guys since you taught me to play."

We played until the morning sun began to rise, and he sang his best, which was always enough. When it became clear that neither one of us could keep our eyes open for much longer, we placed the guitar away and lay in bed. My head was on his chest, and he held me so close.

"I love you," he whispered, as I started to drift to sleep. "I love you so, so much."

There was nothing more special than being able to speak those words back to him.

39

Maggie

The next morning Brooks and I drove together to return the boat he rented out. We were playing the guessing game of how much he'd end up owing for keeping it way past the date it was meant to be returned. Our current guesstimate: a-whole-freaking-lot.

"So, I was thinking. I'm probably going to have to start seeing a vocal coach and actually taking the steps toward recovery soon. That might mean I have to go out to Los Angeles for a while. To meet with the guys, to start working toward rebuilding my career. I know you have school—"

"It's all online," I cut in. "I can do it anywhere, and if need be, I can fly back home at any time."

"You'll come with me?" he asked, surprised.

I took his hand into mine and squeezed it twice. A sigh of relief left him.

"That makes me happy. It's easier with you, you know? Everything's easier."

We pulled up to James' Boat Shop, and I couldn't stop smiling at the howling old dog on the front porch. As we walked up the steps,

I moved over to him and started petting him behind his ear as he stopped his yapping. *Good boy.*

"I've been here a few times, and that's the quietest I've ever heard him," Brooks joked. When we walked into the shop, we were greeted by a man who looked to be our age, maybe in his mid-thirties.

"Hey, Brooks, it's nice to see you again," the guy said, walking over to Brooks, patting him on the back. "But I don't think we've met." He held his hand out to me. "I'm Michael. I run this place with my father."

I shook his hand. "Nice to meet you. I'm Maggie."

"My dad said if you want, you can walk around the dock and check out a few of the boats. He's finishing up a phone call right now. He said he'll meet you out back if that works."

"For sure, that's fine. Thanks, Michael," Brooks said.

Brooks took my hand into his, and we walked around the back, waiting on the dock, studying the boats.

"Does this bother you?" I asked. "Being this close to boats? Should we go wait in the front of the shop?"

He shook his head. "No. It more so only bothers me when I'm dreaming. I'm okay."

"Okay." I glanced down at our hands and grinned. "This is weird, huh? We're outside holding hands. We're outside together."

He pulled me close to him and brushed his nose against mine. "It's amazing, isn't it?"

It was more amazing than he'd known. I'd dreamed of that day for so long.

The door to the shop swung open, and an older man came out of the building smoking a cigarette. The dog in the front of the store started howling again. "Goddammit, shut up, Wilson! Shh! Shh! Freaking dog."

My body tightened up. Brooks narrowed his eyes at me. "You okay?"

Shh… Shh…

I nodded my head. "Yes. I'm fine. Sorry. Sometimes I just have flashes."

His forehead wrinkled and he lowered his eyebrows as he studied me.

I gave him a tight smile. "I'm fine. Really."

"Okay," he said warily.

The man started in our direction, and I wrapped my arm around Brooks' waist pulling him closer to me.

The closer he grew, the more my stomach tightened. He stopped midway and stomped out his cigarette, then waved us over. "Hey, sorry about the wait. Long phone call, you know, business and all. How about you two head inside with me and we'll get all of the paperwork done in my office."

We started in his direction, catching up with him. He held his hand out to me. "Hey, I'm James. Nice to meet you."

I shook his hand, and the smell of tobacco danced beneath my nose. An unsettling feeling took over my gut. He led us to his office and closed the door behind him. Wilson was still barking, and James shouted once more. "Shh, Wilson! Shut it!" He massaged his temple and apologized. "After all these years that dog still won't shut up. Anyway." He plopped down in his chair and gave Brooks a tight smile. "I wish we were meeting on better terms. I'm sorry about your accident. It's unfortunate when freak accidents take place like that."

He rolled up his sleeves, and my eyes fell to his forearm, studying his tattoos.

The air in the room was getting thicker, and I swore the walls were moving in on me. He reached in front of him and grabbed two pieces of black licorice.

My mind started spinning faster and faster. I felt his hold on me. I felt his hands around my neck, his lips against my ears, his body on top of mine.

I pushed my chair back and stumbled to stand. "No," I murmured, moving away from his desk. "No…"

James stared at me with narrowed eyes. "Uh, are you okay?" His glare shifted to Brooks. "Is she okay?"

Brooks stood up and walked in my direction. "Maggie, what is it?" The closer he came, the more my body shook. I shut my eyes, shaking my head back and forth. *No. No.*

Not only could I see him, but I felt him. I felt his face against my face, his skin against my skin, his lips against...

"Maggie, it's okay," Brooks said, his voice soothing. "You're just having a panic. It's okay, everything's all right."

"No!" I shouted, my eyes shooting open. "No, it's not okay. It's not okay. It's..." I felt cold. I felt sick. I was going to throw up. I knew I'd throw up.

Within seconds my past and present crashed together, and I blinked.

A man was there with another. A woman. She kept telling him no, saying she couldn't be with him anymore, and he didn't like that. "We have a life together, Julia. We have a family."

I blinked again.

Brooks grew closer to me, his eyes filled with worry. "Maggie, talk to me." James stood from his chair and raced his fingers through his hair, walking my way.

Blink.

He screamed at her, his voice cracking. "You fucking whore!" he shouted, slapping her hard across the face. She stumbled backward and whimpered, her hand flying to her cheek. "I gave you everything. We had a life together. I just took over the business. We were getting on our feet. What about our son? What about our family?"

Blink.

Wilson started howling, and James shouted over and over again, shushing the dog. "Michael! Get that damn dog to be quiet!" His eyes moved over to me. He wouldn't take his eyes off me.

"Don't look at me," I whispered.

Blink.

My hands clamped up, my mind spun. I stumbled backward, breaking each and every branch my flip-flops hit along the way. My back slammed against the closest tree trunk as the devil's chocolate brown eyes danced across my body.

Blink.

Michael came into the room. His eyes narrowed when he looked my way. He seemed confused. Everyone was confused. Everyone yelled. Everyone shouted over one another, trying to figure out what was happening to me. I didn't know what was happening to me.

"She's sweating like crazy. She's going to pass out."

My throat was tight. He was choking me. The devil was inches away from me, and I could feel his grip around my neck.

Blink.

He placed a hand around my neck, choking me, making it harder and harder to breathe. He cried. He cried so much. He cried and apologized. He apologized for hurting me, apologized for pushing a few fingers into the side of my neck, making it harder and harder for me to find my next breaths. He told me he loved her, told me love did it to him, to her. He swore he'd never hurt her. He promised he wouldn't hurt the woman he already killed.

Blink.

James' hand lay against my skin, and I shoved him away. "No!" I fall backward, into the corner of the room. "Don't touch me." My hands flew to my ears, and I slid down against the wall. "You did this! You did this!" I screamed, my throat burning, my heart pounding against my ribcage. "You did this!"

Blink.

"You weren't supposed to be here, but now you are," he said, lowering his face down to me. "I'm sorry. I'm sorry." He smelled like tobacco and licorice, and his forearm had a big tattoo of two praying hands with a person's name beneath it. "How did you get here?" he asked.

Shh...

Shh...

I felt dirty.

I felt used.

I felt trapped.

Did Brooks see it? Did he see the tattoo? Did he smell the tobacco? Did he notice the licorice?

Blink.

I shut my eyes. I didn't want to feel. I didn't want to be. I didn't want to blink anymore. I kept my eyes closed. I didn't want to see, but, I still saw. I saw him. I felt him. He was still a part of me.

Everything grew darker.

Everything became shadows.

Everything went black.

Then, I screamed.

"You killed her! You killed her! *You killed Julia!*"

Brooks

The space filled with silence. Maggie shook in the corner and wouldn't stop crying. Michael was staring at his father, and James' eyes were on Maggie.

"What did you just say?" Michael asked, confused.

Maggie's hands were pressed to her ears, and I could almost feel her fear. Her lips parted to speak, but no sound came out.

"Listen, I don't know what's going on, but it might be best if you both go," James said with a weighted sigh. He walked over to Maggie and placed his arm on hers to lift her up.

She started shaking more, curling into a ball. "No! Please, don't," she cried.

I hurried to her side and slightly shoved him away from her. "Back up please."

"What's happening?" Michael asked, his brow bent. "What's wrong with her? Should I call for help?"

"No," James said. "I think it's best if they just leave. It's obvious she's having some kind of mental breakdown."

"It's not a mental breakdown," I snapped. "She's just..." My words faltered and I shifted my attention to Maggie. "Maggie. What's happening?"

"He killed her," she said. "He's the one from the woods."

I turned to James and in a split second I saw the fear in his eyes.

"She drowned in Harper Creek. I saw her. I saw you drown her," Maggie cried.

"You don't know what the hell you're talking about, little girl, so you best stop talking."

"You killed your wife," Maggie said as she began to stand up. "I saw you. I was there."

"Dad?" Michael whispered, his voice shaking. "What is she talking about?"

"Hell if I know. She's obviously delusional. She needs to be evaluated. I'm sorry, Brooks, but I need you to go. I don't know what sparked her panics, but you need to get that girl help. I'll even cancel out your charges for the boat. Just get that girl some help."

"Tell the truth," Maggie said, standing taller each second. "You tell the truth. Tell him what you did."

James walked over to his desk and sat in his chair. He lifted his telephone and waved it in the air. "That's it. I'm calling the cops. This is getting out of hand."

Maggie didn't say a word. Her arms crossed, and even though she shook, she didn't fall. "Fine. Call them. If you didn't do what I know you did, dial nine-one-one."

James' hand began to shake, and Michael's eyes widened with horror.

"Dad. Call them. Dial the number."

James slowly placed the phone down on the desk. Michael almost collapsed to the ground. "No. No…"

James looked at Maggie, defeated, stunned. "How? How did you know?"

"I was the little girl who saw the whole thing."

"Oh my God," James began sobbing, covering his eyes with the palms of his hands. "It was an accident. It was all an accident. I didn't mean to…"

"No." Michael kept shaking his head. "No, Mom left us. Remember? She ran off with someone else. That's what you told me! That's what you swore happened."

"She did. Well, she was. She was going to leave us, Michael. I knew she was going to leave. I found phone calls from some guy in her phone, and she shrugged it off. We got into a fight, and she stormed off into the woods. Oh my God, I didn't mean to do it. You gotta believe me." He stood and rushed to his son's side. "Michael, you gotta believe me. I loved her. I loved her so fucking much."

I stepped in front of Maggie, uncertain of what James might do. He seemed deranged, the way he paced back and forth running his hands through his hair. He hurried over to his desk, unlocking drawers and pulling out paperwork.

"Dad, what are you doing?" Michael asked, flabbergasted.

"We gotta go, Michael. We gotta get lost for a while. You and me, okay? It's always been you and me. We can start over. I made a mistake, but I've dealt with the guilt. I've lived each day with the guilt of what I've done. We gotta go now."

"Dad, calm down."

"No!" James' face was red. He kept rolling his shoulders and blowing out short breaths of air. "We need to leave, Michael. We have to…" His words faltered as he started to sob uncontrollably. "I held her, Michael. I held her in my arms. I didn't mean to…"

Michael approached his father with his hands raised. "It's okay, Dad. Come here, come here. We'll go. We'll go." He wrapped his arms around his father and pulled him in close. "You're okay, Dad. You're fine."

James continued to cry into his son's t-shirt, saying words that were unrecognizable.

When Michael looked over at me, he nodded toward the desk telephone, and mouthed, *"Call the police."*

By the time James realized what was happening, it was too late. His son held him in a bear hug and wasn't going to let him budge.

The cops arrived, and after some explanation of the situation, James was taken into custody. The whole time Maggie stood tall. She spoke to the police officers with poise and strength. Her words never tumbled, and her voice hardly shook.

When the police car with James inside drove off, a heavy breath left her body. "He's gone?" she asked me.

"Yeah. He's gone."

Her body almost collapsed to the ground, but I caught her. I held her up as she cried and cried, but I knew her tears weren't from fear anymore.

They were the tears of her freedom.

After the events unfolded, the police sent out a search team to search Harper Creek. It took five days before they discovered Julia's body. The discovery weighed heavy on many people—all of Harper County. Maggie's family dealt with the revelation of what had happened the best they could, which meant standing by one another through all of it. I wasn't too worried about them—they'd come out on the other side stronger for their dark days.

Yet the person I felt the most for was the son who believed his mother walked out on him. The son who lived a life with a father who in a blink of an eye became a monster. Michael had a long road ahead of him, and I wasn't sure how he'd deal with the truths that unfolded in front of his eyes.

I'd prayed he'd find peace as he stood in the eye of the storm.

41

Maggie

I was due in court, but my feet wouldn't budge.

I wore a black laced dress, yellow flats, and my hair was curled, along with my eyelashes, thanks to Cheryl.

"You have to look presentable in court, Maggie. There are always cameras around, especially when you leave the building. With a story as big as this one, there's going to be reporters," she explained as she curled my hair.

Since she'd finished making me camera appropriate, I'd moved to my floor-length mirror, and I hadn't stopped staring. Everyone was worried about me after what had happened at James' Boat Shop. They'd thought I'd fall back into my fear, back into my silence—which was somewhat true. I hadn't spoken much since James was taken into custody. I hadn't said a word at all about what I witnessed in those woods, even though they knew it had to be awful watching a woman die and believing you were next.

When I was called to testify against James, I quickly agreed. I knew how important my side of the story would be. I knew how important it was to finally speak not only for myself, but for Julia. For Michael.

I was ready. I was ready to go to the courthouse. There was only one small problem: my feet wouldn't move.

Brooks showed up and stood in my doorway. He wore a navy blue suit with a checkered light blue tie. His small smile made me grin. He didn't say anything, but I knew what he was thinking.

"I'm okay," I whispered, going back to smoothing out my dress.

"Liar," he said, walking over to me. He stood behind me and wrapped me in his arms. We stared at one another in the mirror. Brooks rested his chin on my shoulder. "Tell me what it is. What's going on in that head of yours?"

"It's just…I have to sit across from him today. I have to sit knowing what that man did and try my best not to react. When I saw him before, everything happened so fast. It was all a flash, but now I really have to face him. He was the one who dealt me my hand; he was the one who stole my voice from me. How do I deal with that? How do I stand in front of the man who stole my voice all those years ago, and how do I ask for him to give it back?"

"You don't ask," Brooks said. "You take it. You take back what he stole from you without permission. Without guilt. It's yours. The only way you take it back is by telling your story. You have a voice, Maggie May. You always have. Now it's just time for the rest of the world to hear it."

"Can we listen to a song maybe?" I asked, still nervous.

"Always." He took out his phone and grabbed a pair of earbuds, handing me one. "What do you want to hear?"

"Play something that will drown me," I whispered.

So he played me our song.

I told my story. Every piece, every inch, every scar. My family sat in court listening. Mama cried, and Daddy wiped her tears. Cheryl and Calvin didn't look away from me for a second's time. I wasn't certain

I would've been able to speak so loud without their quiet support coming my way.

When I finished, I met my family in the hallway, and they told me how strong I'd been, going through everything I experienced. The doors to the courtroom opened minutes later, and Michael walked out. His eyes were heavy, and I could see it—the weight of the world on his shoulders. He walked in my direction and gave me a smile that transformed to a frown within seconds. His hands were stuffed in his slacks.

"Hey, sorry. I know I'm probably not supposed to talk to you, but I just wanted to say what you just did was brave. I couldn't even begin to imagine what you went through your whole life. I'm so sorry for what happened to you."

"You have no reason to be sorry. You're not your father's mistakes," I told him.

He nodded understandingly. "I know, I know. But still. Your life was stolen from you. And my mom…" He snickered nervously. "I thought she walked out on us. I spent all my life confused and hating her, because every memory I had of her was filled with love. I couldn't for the life of me understand why she'd leave."

"If she had a choice, she would've never left your side," Mama chimed in. "Trust me, I know."

Michael thanked my mom and started to walk off until he heard me calling after him.

"She didn't suffer," I lied. "It was fast, painless. It was over in seconds. Your mom didn't suffer."

His shoulders appeared less heavy as I spoke to him. "Thank you, Maggie. Thank you for that."

After years of not speaking, I understood the importance of words. How they had the power to hurt individuals, yet they also had the power to heal if used correctly. For the rest of my life I'd try my best to use my words carefully.

They had the power to change lives.

The next day I headed over to Mrs. Boone's house with tea and turkey sandwiches. She rolled her eyes when she made her way to the door and then invited me inside to eat.

"I saw you on the news yesterday," Mrs. Boone said. "You could've used a bit more makeup. You were on television, not at some pajama party, Maggie."

I smirked. "Next time."

"Next time..." Mrs. Boone huffed, shaking her head. "I'd think you were kidding, but you and your boyfriend might be the most dramatic people I've ever met, so I wouldn't put it past you for there to be a next time," she said, drinking her tea. "And you are awful at picking out tea. This is disgusting."

I laughed. "Now you know how I've felt all these years."

She looked up from her cup, and her hands began to shake. "Your voice isn't as ugly as I thought it'd be." She smiled and nodded her head, pleased. A semi-compliment from my favorite frenemy was the best. She picked up her sandwich and took a bite. "I knew you would talk someday. I knew you'd be able to do it."

The two of us talked for hours about anything and everything that came to mind. We laughed together, which was the best feeling ever. When it began to get late, Mrs. Boone used her walker to get to the front foyer. Whenever her nurse tried to help her, she told her to piss off. Which in Mrs. Boone's world meant, 'thank you.'

"Well, you take care, Maggie May, and take a break from tragedy, all right? It's time for you to go and live the life you deserve with that boy who looks at you all googly-eyed. But don't be afraid to stop by any time you need a break from your adventures for some tea." Her eyes met mine, and she gave me the sweetest grin I'd ever seen. "Or you know, just to talk to an old friend."

"I will do." I smiled. "I love you, Mrs. Boone."

She rolled her eyes, wiped away a falling tear, and replied, "Yeah. Whatever."

Which in Mrs. Boone's world meant, 'I love you, too.'

As I crossed the street, I noticed all of my family members sitting on the front lawn, staring up at the house. "What's going on?" I asked, walking over to them. Cheryl was resting her head on Calvin's shoulder, and Daddy's arms were wrapped around Mama. I sat down beside my siblings and stared up.

"We're saying goodbye," Daddy said.

"What?" I shook my head. "You're selling it?"

He nodded. "We all think it's time. This home has been a place of new beginnings for us, of laughter, of love."

"But also of a lot of pain," Mama said, giving me a small smile. "And we think it's time to start again. To find new places, new sights. It's time for us all to let go of the past and find our future."

I didn't argue with them, because it felt way past due, but still there was a sadness that came with the idea of letting go of the house that saved me from myself.

The house sold in fifty-five days after it was listed on the market. Brooks and his band went off to Los Angeles to start rebuilding their music, and I promised I'd meet him out there once everything was in order with the house.

On the final day of our move, the sky was dark and rain fell over Harper County. Two U-Haul trucks were parked in our driveway, and we'd been loading up the trucks for hours. When the last box was packed, I asked my parents for a few minutes to say goodbye.

My once packed room was emptied of all of the history. My hand fell over my heart as I listened to the raindrops pound against the windowsill. I wasn't certain how to begin to say goodbye. The ache in my chest was reminding me of all the moments those walls brought me. It was the first place I learned what family meant; it was the first place I fell in love, and no matter where life took me, that yellow bricked house would always be home.

I was on the verge of tears when I heard my favorite five words. "You okay today, Maggie May?"

"You're supposed to be in LA," I said, smiling as I turned to see Brooks standing there with his hands behind his back. His hair and clothes were soaking wet from the rain, and he had the biggest smile on his lips. "What are you doing here?"

"Well, you didn't really think I'd miss saying goodbye to the house that gave me you, did you? Plus"—he stepped into my room, brought his hands from behind his back, and held up the dry-erase board with his words written in permanent marker—"I made a promise to a girl a few years back, and I think it's time we cashed in on it. I want to show you the world, Maggie May. I want to take you on the biggest adventure of your life."

I smiled, walking over to him. What he didn't know was that he was the biggest adventure of my life. He was my favorite journey, my anchor that always led me home. He placed the board on the floor and took my hands into his.

"I'm ready for that. I'm ready for our lives together, Brooks. I want you, and only you, for the rest of my life. I'm ready to let go of this place now."

He smiled. "Are you sure?" He glanced around the emptied space.

I curved into his body as he held me close.

I bit my bottom lip. "Maybe five more minutes," I whispered.

He kissed my forehead, and softly spoke. "Let's make it ten."

When it came time to leave, Brooks grabbed the dry-erase board and held my hand as we walked out of the house. The rain was still falling heavily, and I started to hurry toward the car, but Brooks made me stop. "Maggie, wait! I forgot to tell you the only requirement to my promise of helping you complete your to-do list."

"And what's that?"

He flipped the board over, and I read the words.

Marry me.

"What?" I chuckled nervously.

"Marry me," he repeated. Water crystals dripped down his nose and slid to the ground.

"When?" I asked.

"Tomorrow," he replied.

"Brooks." I laughed taking his hands into mine.

"And the day after that. And the day after that one, and the one after that, too. Every day, Maggie May. I want you to marry me every single day for the rest of our lives." He pulled me closer to his body and the chilled rain somehow felt warmer in that moment. In that moment we became one unit in the pouring rain. His skin on my skin, his heart beating with mine, our souls linked together from that day forth. He grazed his lips against mine, and softly spoke. "Say yes?"

I squeezed his hands twice.

And we kissed beneath the rain.

That was it.

That was the big moment. That was what my father always told me would someday happen. Brooks was the moment I'd been waiting for all my life.

This time is forever.

EPILOGUE

TEN YEARS LATER

"It's too loud," Haley shouted from the front row of the arena. She'd just turned six two weeks prior, and it was her first time seeing The Crooks live in concert. Brooks and the guys were celebrating their twentieth anniversary in the arena center fifteen minutes away from our house, and Haley asked if it could be her birthday present.

"It's not too loud, you're just a baby," Noah mocked his younger sister.

"No, it's a bit loud," I replied. I reached into my purse and pulled out a pair of pink soundproofing headphones, and placed them on my daughter's ears. "Better?" I asked.

She smiled wide and nodded. "Better."

As the lights began to fade, Haley and Noah both started jumping up and down. When the band entered the stage, the kids seemed seconds away from losing their minds. Their eyes were wide with wonderment as they stared up at their papa.

Their hero. My love.

"Hey, Wisconsin," Brooks said, wrapping his right hand around the microphone. "If you have ever been to one of The Crooks concerts, you know that we've never opened a show with a speech, but tonight is a bit different. Tonight marks the twentieth anniversary of the band, and tonight we are back in our home state to celebrate. So the guys and I thought it would be best to dedicate this show to the one person who made our dream come true all those years ago. There once was a girl who uploaded a few videos online, and she was the reason The Crooks were discovered. Hell, she even named the band."

"We love you, Maggie!" the twins shouted in unison.

"Love you, sister," Calvin said, smiling my way.

"They're talking to you, Mama!" Haley said, amazed.

I kissed her forehead. "I know, baby. They are pretty amazing, aren't they?"

She sighed, stars in her eyes. "Yeah, Mama. Daddy's amazing."

"So the first song isn't a song by The Crooks, but it only seems fitting to perform this hit on a night dedicated to my heart, my soul, and my best friend," Brooks explained. "This is an oldie, but a goodie, and I welcome you all to sing along. This is "Maggie May," by the amazing Rod Stewart."

Calvin started playing the introduction on the guitar, and within seconds Brooks wrapped his hands around the microphone and began singing directly to me. The kids kept cheering, shouting his name over and over again.

"I'm gonna be a rock star, just like Daddy," Noah shouted, jumping up and down.

The show was amazing as always. After the final performance, Brooks said, "Thanks to everyone for coming. We are The Crooks, and we are so damn happy you allowed us to steal your hearts tonight."

Brooks

"Daddy, I thought you were really good tonight!" Haley said, yawning. She had those same blue eyes as her mama and the same beautiful smile which made me bend to her every need. Her arms were wrapped around my neck as I carried her to her bedroom. Even though I'd toured the whole wide world and seen so many sights, there was nothing better than being home with my loves.

"Yeah? You think so?"

She nodded. "Yeah. I think Mama sings better than you, but still, you were good."

I cocked an eyebrow. "Oh, is that so? You think Mama's a better singer?" I laid her in her bed and began tickling her. "Say I'm the better singer! Say it!"

"Daddy!" She giggled. "Okay, okay. You're the better singer! You're the better singer!"

I laughed and kissed her forehead. "That's what I thought."

"Daddy?" Haley asked.

"Yes?"

"Secret time?"

I nodded. "Secret time."

She moved in closer, pulling me in for a secret, and whispered, "I lied about you being a better singer."

The tickle war began again and continued until we were both out of breath. I picked up the cat roaming around the room and placed him at the edge of Haley's bed where he slept each night. "Okay, it's time for you both to get some rest." I kissed her nose. "And, Haley?"

"Yes, Daddy?"

"The world keeps spinning because your heartbeats exist."

I headed out of her bedroom after turning on her nightlight, and when I stepped into the hallway I saw Maggie coming from Noah's room. We smiled at one another and walked downstairs together.

"Is Skippy in there with him?" I asked.

She nodded. "And Jam is with Haley?"

"Yup."

When Maggie walked into the living room, I went over to the light switch and dimmed the lights. She smiled my way, bit her bottom lip, and moved over to the jukebox that Mrs. Boone had given us years ago as a wedding gift. She picked her favorite track—our song.

As the music began playing I took Maggie's hands and pulled her closer to me. Our lips brushed against one another, and I gave her a light kiss before whispering, "Dance with me?"

She always said yes.

Moments.

Humans always remember the moments.

We recall the steps that led us to where we were meant to be. The words that inspired or crushed us. The incidents that scarred us and swallowed us whole. I've had many moments in my lifetime, moments that changed me, challenged me, moments that scared me and engulfed me. However, the biggest ones—the most heartbreaking and breathtaking ones—all included her.

It all ended with two kids, a dog named Skippy, a cat named Jam, and a woman who always loved me.

A Note from the Author

Okay, okay, I know I just told a story, but I'd like to tell another one right now. Don't worry, it's shorter. Nowhere near eighty-thousand words. This one's a bit more real, and a bit more personal, but here goes. The Silent Waters was a tough book for me to write. Unlike Maggie May, I wasn't mute as a child, yet I hardly spoke. In elementary school, I was super talkative. By third grade I was outgoing, and wild. I loved people, and they seemed to like me, too. Except for one girl, let's call her Kelly. Kelly and I rode the school bus together, and one day Kelly said she was going to be eight feet tall some day!

Eight feet tall! Could you imagine?

"That's so tall," I replied. "You'd be bigger than the whole world!" I exclaimed.

Kelly's eyes narrowed. "What did you just say?"

"I said you'll be bigger than the whole world!"

"Did you just call me a hoe?" she snapped, angered. Her anger threw me off—what had I said? What did I do wrong?

You see, I had a speech impediment. There were certain letters I couldn't pronounce, and certain words came out of my mouth which didn't sound like the words I held in my head. Still to this day, there are things I can't pronounce correctly when I get nervous. It's pretty embarrassing how fast this twenty-nine-year-old can feel like that third grader again in a blink of an eye.

I said *whole*—she heard *hoe*.

And she never let me forget it.

I didn't even know what a hoe was. I was in the third grade. I pretty much only knew what *Boy Meets World* taught me, and Cory never said the word hoe to Topanga.

Kelly didn't forget it, though. She made my life a living hell, talking about my speech, bullying me on the school bus, and pinching my ears saying, "I want to see how red the Cherry's ears can get!" It was crazy how fast other kids joined in on mocking my words. It was awful. I'd go home crying, and my mom didn't know how to fix it, other than marching to the school district and going Mom-mode demanding things be changed. P.S. It worked. (Thanks, Mama!)

But by that point, I already changed.

I lost my voice.

I became super self-aware of the words I used, therefore I hardly used any. I was a freak, a weirdo who couldn't speak correctly. My voice wasn't worthy of being heard.

In middle school, I was voted the quietest girl in the yearbook. When we had to read out loud in class, I remember having panic attacks and shaking. When I knew we were going to be reading out loud, I stayed home sick. If I couldn't stay home, I'd go to the nurse's office after splashing hot water on my forehead to fake a fever. If I did have to read out loud, I'd think about it for days and weeks after the fact, imagining the words I pronounced wrong, and the classmates who probably laughed at me.

I was shy to the point where teachers questioned if I had a learning disorder. My mother was told I'd never be able to communicate in a normal fashion due to my shyness and my speech, but she said she couldn't afford to believe that. You see, I was so talkative at home. My home was my safe haven. Those walls were where my voice was heard. It was the only place I could be myself after spending eight hours in a school building trying my hardest to *not* be me.

My older sister, Tiffani, doesn't know it, but she helped me find my voice. She was this amazing cheerleader who was popular and fun, and I looked up to her so much. One day, she told me I should try out for the wrestling cheerleading squad—yes, that's a thing.

I tried out, and I made the team.

I was able to stand in crowds, and even though I was terrified of what people thought of me, I still gave it my all. I started talking more in school. I started laughing more, too. Putting myself out there was the best thing in the world. One day, during my senior year of high school, a boy turned around in his seat and said to me, "I liked you better when you didn't talk."

For a split second I wanted to retreat back to my mute cave, but instead I thought, '*Be strong like Tiffani.*' So, I replied, "That's funny, because I never liked you."

Sass. I discovered sass.

My voice had sassiness sometimes! Which, later in life would probably get me in trouble, but that's another story.

This is why The Silent Waters is so close to my heart.

I was Maggie May, and she, in a way, was and still is me. I still sometimes have panic attacks, mostly before I publish a novel, or before I fall in love, or before I make any big life decision, because in my mind I'm still that third grader who feels as if I'm being judged. What if I screw up? What if I'm not worthy of love, or success, or living my dreams?

But then I breathe and remind myself that it's okay to be me. It's okay to be scared some days, and fearless the next. It's okay to be afraid of having a voice, and still using it each day. It's okay to be a little cracked, and yet, still whole.

So, this book was written for me, yet not only for me. This is for all of the Maggie May's of the world who sometimes feel so lost and alone. It's for the ones who feel invisible. It's for the ones who have panic attacks in their dark bedrooms at night. It's for the ones who cry themselves to sleep, and wake up the next morning with tear stains still against the pillowcases. This book is yours. This book is your anchor. This book is proof that you, too, will find your voice. You are worthy of love, and success, and your dreams coming true. Never stop speaking, even when your voice begins to shake, okay? Never give up on yourself. You are important, you are loved, and your beautiful voice matters.

About the Author

Brittainy C. Cherry is an Amazon #1 Bestselling author who has always been in love with words. She graduated from Carroll University with a Bachelor's degree in Theatre Arts and a minor in Creative Writing. Brittainy lives in Brookfield, Wisconsin with her family. When she's not running a million errands and crafting stories, she's probably playing with her adorable pets.

Other novels by Brittainy C. Cherry include: *The Air He Breathes, The Fire Between High & Lo, Loving Mr. Daniels, Art & Soul,* and *The Space in Between.*

You can find her on Facebook at:
www.facebook.com/BrittainyCherryAuthor

Acknowledgements

Writing a book is really hard, but writing the acknowledgements is the hardest. I always feel as if I'm going to forget someone, and then it will be in print that I forgot that person—which is terrifying.

But alas, here goes. Firstly, I'm going to thank Danielle Allen—my soul sister. Thanks for always being there for me. You've brought more tears from my eyes from laughter and appreciation than anyone I'd ever known. Thank you for being a true friend.

To my tribe. You each know who you are, and I am a stronger woman for crossing paths with you all.

To Allison, Alison, Christy, Tammy, and Beverly—the best betas in the world. This one was TOUGH. Thanks for the honesty and the support to help me make this story into what it is today.

Thank you to my editors Caitlin at Editing by C. Marie, and Ellie at Love N Books, and Kiezha for going above and beyond on this book. You make me sound better than I actually am, and I owe you the world!

To my proofreaders, Virginia and Emily—there are no words to describe your talents and your eye for detail. Thank you for catching those last minute mistakes.

A big thank you to Indie Solutions by Murphy Rae for formatting the novel, Staci Brillhart for the amazing cover design, and Luka Ditella for being an outstanding cover model.

To the readers, bloggers, family, and friends who not only support my writing, but speak about it to others without shame and embarrassment—thank you. Thank you for allowing me to live this wild dream and giving me reasons each day to smile. Thank you for hearing me, even when my voice shakes. Thank you for believing in me, even when I want to retreat and hide. Thank you for your love. Thank you for your energy. Thank you for being you. The world keeps spinning, because your heartbeats exist.

Other Books by Brittainy Cherry

The Elements Series
(All Standalone Novels)

The Air He Breathes

The Fire Between High & Lo

Keep an eye out for the final novel in The Elements Series—
based on Earth—coming Spring 2017.